HOT SPRINGS

HOT SPRINGS

GEOFFREY BECKER

TinHouseBooks

Published by Tin House Books, Portland, Oregon, and New York, New York

Distributed to the trade by Publishers Group West, 1700 Fourth St., Berkeley, CA 94710, www.pgw.com

Library of Congress Cataloging-in-Publication Data

Becker, Geoffrey, 1959-

Hot springs : a novel / Geoffrey Becker. -- 1st U.S. ed.

p. cm.

ISBN 978-0-9820539-4-2

1. Parenthood--Fiction. 2. Self-actualization (Psychology) in women--Fiction. I. Title.

PS3552.E2553H68 2010

813'.54--dc22

2009038276

A portion of this novel has been adapted from a short story, "Hot Springs," originally published in *Ploughshares* magazine.

First U.S. edition 2010

Printed in Canada

Interior design Janet Parker

www.tinhouse.com

"What did I know, what did I know
of love's austere and lonely offices?"

—ROBERT HAYDEN

PROLOGUE

Bernice was ten when her mother walked around the block naked. It was the week before Christmas, the night after they'd set up the tree (her father swearing and muttering as he tried to keep it straight in its stand). School was out, and she had a rabbit named Mr. Ed, and she was supposed to be getting an easel. That was what she always got—art supplies. Her friend from school, Casey Littlejohn, was getting a bicycle, but Casey lived in a different neighborhood, one with yards and quiet streets, where it was safe for a kid to ride a bicycle. In Bernice's neighborhood, you had to be more careful. One day, in front of Tony's Market, a man in a blue jacket with a neatly trimmed beard had asked her if she wanted to be in a movie; she'd just shaken her head and kept walking. Another time, robbers had held up the liquor store at the end of the block. She hadn't seen this happen, had only heard about it later—she imagined comic figures in black masks running out with canvas sacks of money. And when her dad had left his grill out on the porch one night after cooking them all hamburgers for dinner—they'd been so charred and dry they were nearly impossible to eat, even drowned in ketchup—it was gone the next morning, and he announced that he was retiring from barbecuing.

She'd seen other things. A woman with no legs carried out crying and cursing from her house by two policemen. A man with a stomach so huge part of it bounced against his knees. In addition to thieves, she was beginning to understand, the world was full of misfits and grotesques who hid away most of the time, but who occasionally had to go out like anyone else to pick up a loaf of bread or mail a letter. You could see them, if you kept your eyes out. It was like watching for shooting stars, which she'd done with both her parents one night on their roof, the three of them climbing out the third-floor window, she in her nightgown, her father holding a star chart of the summer skies he'd pulled out of *National Geographic.* Most of the time there was nothing to see, but if you were patient, every now and then something emerged from the darkness and scooted across your field of vision.

This was something like mice, which she didn't mind, but not at all like rats, which disgusted her. Mice lived in their big kitchen, and at night they came out and foraged for crumbs. Her dad killed them with traps he baited with peanut butter and placed under the sink, but Bernice always rooted for the mice. Rats, on the other hand, didn't scoot—they didn't have to. They took their time, and she often saw them in the alley behind the house, because at the end of the block was an apartment building with multiple overflowing garbage cans. "All-you-can-eat buffet," her dad called it.

The day of her mother's naked walk, they'd seen a movie together that she didn't understand at all. It was called *Smooth Talk*, and in it a girl stayed home instead of going to a cookout with her parents, and then let a dangerous-looking hoodlum and his buddy into her house. In the theater, her mother had started to cry, and Bernice wasn't sure why—the story was more mysterious than anything else. She had no idea why anyone was doing anything, and she felt strongly that it was somehow for adults—that it was hopeless for her even to try to understand. She'd spent a lot of the movie thinking about her envelope-lining collection, and the new addition she'd made to it just that day, which had come from inside a letter her father had received from Japan. She kept these cut squares of paper from security envelopes in a small leather album, and she now had over seventy different examples, and she thought they were beautiful the way wallpaper could be beautiful, the way rain on the roof could be, repetitive and calming.

During dinner, she'd counted the glasses of wine. She did this because she'd recently learned the meaning of the term *alcoholic* and was curious to figure out if it described her parents, who drank every night. At school, a man had come and given them a lecture called "Ethyl Is No Lady." Ethyl was alcohol, it turned out. During the talk, Casey Littlejohn kept poking Bernice, whispering "Luuuuucy!" Bernice and Casey Littlejohn thought *I Love Lucy* was the greatest show that had ever been on television, and their favorite name to say out loud was Ethel Mertz. Both of her parents had five glasses of red wine. She thought this was probably a lot, but at least neither of them planned to drive.

After dinner, which was quiet—just the sounds of their chewing, the tick of flatware on plates, the occasional clanking of the broad-shouldered steam radiator that hunkered along the interior wall behind her father's chair—she went to the parlor to practice piano. They had an old upright that wouldn't stay in tune, but she liked it, liked the sourness of it the same way she liked bitter vegetables that none of her friends had even heard of, Swiss chard and kale and beet greens. This was the thing she and her mother had in common. One of things, anyway.

Her father went upstairs, as he always did. Bernice worked on the Minuet in G. It wasn't going well, but her grandmother was paying for lessons, and she felt some responsibility to try to get at least one piece learned. From the hallway, she heard the click of the front door opening. Then she heard it close again, quietly. A few moments later, cold air slipped into the room, settling around her feet.

At first, she thought she'd keep playing. But after a moment she stood and hurried to the window, climbing up onto the ledge so that she could peer out over the top of the lower shutters, which were closed. What she saw filled her with dread. Her mother was walking out to the sidewalk, nude except for her running shoes, the reflective strips of which flickered in the thin light from the street lamps. Her boyish body was right there on public display for the neighborhood: her flat bottom; her small, white breasts; all her most secret places. She paused for a moment and looked at the house, and their eyes met. Her mother smiled and waved, then gave a thumbs-up, fluffed her hair, and proceeded to walk down the street.

Bernice wasn't sure what to do. She felt panicked, but more than that, she was afraid that if her father found out, it would somehow be the end of everything. Bernice sensed that her family was held together so lightly it was almost certain to someday come apart like a cheap toy. Her dad had been her mother's teacher before they fell in love. He was twenty years older, and he sometimes seemed so frustrated with her that Bernice saw her mom as just an overgrown kid who might even be better off coming to school with her rather than staying around the house all day.

She was gone about five minutes. Bernice watched her come up the porch steps, then left her post at the window and stood at attention in the parlor entrance. Her mother reentered the house, accompanied by a draft of frigid air. She pushed the enormous oak door shut behind her, the heavy central glass pane rattling loudly in its frame. Her skin was bright red. She stood with her back to the radiator in the entrance hall, rubbing her hands together. She seemed pleased with herself.

"Mom?" said Bernice.

"Pretty," said her mother, and for a moment Bernice thought this was directed at her, but then she realized her mother was looking past her, to the Christmas tree directly behind, which glittered in the corner by the far parlor window, covered in bright ornaments.

Bernice turned and looked, too. She knew exactly which presents were hers. The easel was obvious, wrapped in candy-cane paper, a lumpy object too big to fit under the tree and so leaned up against the wall beside it. With her father's help, she'd bought her mother a book called *The History of Photography* from a discount catalog, something she felt reasonably certain qualified as the worst present ever given anyone. She dreaded the moment when her mother would open it.

She turned back. "He doesn't know," she said, at length.

"He doesn't?" asked her mother.

"I don't think so. We don't have to say anything."

Her mother's eyes lit up. A secret. She loved secrets. The cold air had turned her cheeks alizarin crimson. "Do I have a kimono?" her mother asked. "I don't, do I? I should have one. Everyone should have a kimono. But no. Instead, we have bathrobes." She grasped her breasts with both hands, as if reminding herself that they were there.

"I can get your bathrobe," said Bernice, happy to have something to do. "You stay right here."

"No kimono," said her mother.

She went up to her parents' bedroom and got the big blue bathrobe out of the closet and brought it back down. Her mother was still naked, still by the radiator, waiting, humming to herself.

She took the robe and put it on. Then she bent her knees so that her face was even with Bernice's. Her breath had a sour, almost medicinal quality to it, and Bernice didn't like the way her eyes looked at all. "Do you know what that was like?" she asked. Her expression suggested that a part of her was still outside. "It was like sailing around the world."

"Did anyone see?" Bernice asked.

"Did anyone? I think so. I hope so." She touched Bernice's nose. "Don't worry so much. It will give you lines around your mouth later in life."

"Who? Who saw?"

"I don't know," she said. "A better question would be, *what* did they see?" She stood. "Do you want to stay up all night with me?"

"No," said Bernice.

Her mother scrutinized her, then smiled in a way that made Bernice feel peculiar, as if she were being forgiven for something she didn't even know she'd done. "Of course not. All right then, up to bed."

"It's too early," Bernice said. "I want to watch television."

"You're a shining star," said her mother. "That's what you are. And you know what? I could have just kept on sailing. Honestly. Except for you. You brought me back." Then she stood up, went into the kitchen, and set about making tea.

»»»»»»

He didn't know, and Bernice never told, but she didn't have to. Christmas came and went without much in the way of further incident. They all played their roles, pretended at being a normal, happy family. But her father was on to her mother. How could he not be? She'd been his best student—at least that was the story—and they'd fallen in love, and now she was going crazy. Or maybe she'd always *been* crazy, and that was why she was his best student, and it was what he'd loved about her. Bernice didn't know, and she found the circularity of the puzzle dizzying. One thing led to another, didn't it? Perhaps it was the burden of being his best student that had started to *make* her crazy. Perhaps it was no longer being his student, and hence no longer being the best, that was the problem.

Sometimes her mother went out at night and didn't come back until very late.

Sometimes she wore black lipstick.

She liked to sing along, very loud, to Elvis Costello records, and also sinister-sounding blues ones.

One day, Bernice found that the crotches had been snipped out of all her underpants. That night at dinner, her mother started giggling and had to be excused.

Sometimes Bernice could hear her sobbing in her studio, when she was supposedly working on her paintings. (Her father did his painting outside the house, in a rented space downtown.) Bernice imagined what Casey Littlejohn would say about that. *Wimp*, maybe? *Froot Loop*, more likely. Bernice had made the mistake of telling Casey about the underwear incident, and now she lived in constant fear that Casey would someday stop being her friend and let it get around to the whole school, at which point Bernice's life, as she knew it, would essentially be over.

And then, less than three months after the naked walk, her mother solved everything by moving out. This came as a complete surprise to Bernice, although she had sensed that something was up.

Often she heard her parents fighting down in the dining room after she went to bed, their voices drifting up the stairwell, the individual words losing definition and becoming more like the distant sounds of animals, or perhaps the moaning of unhappy ghosts.

Her father came to pick her up from school. On the way home, he suggested they stop at Safeway and get Berger cookies, her favorite. It was a Monday, and the day before, in a magical transformation, as if they'd been holding their breath and were now exhaling, all the cherry and pear trees in Baltimore had blossomed at once. Sunlight glanced off the pink and white flowers, and Bernice felt excitement at this clear promise that summer was coming. She liked summer. She loved the sun.

They bought the cookies. He seemed preoccupied, distant. When they got back to the house, he nosed the car too far into the garage and broke a hole into the wooden cupboard that stood against the back wall.

Inside, he got her milk from the refrigerator, then sat with her at the kitchen table. "Your mother," he said, "has gone to live with another man."

"What other man?" Bernice asked.

"Just someone. I don't know, to tell you the truth. A musician, I think. It doesn't really matter. The point is that she doesn't live here anymore. You are not to think about her, all right? It's just you and me, now. We'll get along fine. If she calls, I'd like you to give me the phone. What she's done is inexcusable, and she knows that." He hadn't looked at her the entire time he'd been talking, but now he did. "All right?" he asked. He might have been working out a deal on how much television she'd be allowed, or on what kind of grades she'd need to get an increase in her allowance.

Bernice knew that this was not necessarily her real mother doing this, whatever it was. It was her Froot Loop mother. The underwear snipper. The person who had sneaked in and was wearing her real mother's body like a Halloween outfit.

"I want to talk to her," she said.

"Well, you can't. She's not here." He stood up. "You may need counseling or something like that. If you do, I hope you'll let me know. It's expensive, and I'm not sure whether my insurance will cover it or not, but that's all right. I want you to know that—you can go to counseling if you want to. We'll make that work."

The next weekend, her mother came to pick her up in her green VW bug for Sunday brunch. Her father, after a brief telephone discussion with her mother, had agreed to this. She wore a low-cut brown dress and makeup. Bernice wore jeans and a pink shirt. When she got in the car, she gave her mom a drawing she'd done at school. It was of a screen door with a girl behind it, which was a scene from the movie they'd been to.

"Oh," said her mother, when she saw it. "This is really nice."

"Thanks. It's for you."

She took it and reached around, placing it carefully amid the detritus on the backseat—candy wrappers and empty soda bottles and library books and plastic grocery bags.

They drove to IHOP, where a tall, skinny man was waiting to meet them. His name was Craney Crow. "Just like the song," he said, smiling.

"What song?" Bernice asked.

Her mother laughed. "That's what I said!" They were in a booth in the back of the restaurant, and almost all the people at all the other tables were black. Many of them were dressed up very nicely, and Bernice couldn't help staring, even though she knew it was rude. One woman wore a purple hat with white flowers on it that was so big it looked like a very wide wedding cake.

Craney Crow had nice eyes, but he also had snaggle teeth, olive skin, and a little soul-patch beard. He said "cool" too much. That was what he'd said when her mother had introduced them out in the reception area, where he'd been waiting for them. *Cool.* Craney Crow was a cool cat. He had long, tangled dark hair that Bernice wanted to run a comb through. "It's this song," he said. "People know it."

"What people?" asked Bernice.

He stared right at her. She wondered if he were going to use whatever magical powers he had to seduce her into liking him, the same way he had her mother. "People."

"Not any people I know," said Bernice.

"Shake-a-my, shake-a-my, shake-a-my, shake-a-my, shake-a-my Craney Crow."

"It sounds like a dumb song."

"What songs do you like?"

She sang him a line about standing too close.

"Jesus, she likes the Police. What did you do to her, Eve?" He turned to her mother, picked up his spoon to use as a microphone. "Da doo doo doo, da daa daa daa," he sang.

"I like that one, too," said Bernice.

Their pancakes arrived, along with Bernice's Belgian waffle, and they set about eating. Bernice's mother had asked for a pitcher of hot water with hers, and she poured it over the top of the stack.

"She wants to make 'em bigger," said Craney Crow. "You put hot water on 'em, they inflate."

The pancakes did seem to grow an extra third or so in size. Her mother offered the pitcher. "You want to try it?"

Bernice shook her head, then watched as Craney Crow did the same thing to his. "It's a Devereaux family recipe," he said, grinning.

"I thought your name was Crow."

"That's my first name. It's actually spelled with an *e* on the end, not that it matters. Family thing. Craney is my nickname, and

Devereaux is my last name. But most people just call me CC."

She wondered if she were somehow now included in this man's family. She didn't like the idea at all. She imagined a bunch of birds hopping around a kitchen squawking at each other.

"CC is a musician," said her mother. "It's better for me not to be with another artist. You can understand that, right? It's like two trees next to each other in the forest, fighting for a view of the sun. The one that gets the sun is going to flourish, but the other—it's going to wither away."

The pancake thing was grossing her out, and she didn't like the word *flourish.* She hated that her mother was changing, or trying to act like she was changing, into some totally new person. Bernice poked into the crevices of her waffle with the side of her fork, trying to create pathways for the syrup to enter.

"So, is everything OK?" asked her mother.

"Oh, yeah," she said, aware that this moment, right now, was probably the point of the whole outing. "Everything's fine."

"Because, if there's anything you want to ask me, you can. I'll try to answer."

She looked up at CC and noticed that he was eyeing her in what she supposed he thought was a friendly way, but he sort of gave her the creeps. "I'm fine," she said.

The waiter brought more coffee and CC told a story about his drummer getting sick on oysters, and then it was later and she was back in the rattling VW watching the brick row houses stream past while her mother hummed loudly the way she always did—today she kept going, "What's the matter with the mill? It done broke down!"—and then they were back in front of the big house she now shared with just her father and her rabbit, and she was watching her own sneakers as she stepped out onto the curb.

"Can I get some sugar?" asked her mother, and Bernice turned and kissed her quickly on the cheek, then headed up the stairs onto the front porch. She waited until she was inside to start crying, and when she did, it didn't make her feel better at all. There had been something she was supposed to do, and she hadn't known what it was, and it wasn't fair, but she still felt her failure in every bone and nerve. In her room, she climbed into bed with all her clothes on, shut her eyes tightly, and tried to think of the happiest thing she could, which at that moment was the beach at Ocean City, where they had gone as a family for a few days the previous summer. Piece by piece, she assembled it for herself: the cries of seagulls, sand underneath her towel indented to conform to her body, the sun hot against her skin, the nearby rush and retreat of the waves, the distant smell of hot dogs.

ONE

Just north of Truth or Consequences, Landis heard the unmistakable bang of metal punching through metal deep inside the engine. Lights came on all over the dash, and then they were coasting along dead. He pumped at the brake pedal, which had lost its power assist, and aimed toward the shoulder.

"What did you do?" Bernice said, once they'd come to a full stop.

"I didn't do anything. We threw a rod, I think. I told you there was a rattle."

"So, this is my fault?"

"I didn't say that." He sighed. "It's no one's fault."

Emily, who had been asleep, rubbed her eyes and sneezed.

"Oh, baby," said Bernice. "You want a tissue?"

Emily nodded. She had dark brown curls and blue eyes, a high forehead, and sharply defined eyebrows, and wore a detached expression that suggested she was constantly in a state of remembering something that had happened elsewhere and at another time. She had on blue and white Oshkosh overalls and a light green undershirt, an outfit Bernice had selected for her early that morning at the Hardings' after poking around to see where the child's clothes were kept.

Bernice leaned back and wiped Emily's nose clean, then balled the tissue and tossed it to the floor. "You're thinking 'I told you so,' aren't you?"

"Not at all."

"I know you are. Can it be fixed?"

He turned the key. There was a clicking from the solenoid, but that was all. "With a new engine." Landis stared out at the huge rock formation that slept off to the side of the highway, rising up layered and dark out of the flat desert landscape. "That's Elephant Butte," he said. "It's on the map."

"I know all about it," she said. "Now, don't you think we'd better see about getting a hotel room?"

The temperature was nearly one hundred degrees out, and with the AC off, the car was quickly becoming an oven. He turned to Bernice, in her jeans and white tank top, her bright-lemon dyed hair standing up off her head as if some comic-book artist had drawn it that way. He loved her. But she scared him a little, too.

»»»»»»

He worried that a state trooper would come along, but it was a cowboy who stopped and asked if they were OK. Twenty minutes later, they were getting a tow into town. They stayed in the car, the three of them, tipped backward in their seats as if they were headed up a roller coaster; at any moment, Landis expected his breath to be sucked away when they reached the top and went spilling over. Instead, the windshield remained full of bouncing blue sky.

The mechanic had gone home for the day, and the boy who'd towed them took Landis's forty dollars and wrote down his name on a grimy legal pad by the register.

"Where you staying at?" he asked.

"What you got?" Landis said. He could hear Bernice outside with Emily, trying to kick a soda out of the Pepsi machine.

"Oh, there's a bunch of motels. Where you are, here, this is a resort town."

"*Last* resort, don't you mean?" said Landis.

"Used to be people come here for the hot springs."

"And now?"

The boy adjusted his dirty cap. "Just to say they been."

"Sounds like my wife's having a little trouble out there."

"I'll bet she is. There ain't no soda in that machine."

Landis didn't find this surprising. The whole town seemed to him as if it had been emptied of its contents. Or maybe more like a stage set—one of those fake towns you could visit for six bucks, where desperadoes shot it out with lawmen in the middle of the street every day at noon.

"Any of these cars for sale?"

The attendant looked dubiously out toward the side of the lot where, next to the wrecker, there were three parked cars, one on blocks. "The Nova, maybe. You'd have to talk to the owner. He went down to Hatch today."

Landis had four hundred dollars in cash with him, along with a maxed-out Discover card. He wasn't sure about Bernice. He knew there was a roll of bills in her purse, but he had no idea how much it came to.

They checked into the Hot Springs motel, two blocks down the street, and took naps. When they awoke, they went to the Fiesta Cafe for dinner. After their orders arrived, Emily leaned her head forward and clasped her hands together. Bernice rolled her eyes and batted at the flies hovering over her chicken. "Thank you, Lord," Emily said in a quiet voice, "for the bounty we are about to receive."

"Bounty," said Landis. "That's one way of looking at it."

"There used to be a candy bar called Bounty," said Bernice. "I can't tell you what was in it, though. Probably coconut. Do you like coconut?"

Emily didn't answer.

"This town was named after a television show," Landis said.

"I'm not allowed to watch television," said Emily.

"Yes, you are," said Bernice.

"No, just videos."

"There's a town in Montana that changed its name to Joe." It occurred to Landis that trying to explain this further would be more trouble than it was worth.

"They should have called it Hollywood Squares," Bernice said. "Or Star Trek."

They turned their attention to the food. Emily had a bowl of macaroni with butter on it. She ate half, then pushed it aside and drew quietly on her place mat with a Bic pen. Landis tried to get her interested in the mini-jukebox that hung over the table, but with no success. Bernice took the pen and did Emily's portrait on a napkin. After coffee and pie and milk, the three of them walked through the still, hot air back to the motel.

The mirror over the dresser was missing about two inches of the upper left corner. The dresser itself was covered in cigarette burns. "Look," said Bernice, "a rotary phone. You don't see that every day." She turned the television on to the cartoon channel. Emily, clutching the plush penguin they'd bought her at a rest stop outside of Albuquerque, climbed up on the bed to watch. Bernice stared hard at her.

"What?" said Landis. "Something wrong?"

Bernice turned to him and squinted. "You're kidding, right?" She went over and touched Emily's face with the back of her hand and held it there. "She's burning up. I knew she was hot, but I thought it was just the weather. I thought she'd cool off once we got her into better air-conditioning. Come on over here and feel her."

Landis touched her forehead. "Maybe she should take something?" he suggested.

Bernice brought over a glass of water, but Emily wouldn't drink. Her cheeks were red blossoms against her white face, as if she'd been slapped.

"Please, honey? I think you have a touch of the flu. We have to put out the fire."

Emily shook her head.

"Hey, little girl," said Landis, "listen up. Drink that water."

Bernice set the glass on the night table. "Never mind. Go on and watch the show." She motioned to Landis to join her outside, and the two of them stepped out the door.

"We need another car," he said.

"I know you think this is my fault, but it's not." She lit a cigarette. "You drive too rough."

He watched a bug bang itself against the floodlight attached to the side of the building. Getting into a big fight with Bernice wasn't worth it. He had suggested using his truck, but she'd insisted on her Hyundai, because it was a family car, and because it was illegal to drive a kid around in a truck. He'd distrusted the thing, but conceded her point.

Bernice sucked deeply on her cigarette, then tossed it. "I'm going to go sit with her. It's no fun being sick."

The door clicked shut. He stared for a moment at a dark cloud shaped like a hand floating in the purple sky. Bernice had a friend in Tucson. She and Emily were going to stay with her at first. Landis would ride the bus back to Colorado Springs, take care of details—finish cleaning out her apartment and his trailer—then drive down in the truck in a few days. After that, they would start their new life together.

»»»»»

He'd met her six months ago at Midnight, the club downtown where he was substitute soundman. Their first date was the movies, followed by cheap Mexican food and not a lot of talking. That was OK with Landis, as talking made him uneasy. It had been his experience that people gave him more credit the less he said. They agreed to see another movie the following night—the latest Bond—and afterward went back to his trailer with a bottle of Hornitos. There she told him her story about how she'd been living in Atlanta and gotten pregnant. She'd answered an ad from a childless couple, come out to the Springs, and stayed with them.

"They prayed for me and the baby every night—I could hear them up in the living room, just kind of murmuring. After I gave birth, I got out as fast as I could, to Florida, where I beach-bummed, waitressed, took some classes. But I always knew I'd come back. I kept a key."

All fall, she explained, she'd been going to the house. She'd park a block away, sneak in, eat leftovers from the fridge, watch a little TV, look at the pictures of Emily. She'd even managed to get hired at the Coffee Connection across the street from where Emily was in day care. She could step outside and watch the children playing in the yard. "It's Christian day care, of course," she told him. "Whatever that means. They both work in town, but Tessa isn't full-time. She drops her off Mondays, Wednesdays, and Fridays." Emily liked to sit by herself, Bernice told him. The child was leading the wrong life, and even if she didn't understand that, exactly, she *sensed* it, and it was making her unhappy.

It was nearly 4:00 AM, and they both still had on all their clothes. This was not what Landis had envisioned, but he was coming to the conclusion that Bernice wasn't much like other girls he'd known.

"They are brainwashing her. It isn't right. They bought my daughter from me because they couldn't have one of their own, and now they are killing her mind, one day at a time. If there is a God, I think it's pretty clear he did *not* mean for these people to have children."

"What are you going to do about it?" he asked.

"Take her back."

"Excellent idea."

Her eyes narrowed. "You don't believe me?" She lifted her hand to her mouth and bit into the fleshy part at the base of her thumb.

"Hey," said Landis. "What are you doing?"

She didn't answer, just looked out at him over her hand, which she continued to bite. After a few seconds, when blood appeared, she stopped. "Most people couldn't do that to themselves," she said.

"Most people wouldn't want to."

"You're looking at a woman with a purpose." She grinned, the traces of red on her mouth like smeared lipstick. Then she took off her T-shirt and wrapped it around her wrist. Landis tried not to appear to be staring at her breasts. "Will you help?" she asked.

"No way in hell," he told her.

»»»»»

Bernice was on the motel bed now, next to Emily, watching *Scooby-Doo*. "Remember Lucky Charms?" she said. "Those marshmallow pieces made your teeth hurt."

Landis saw that she'd wrapped Emily in a blanket. "If she's cold, we don't need this." He went over to the air conditioner and switched it off. It shuddered, did a miniature version of the noise the Hyundai had made, then fell silent.

"She was shivering, and her fever seems worse. I don't like this at all."

Emily poked at a cigarette hole in the blanket and said, "I can do the minor prophets."

"This ought to be good," said Landis, sitting on the edge of the bed to listen. "I'm a sucker for the minor prophets."

She closed her eyes. "Amos, Obadiah, Jonah, Micah, Nahum . . ."

"Bert, Ernie, and Kermit." Bernice stood up. "I'm getting you an aspirin."

She went into the bathroom and fumbled through her bag. From where he was, Landis could see her reflection in the mirror, her smooth strong arms tanned and pretty against the white of her T-shirt. She came back in with a half tablet in her hand.

"Don't you give kids Tylenol?" asked Landis. "I think aspirin might be bad for them."

"Ever hear of baby aspirin?" she said.

"Seems like they just give that to old people."

Bernice held the pill in front of Emily's flushed face. "Anyway," she said, "this *is* Tylenol. I just said aspirin."

Emily turned her head and looked at Landis for a moment, then brought her attention back to Bernice. She swallowed the half pill, washing it down with water Bernice gave her in a plastic cup.

"The water tastes bad," she said.

Landis got up and peered out the side of the blinds. He could see across the parking lot to the lobby, where a fluorescent light illuminated the Vacancy sign. There were two other cars in the lot, both of which had been there when they'd arrived. He wondered if they belonged to guests, or if they were always there. He tried to put himself in the Hardings' position. They would have called the police pretty early this morning—Bernice said they got up around eight. The police would have asked who they thought might have taken the child. Would they think of Bernice? It hardly mattered. Even if Landis and Bernice could somehow manage to return Emily without getting caught, the child could identify them.

"I can get us a Nova, I'm pretty sure," Landis said. "Then I think maybe we should turn around and take her straight back. Drop her off on the corner, give her a push in the right direction, and run."

Bernice stood silently in the middle of the room, her hands in the back pockets of her jeans. "Are you backing out on me?"

"No, of course I'm not."

"Do you think I'm crazy?" she asked.

"I don't know. No."

"But you think it's possible, right?" She came over and leaned against the wall beside him. With the air-conditioning off, the room had quickly grown stuffy. The walls were permeated with old cigarette smell. "I need to hear from you that except for the engine blowing up in my car, and for Emily getting sick, this was an OK plan." She pushed up against him and touched his arm with her hand. "Please? Can you just say that?"

In the various conversations they'd had about this through the spring and early summer, he'd tried to talk to her about alternatives. The courts, for instance, regardless of the papers she'd signed. But she wouldn't listen, claimed he didn't know what he was talking about. "You think knowing how to run a PA system qualifies you to give legal advice?" she'd said.

And then they'd stopped talking about it, except that it was always there, an underlying hum in the system that would not go away. She was the strangest girl he'd ever known, and time and again, he'd thought that if he were smart, he'd have nothing more to do with her. But then he'd see her, with that infectious smile, that look in her eyes that suggested imminent sex, an electric surge that seemed to radiate from her and make everything in her vicinity vibrate. Some days they made love four, five, six times, doing it in her unmade bed and on the floor and just about anyplace, until both of them had reached a point of exhaustion, until Landis was so sore it hurt to button his jeans. But then she'd disappear for a day or two, and he wouldn't know what to think. He'd feel her absence in his whole body, like a fever. As long as her plans about Emily had remained hypothetical, he hadn't figured there was much to worry about. People lived with all sorts of stories they told themselves.

"I know what I'm doing," she'd promised him last week. They were at his trailer, in bed, listening to the coyotes. "It's all going to work out fine. You have to trust me." She had leaned over the wall of Little Angels to talk to Emily. "I just said, 'Hi.' Know what she said? 'It's you.' I asked her, 'You, who?' And she said, 'My real mommy.'"

"And what did you say?" Landis asked.

"I didn't say anything." Bernice was beaming. "I put out my finger and she gave it a squeeze." She held up the finger to show him.

"Don't you think she might say something about this to the people?"

"No, no, she won't. She knows it's a secret."

"Kids aren't great with secrets."

She'd wrapped herself around him and hugged him hard, and he realized with some surprise that by not ever consciously making a decision, he had in fact made one.

"It was an OK plan," he said now.

She went into the bathroom and began running water into the tub. "Go get some ice," she said. "Get a whole big bag."

He was gone less than five minutes. When he returned, Bernice had put Emily in the tub. He reached a hand in and quickly pulled it out. "That's cold."

"What do you think the ice is for? We need to get her fever down."

"That can't be right. Look at her." He put the bag down in the sink. Emily's naked body was magnified and flattened by the bluish lens of the bathwater, and she was clearly shivering. Her eyes were shut tight. Landis reached in and scooped her up in his arms. Water splashed all over the floor and all over him. She was so light. He grabbed a towel off the rack, wrapped it around her, brought her back into the room, and sat her on her bed. Behind him, he heard the bathroom door click shut. He dried her off and put her T-shirt back on.

"Did I do that OK?" he asked.

"You forgot to dry my toes," Emily said.

He dried her toes.

"And I want underpants."

"Right." He found them on the floor, handed them to Emily, and looked away as she pulled them on. Then he tucked her in, leaving the towel under the back of her head where her hair was still wet.

Landis knocked, entered the bathroom, and found Bernice staring into the mirror over the sink. "I've ruined everything," she said. "I'm an unfit mother."

"Shhh. Nothing's done that can't be undone."

"It isn't? Do you know what you are saying? Are you even in the same movie as me? Because mine is a bad gangster one, and it ends in a hail of bullets."

"Just stop it. Everything is under control. We've got a little money. We've got Emily. What we need is to get some sleep."

They went quietly back into the bedroom. Emily's face was still flushed, her closed eyelids fluttering like tiny moths. He couldn't tell if she was asleep. She was a strange one, he thought, just like her mother. Any other kid would have been screaming in that ice water. Landis took the towel out from under her head and hung it on a chair. "She's still hot," he whispered.

Bernice took off her clothes and got into the other bed, facing away from him. As Landis undressed, he inventoried his body: his chest, hairy and beginning to gray; his appendicitis scar; another scar on his left thigh where a disturbed woman had stabbed him on a Greyhound ten years ago; the flat feet he'd inherited from his father. There'd been a time in his life when he was impressed by his body, the fact that he had muscles, the full head of long hair that made him look like a rock star. Now, he was just glad nothing embarrassed him too much.

He eased into bed and slipped his arms around Bernice. "Who was he?"

"Who was who?"

"The guy. Her daddy."

"I've told you before, I don't want to say. It doesn't matter."

"If it doesn't matter, why not tell me?"

"Just some kid I liked for a while. He was a baker."

"A baker? Really?"

"Really."

"What did he bake?"

"Muffins. Bread. Cakes. Pies."

"So what happened?"

She rolled over onto her back. "I was a part-time cashier at the bakery. I saw the ad in *Creative Loafing* and I called."

"Where is this baker now?"

"Married his high school sweetheart. That was his plan all along.

Let's not talk anymore, OK?"

"You never told him?"

"No. It didn't involve him."

"It didn't? How can you say that?"

"I'd flunked out of school. I just did this thing. It was my business."

"If it was me," he said, after a while, "I think I'd want to know."

There was a rustling from the next bed, and Emily got up and padded into the bathroom. The toilet flushed. When she came out, she did not return to her bed, but went to theirs and got in next to Bernice, who backed up to make room for her. Landis pressed up against Bernice's back and put his arm over her, his fingers just brushing against Emily's hot shoulder. As he lay there trying to gauge from their breathing whether either of them was asleep, the girl took his hand and squeezed it, lightly at first, then harder. She was making sounds. He thought about what he had prayed for as a child—a dog, a ham radio, his parents to stop the yelling that went on night after night. That was the thing about kids—they believed if they just asked the right way, they could get the things they wanted, all of them.

»»»»»

In the morning, Emily's shirt was soaked and clammy with sweat, but her fever was down. "It was the bath," said Bernice, proudly.

Landis left them to clean up, walked back to the repair place, and struck a deal with the owner: the much newer Hyundai, plus a hundred cash, for the Nova. It was fifteen years old and on its second engine, and there was rust lacing the metal around the wheel wells, but it ran, the tires were decent, and the radio worked.

"Never thought I'd have a Korean car," the owner mused. He was a fat, red-faced man of about fifty, with thick eyebrows. From the adjacent service bay came hammering sounds as the boy who'd towed them yesterday attempted to remove a tire from a rim. "But I used to say that about the Japs, and look at them now. That Nova's a Jap car. I had a real Nova, a '69, with a 350 V-8. That sumbitch could fly. Traded it for an El Camino. Shouldn't have. Did you know the bombs Japan dropped on us at Pearl Harbor were made out of steel we sold them?"

"I guess what goes around comes around," said Landis, fingering a collection box for cerebral palsy on the counter. "I'll be back in a few minutes with my wife to sign over the title."

"I'll bet that car is made of steel from bombs we dropped on Korea. I wouldn't be surprised."

"Swords into plowshares," said Landis. "Or sedans." He thought about Emily. How long would it be before she asked to go home? It surprised him that she hadn't already, but there was something between her and Bernice, an understanding, that he would probably always be excluded from. He supposed he didn't mind that much.

"My point exactly. If you ask me, what with these terrorists, the world's finally come into focus. Good guys and bad guys—that's all there really is. It's nice to have an intelligent conversation like this from time to time." The owner wiped sweat off his face with the back of his hand. It occurred to Landis that the last thing he ought to be doing was making an impression on people. He found a penny in his pocket and stuck it in the box.

"Well, I'll go get the plates off that one," the man said.

Landis followed him out into the sun. A mangy yellow dog watched him from the shade beside a Dumpster. As he headed back up the street to the motel, he reminded himself not to forget to transfer the booster seat they'd bought last week, the two of them shopping the baby section of Walmart like any other responsible set of parents.

TWO

"I know what it is," Emily told Bernice on their second day at Gillian Cooper's apartment. "I swallowed a demon."

"You did no such thing," said Bernice. They were out by the pool, Bernice sunning in a green plastic chaise, Emily sitting up beside her with a white Diamondbacks sun visor shading her face. "There's no such thing as demons."

"One slipped into my mouth while I was sleeping. Now it's cooking me from the inside." She seemed downright pleased.

Bernice picked up her Diet Pepsi and handed it to the girl. "Here, drink some of this. You do not have a demon in you, and you're going to be fine." In fact, Bernice was worried, as the child clearly still had a fever. Landis had left yesterday—she and Emily had dropped him at the bus station downtown—and she still hadn't heard from him. She tried to tell herself that she would, that for some reason he just couldn't get to a phone—he'd stopped service on the one at the trailer last week—but deep in her heart she knew she'd blown it. He was gone, run off, back to the life he'd had before meeting her. She thought it was a cheap and cowardly trick to leave the way he had, acting like he really wasn't, like it was all still OK between them.

"We need to go to church," said Emily.

"We do not." She held out a tissue. "For one thing, it's Friday. Blow real good, OK?"

Emily did this, solemnly handing it back when she was done. The whites of her eyes were the color of robins' eggs. "It's OK. I can pray in my head."

"You better not." Bernice watched another mother with her child on the opposite side of the pool. The woman was Mexican-looking, her daughter a round-stomached little windup toy, brown as a Brazil nut, wearing a yellow plastic water wing on each arm.

"I can talk to him. I can talk to him for you!"

"Who?"

"Jesus."

"You know what, honey? Instead of Jesus, I wish you'd talk to Jerry."

"Who is that?"

"Think of a nice, fat man with a beard and sunglasses kind of like Mr. Landis wears. Sort of Santa Claus, only with a guitar. He died, too. Instead of talking to Jesus, you talk to Jerry, OK?"

Emily was quiet. It was hot out by the pool, but Bernice wasn't ready for the air-conditioning again. At least out here the air was real. Gillian's apartment was small and smelled of carpeting, and all the furniture was glass or acrylic. It was bad in there—deeply unnatural. Right now, Gillian was away at work.

"I'm not afraid to die," said Emily.

"Stop it," said Bernice. "No one's dying." She closed her eyes. This wasn't so easy. She hadn't planned on being abandoned. "Hey," she said, brightly. "What about we go get some ice cream?"

»»»»»»

The Albertsons supermarket was only a few hundred yards away, but there was no practical way to walk to it—you had to cross eight lanes of traffic with no pedestrian light, and the line of cars never let up. It amazed Bernice that it had come to this—a world where you couldn't walk, even if you wanted to. She got into the Nova, which despite being parked under one of the sun awnings that stood along the outside edge of the parking lot, still contained air as hot as a blast furnace. She cranked the feeble air conditioner and rolled down her window, then got back out and strapped Emily into her seat. For some reason, the word *toenail* had been stuck in her head all day, and she thought of it again. *Tucson, toenail, tough, turban.* She wondered if her brain was getting baked.

Inside, the supermarket was so cold she immediately got shivers. Emily held her hand as they walked first to the liquor section, where Bernice picked out a green bottle of premixed margaritas for herself. Then they wandered past meats and the huge pharmacy area over to dairy and cakes and bread. The smell made her dizzy. Bernice did her best not to meet people's eyes. She had no idea what the Hardings might have done in terms of putting out the word, but it wasn't like they didn't know her face. She tried to remember if they had any photographs around the house with her in them. She didn't think so. But there were police artists who could draw you from descriptions. People got caught that way all the time.

"What kind of ice cream is your favorite?" she asked.

Emily stared at the big freezer doors. "Green," she said.

"Honey, there is no such thing as green ice cream. We could have chocolate or vanilla, or Chubby Hubby, or just about anything. Green would be lime, and that wouldn't be a good flavor for ice cream. Sherbet, maybe. Is that what you're thinking of?" Bernice opened the freezer and reached in. "Except I don't like sherbet. Fudge ripple?"

Emily pointed to the shelf below.

Bernice picked up a plain-looking carton with old fashioned writing on it. "Pistachio," she said. "You can read that? What else can you do? Wow." She put the carton in the basket she wore over her arm. They made their way back to Health and Beauty, and she picked through the various hair products. "What do you like? Red? Auburn? You like my color? Blonde?"

"Uh-huh," said Emily. She had a bit of a runny nose starting up, and Bernice put down the basket, dug a tissue out of her pocket, and mopped it for her.

"We're going to turn you auburn. It's a great color. I had nothing but fun when I was auburn." She looked up and down the aisle, but they were alone.

"I think I like my hair the way it is," said Emily.

"I know you do." Bernice touched her hair, enjoying how thick it was. She imagined Tessa Harding doing this same thing. She couldn't believe she'd allowed herself to miss so much of Emily's life, but while she could not unmake the past, or ever really alleviate her guilt, she could still maintain some purchase on the future. She straightened the visor, which was falling down over the child's eyes. "We need to make you look different."

"Why?"

"Because people are going to be trying to find you."

Emily coughed, a tiny, abrupt sound.

"I mean, maybe. Don't worry about it. OK, let's get out of this icehouse." Bernice took her hand and they made their way to the front, where only two registers out of ten were open. They stood behind a woman who was buying three cases of store-brand cola and four bags of cat litter.

"Well, hello," said the woman, looking down at Emily and ignoring Bernice entirely. "Aren't you a lovely child? Would you like a soda?" She was pear-shaped, in a violet tracksuit, and had a nose that seemed too small for the rest of her face. Her sandals were gold, and her nails were painted a vivid shade of red. Tough Tucson toenails. Bernice imagined those toenails plowing their way through thick pile carpet in a hideous house with a private pool and a TV in every room.

"No," said Emily. "I wouldn't."

"You tell her," said Bernice.

"I guess politeness is no longer something that gets taught to children," said the woman, looking at Bernice like her head was smoking.

"I guess some people don't know when to mind their own business," said Bernice. "What makes you think she'd want a cheap, warm soda? We have drinks at home."

"I'm sure you do," the woman said, eyeing the bottle in Bernice's basket. She turned away and began lugging her colas up onto the belt.

"I don't want my hair dyed," said Emily. "I like it how it is."

Oh, Christ, Bernice thought, here it comes. Sure enough, the woman turned around again. "You're not dyeing that child's hair, are you?"

"Not this minute."

"But you are later?"

"Maybe."

"Then what? Will you get her a tattoo?"

"If she wants one, she can have one. She can have two."

"That's criminal," said the woman. "Putting chemicals on a little girl's head."

"Hey, how'd you like one of those cans shoved up your ass?" asked Bernice, stepping forward. She knew the switch had been thrown—she could feel herself losing control. She wished Landis were there.

The two security guards were beside her before she even understood that the woman had complained, or perhaps she hadn't and the checker had summoned them with some secret button. They were polite, but insistent. "We're going to have to ask you to leave," said the larger of the two. He had acne-pitted cheeks, a moustache, and looked like a character from a Western movie.

"Not without my ice cream," she said.

"She threatened me," said the woman with the sandals. "Keep her away from me."

And then they had her, each with a firm grasp on one of her arms. Emily dutifully tagged alongside. The ice cream and hair dye and the margaritas had been taken from her. She felt the hot air of the parking lot, saw in the distance a horizon of low mountains and craggy rocks pointing up like broken teeth. "Hey," she said. "This isn't right. You can't do this. I'm a mother."

"We're sorry," said the one with the moustache. The other was shorter, darker, possibly Native American. He hadn't said anything, and he didn't seem very interested in any of this. "I'm going to have to ask you not to come back."

Bernice shook herself loose from him. "You get your kicks doing that?" she asked. "Pushing women around? What if I told them inside that you touched my breast just now?"

He shrugged. "I didn't. Anyway, you're not going back inside. That's the whole point."

"You don't understand," said Bernice. "My daughter wants pistachio ice cream. That rhinoceros in there insulted me."

"I'm sorry, Ma'am." He looked down at Emily, who was standing in the sun with her hands folded in front of her. He smiled. "What's your name?" he said.

"Don't start," said Bernice, taking Emily's hand and hauling her off toward the car. "Let's go find a store that isn't run by fascists."

They drove over to Oracle, the next big intersection, where there was another shopping center, but they didn't have pistachio ice cream in the smaller, crummier market there, so Bernice chose chocolate, which was what she'd rather have had anyway. They sold premixed margaritas, too, for a dollar more, but she bought a bottle anyway, figuring it was worth it, considering the way her day had gone so far. She decided maybe the lady had been right about the hair dyeing, and she didn't even look for another box. Perhaps they should have thought up something clever to put the Hardings off track, like smashing the TV or writing odes to Satan on the bathroom mirror. Instead, they had taken clothes and even Emily's toothbrush. And they hadn't left a ransom note. Kidnappers always wanted a ransom. Changing Emily's hair color wasn't likely to solve much.

She found her way back to the Linda Vista apartments, turning in just after the bouquet of colorful balloons tied to the sign that advertised First Month Free!, negotiated the speed bumps in the asphalt and circled around to the back, past the recycling station, to 13F. It was like being a bee and knowing which square of the honeycomb was yours. Each building was exactly the same light-colored fake adobe, with metal stairs outside that thunked as you climbed them. Sprinklers embedded in the ground came on and off unpredictably in a weak attempt at keeping the lawn areas between the sidewalks green.

"You want to watch some TV, or go back out by the pool?" she asked Emily, once they were back inside. She had been surprised by how characterless Gillian's apartment was, like a hotel room. If this was life as a professional person, Gillian could have it. She worked for some data company these days, and on weekends she golfed. There were clubs in the hall closet, along with a mostly deflated silvery heart-shaped balloon that said Be My Valentine! on it, with a blue ribbon tied to the end. Gillian's boyfriend, Kirk, was a systems consultant, whatever that meant. Bernice suspected it meant he ironed his jeans.

Emily stiffened slightly, as if considering a complicated question she'd been asked, then threw up on the white living-room carpet.

"Damnit," said Bernice. She hesitated between the urgency of getting to the child and that of getting to the paper-towel dispenser in the kitchen, then decided on the dispenser. She tore about fifteen sheets off and hurried over, handing a big hunk to Emily and pressing the rest onto the soft pile in front of her. It stunk and was hot under her hand, but there wasn't much substance to it—Emily's diet had consisted almost entirely of pasta with butter on it, peanut butter on Saltines, water, and an occasional slice of American cheese. "She likes the beige foods," Landis had commented.

Bernice turned her attention to Emily, whose face was hot and devoid of color. "Do you want to lie down, sweetie?" she asked. "What happened?"

"I don't feel good," she said.

"Well, I guess that's pretty clear. Couldn't you at least have tried for the toilet? This isn't our house. We're guests here, and we need to be the kind of guests that people are happy to have around, because we don't know how long we might need to stay."

"I don't want to stay here," said Emily.

"Not permanently. Permanently we'll be someplace really nice, where you can have your own room just like you're used to, and Mommy can have a nice work space to do art." As she was saying it, it occurred to her that the vision she'd had all along for them was basically the Hardings' house, only without the Hardings in it. A modern house with all the amenities and high ceilings and a mountain view, with a garage big enough for a workbench and fireplaces on both floors. It was pathetic. They'd never live even remotely that way. Instead, it was going to be more trailer parks, almost certainly. She hated Landis for letting her count on him and then running. She hated herself for being so incompetent that she couldn't even manage to buy her own daughter a pint of ice cream without getting hauled out of the store.

"Shadrach, Meshach, and Abednego," said Emily.

"What. What is it?"

"Went into the fiery furnace. But they praised the Lord and they didn't get burned up."

"You're not in the fiery furnace, so you don't have to praise anyone. Don't make me have to hire one of those deprogrammers."

At this, Emily suddenly looked as if she might cry, and Bernice, seized by love for her, held out her arms. She hugged her tight against her, felt as if she might never be able to let go, as if she were holding on to herself as much as another person. Finally, she picked her up and carried her into the small extra bedroom they were sharing, with its futon and the desk with Gillian's fax machine. She laid her down on the blue comforter and pulled a light blanket over her, gave her a couple of stuffed animals for company.

"I'm going out to work more on that carpet," she said. "You take a nap, all right?"

Emily nodded. "I think I should have a new name," she said.

"You do?"

"So they can't find me."

"Who?"

"Whoever it is who might come."

"But you'll still look the same."

"But I won't be. I'll be Pearl."

"Your new name is going to be Pearl?"

She nodded again.

"I don't know if I like it. It's a little unusual." But she had to admit, changing names wasn't a bad idea. She might even want to change her own. "Can we think about it?"

"Uh-huh."

"We'll let it sit for a while, and then if it still seems like a good idea, we'll go with it." There was a boom box on the desk, and she turned it on to a station that had quiet jazz. "Is that OK?" she asked.

"I like Christian music," Emily said. She'd said this in the car, too. Bernice remembered the mismatch of the Hardings' tastes: David blasted loud rock in his SUV, sometimes sitting in the driveway when he returned from work until whatever inane praise song was on finished; Tessa practiced Mozart on the piano in the dining room every evening.

"I'll bet you do." She played with the dial until she found a country station, which she figured was a reasonable compromise. She turned the volume way down until it was just a twangy murmur, kissed Emily, then went back out to the living room to see how the carpet was looking.

»»»»»»

"I bought more spaghetti. It was all I could think of." Gillian put the bags she was carrying down in the kitchen. Her eyes were puffy and dark, her shoulder-length hair limp and streaky-blonde. She wore a pale pink suit with a low-cut, white blouse underneath it, which contrasted with her tan skin. Gillian was Bernice's one remaining friend from her time in Atlanta. The two had met on karaoke night at Apex, a Virginia Highland neighborhood bar where Bernice had made herself a regular and where they never carded. Gillian had just been laid off by Delta. Thinking she looked sad, Bernice had persuaded the bartender to buy her a free drink, then delivered it to Gillian herself saying brightly, "Who died?" They'd gotten drunk on gin and tonics and sung the Styx song "Sail Away" together, bringing an audience of thirty to its feet cheering when it was over. Despite the fact that Gillian was seven years older, they had become tight as sisters, but then Gillian had left for the Southwest. Bernice understood it was not about her, but she'd still felt abandoned.

Bernice stood and turned off the TV. "Great. Our fave. Something wrong?"

"I'm dumped. By e-mail, no less." She started putting things away. The bracelets on her wrists jangled as she worked.

"That's cowardly."

"Ungrateful bastard." She examined a can of salmon. "Why did I buy this? I'll never eat it. Here"—she held it out—"you take it."

"Take it where?" said Bernice.

"I don't even like salmon. He likes salmon. I just pretended I did. And I pretended so long that I apparently forgot. I forgot."

"Throw it out. Donate it to charity. It's just a can of salmon."

"No, no, don't you see? It's a symbol of how pathetic I am."

"You're not pathetic. You have a wonderful life here. I'm impressed." Bernice looked at the can, which was green with pink writing. "I'm sure he's not good enough for you. And he's obviously stupid."

"He isn't—he isn't stupid. He makes seventy thousand dollars a year, and he plays guitar in a band. He's really talented." She took the empty grocery bags and balled them up, then deposited them in the trash.

"Why do boys all think they have to be in bands? Does the world need all these bands? It's like, just in case you thought they were only Peter Parker, they want you to know they're really Spiderman." Bernice sat on the floor. "I nearly got hauled off to the pokey today."

"What do you mean?"

"I made a scene at Albertsons. A lady started giving me shit about Emily, and I lost it."

Gillian laughed. She took off her jacket and went around the kitchen divider and into the small living room, where she sank down onto the sofa and kicked off her shoes. "God, she is such a cute kid, Bernie. There's so much of you in her." Bernice hadn't told her anything beyond the fact that she and Landis were relocating. "Are you guys going to get married, or what?"

"Maybe. Probably." Bernice wondered if she would ever even see Landis again. "The marriage issue hasn't really come up."

Gillian massaged her feet. Her toenails were neatly painted magenta, even the smallest one, which was barely there. "I'll never get married. I go through one doomed relationship after another. Before this, there was Paco, except it turned out he was cheating on me with two other women. Before that, there was Michael, who wore panties and liked to hang out in gay bars. He said he found it empowering to get hit on."

"What happened with him?"

"Amazingly, it turned out he was gay."

"My last boyfriend before Landis was a Roosky," Bernice said.

"Oh," said Gillian.

Bernice realized that if Gillian had assumed Landis was Emily's father, she probably no longer did. "In Miami Beach. Vaseline. Well, Vasily, technically. But he was a greasy guy. In the hospitality furniture business." She hadn't said his name aloud in months. His intense, light blue eyes had made him seem almost ethereally beautiful—a space alien. She'd drawn a number of portraits of him when she was taking classes up at Broward, and she knew every inch of his face. "Things were going just fine until his business partner showed up from Moscow. I guess Communists figure the whole sharing idea is supposed to extend to women, too." She shuddered. That particular night was one she tried never to think about. They were drunk at his apartment, where she'd been spending almost all her time. She'd hit him; he'd hit her. She left with a black eye. Her boss, Pete, from the Mango Lounge, had let her stay on his sofa for a few nights because she was scared to be alone at her own place. "That was kind of my wake-up call. Life is short. No point in wasting it. Decide what you want and then go after it. That's the one thing I learned from old Vaseline. Lie, cheat, steal—it doesn't matter."

"So, you and Emily moved to Colorado to get away from him?"

"Yeah. Sort of."

"Anyway, I don't know what I want," said Gillian. "That's my whole problem."

"I know what I want," said Bernice. "A margarita."

She made them each one, and they stepped out on the apartment's tiny balcony which overlooked the parking lot. The sky was deepening in color, a pretty vermilion that reminded Bernice of the way the ocean sometimes looked at twilight. They sat on plastic furniture.

"Tequila is the best," said Gillian. "We should go down to Nogales this weekend and get some really good stuff, cheap, bring it back. Have you ever been to Mexico?" She brightened at the prospect. "We'll bring Emily, and we'll go down there and do some shopping! "

"I should tell you what's really happening," Bernice said. "It's not fair if I don't."

"What do you mean?"

"I lied to you just now. We didn't move to Colorado—I did. Emily wasn't with me in Florida. She wasn't with me until just a little while ago, in fact. I mean, she's my daughter and all. It's just that I gave her up for adoption."

"OK," said Gillian.

"I don't think they know it's me who's got her. We didn't leave a note."

"We?"

"Right."

"Landis is in on this?"

"Was. He may have had second thoughts."

"Bernice! Do these people have money?"

"Oh, sure. Big house, two SUVs."

"Then they'll hire a private investigator, at least. And they'll find you. Did you sign papers? I mean, it's all legal?"

"I signed all kinds of stuff. But I'm allowed to change my mind. I don't give a shit about some legal document—she's my daughter."

"I don't think you *can* change your mind."

"Well, I probably wasn't supposed to wait five years."

"What were you thinking?"

"I don't know," she said. She looked at her nails, which were bitten to the nubs. "A lot of stuff. I did nothing *but* think."

Gillian clasped her hands nervously, putting things together. "I can't believe you did this. And I can't believe you came here and got me involved."

"You're hardly involved."

"Then why does it feel that way?"

"I think of you as my friend—maybe my only real one. You *get* me. Hey. 'I'm sailing away,'" Bernice sang. "Remember?"

Three staccato coughs sounded in the guest room. "Is she OK?" said Gillian.

"I should take her to a doctor, I guess. She's got a temperature."

"How bad?"

Bernice didn't answer. She didn't particularly want to know, and she had on purpose not yet bought a thermometer. She remembered temperature taking from her own childhood, and she wasn't sure she wanted to go there yet with Emily. She could just hear the policewoman they'd have testifying against her in court: *The child stated she was subjected to sexual abuse by the defendant, specifically in the form of anal penetration.*

"You don't know the first thing about this, do you?" said Gillian.

"Please, not you, too. I've only had a few days on the job. But I love her and she loves me, and we're going to be fine, no matter what. We'll figure it out as we go along."

"How? How will you figure it out?"

"I've read books. *What to Expect. Parenting for Dummies.* I know plenty."

Gillian stood, then downed the remainder of her drink. "I'll make us dinner," she said, but Bernice knew she was saying something else. She didn't want them there, and that was fine. Bernice didn't want to be anyplace she wasn't wanted.

"Look, I'm sorry to unload all that on you when you're having such a bad day."

"No, no, it's fine," said Gillian. "So, who is he?"

"Who's who?"

"The father."

"Just some guy. It doesn't matter. Ancient history."

"Vaseline?"

"Jesus Christ, no. That's recent. She's *five.* I don't know who he was, exactly. I have ideas."

"Wow."

"Wow, what? Wow, you slut? Wow, I'm sympathetic?"

Gillian looked away. "Nothing."

"Nothing?"

"All right. Here's what I think: You ask for this stuff. You like drama. You thrive on it."

There were people in your life who just knew you. You could pretend all you wanted, it didn't make a difference. "You know what I'd like?" Bernice said. "For her to turn out to be an artist. It ought to run in the family, at least a little."

"I guess that depends on which family. Maybe you slept with a car salesman or something. Or a lawyer."

"I'm going to work on that. It's one of the things I promised her."

"Bernice, you weren't pregnant when I left Atlanta. Let's see. You went out with that English piano player a couple of times, right? Him?"

"You wouldn't know the person. I just got careless, OK? And if I was hooking up a little too randomly, well, all right. I was. Did someone tell you that I had high self-esteem?"

Gillian shook her head and straightened the tiny green table. "Promised her when?"

"Back when it was just the two of us, when I was pregnant. We talked a lot. I did, anyway—she mostly kicked, floated around, and hiccuped. She was the only person I had *to* talk to." Bernice stared out at the parking lot, imagined she saw flames rising from beyond the pale cars. What would make a child think she'd swallowed a demon? "I called her Chili Bean."

"I don't get it. If you knew you were giving her up, what were you doing promising her things? Or naming her. You pick up a stray dog, you don't name it. Name it and you're keeping it."

"Chili Bean isn't much of a name. But, yeah, that was one of the things. I promised her I'd come and get her when the time was right."

"Why didn't you just *keep* her then? Bernice, you aren't making sense."

"I couldn't. That's all." How to tell her? How to explain the absolute certainty she'd had about herself? She'd known she would fail. She wasn't like other people. Sure, she looked like them, she walked around in the world, bought things at stores, ate, made love. But there was something wrong with Bernice, something broken. She knew it. Vaseline had known it. *You don't cook!* he'd shouted. *You don't clean. And now you won't fuck?*

"What is it that you do for a living?" Bernice asked.

"You know that. I work for DataSoft," Gillian said.

"But what do you *do*?"

"It's really not that interesting. We process information for various clients. A lot of it is health-industry stuff. It all depends on the particular contract."

"I don't understand," said Bernice. "I don't. All these people in the world, all of them going to their jobs, sitting at desks—I don't get what they do. I've had jobs, but they all involved delivering food to tables or mixing drinks. Seriously, I feel like there's something I missed, something no one ever explained to me."

Gillian put her hands on the stucco wall of the balcony and looked out and away toward the next group of buildings. "Do you understand how all this makes me feel?"

Bernice bit at her thumbnail. "You? No. Why should it make you feel any way at all?"

"Some of us want nothing more than to have children. Even if it's probably never going to happen, realistically. We still hope. But that's not the point. It's just—"

"What?" said Bernice. She was feeling worse and worse. Gillian was right—she'd only been thinking of herself.

"It's just you, I guess." Gillian turned and looked at her with sad eyes, reminding Bernice of the first time she'd seen her. The skin around her neck was leathery from too much sun. "It's just who you are."

"Could you please do something for me?" Bernice asked, suddenly feeling as if all the air was being sucked from her lungs. She stood up and held out her arms, trembling. After a few moments, Gillian moved toward her. Bernice closed her eyes and felt the softness of Gillian's wet cheek against her face. But it wasn't a real hug—Gillian embraced her the way people do a relative they hope will soon leave.

THREE

Landis spent his first day back in the Springs attending numbly to all there was to be done. His trailer was a mess, and he brought a couple of loads of stuff to Goodwill: boxes filled with clothes he didn't wear, old shoes, kitchen things they'd replace eventually, once they were settled. A waffle iron he'd never once made waffles in went, as did a blender he'd used for a week for smoothies, before he decided they weren't all that tasty. His previous girlfriend, Junebug, had liked them, and he'd always thought of himself as someone open to new experiences. He threw away magazines and old pizza boxes and catalogs from Pottery Barn and Banana Republic that only proved to him that those people had no idea who he was or where he lived.

The bus ride up from Tucson was a reverse version of the same trip they'd just gone on, almost, and in Truth or Consequences, where there was a scheduled stop, he bought himself a coffee across the street from the place where he'd gotten rid of the Hyundai, though he didn't see the car in the lot. Back on the road, with a scheduled arrival time after 1:00 AM, he allowed the vibrations of the wheels to hum him into a light sleep, as if he were attached to a speaker cone and the whole bus were its cabinet. He enjoyed public transportation. He liked how it was this system that was always there, always in motion—man-made, certainly, but even so, more like a tide or a wind—to which you could attach yourself for the price of a ticket and magically get shot out someplace entirely different. A wormhole, maybe. Eyes closed, he imagined trains and buses and planes slowly inscribing an elaborate, hieroglyphic pattern onto the entire country.

His neighbors at the trailer park were mostly gone during the day, but the woman who lived just across from him kept vigil in her lawn chair under her awning, a beer and a cigarette going at all times. Landis hadn't spent much time at home since he'd met Bernice. Her place was larger and nicer. Still, on occasion they stayed at what she called "the spaceship," and they both laughed about this woman, the way they'd hear her abrupt coughing inside following her morning bong hit, before her door clanked open and she came out accompanied by the strains of "Sugar Magnolia" to smoke a cigarette and stare at the sky.

"You outta here?" she called over, now. She wore Ray-Ban Wayfarers that sat askew on her face.

"Yeah," he said.

"Job?"

"That's right," he called back. "New job."

"Where at?"

"Tucson." He felt Bernice kicking him and telling him he was an idiot. There was no point in leaving a big trail of clues behind.

"Where's *she*?"

Landis finished tying up a contractor bag of garbage, stood it up, and walked over to her. He didn't feel like shouting his business, and he thought he probably ought to be polite and act normal, just in case some Columbo-type ever came around asking questions about him.

"We broke up," he said.

"Really?" The woman yanked her glasses down her nose just enough to peek over them in what she probably thought was a sexy way, but Landis couldn't help comparing her thighs, which were pale and dimpled, coming out of a pair of white shorts, to Bernice's. Landis loved Bernice's body, found it almost inconceivable luck that at his age he got to sleep with her. "You guys have a fight?"

"Not a fight. Things just kind of ran their course. You know how it is."

"Oh, yeah, I know. That's my life in a nutshell. Want a beer?"

Landis looked up at the sun—it wasn't yet noon. "No, I believe I'll hold off," he said. "I get started now, the day'll be over before I get anything done."

"I don't plan on getting anything done," she said. "That makes life a hell of a lot easier." She ground out one cigarette and extracted another from her pack of Winstons. "It's a shame we never really got to talk much, and now here you are leaving."

"Well," he said, but could think of nothing to follow it with.

"None of my business, I know, but that's probably for the best. I never thought you two were right for each other. You seem more or less normal, but her—" she brought a red lighter to the end of her cigarette, lit the end, inhaled deeply, then dropped the lighter back on the plastic table and exhaled. "She just didn't seem right. Nervous."

"She's a little high strung. She's from back east." He'd learned that in the West this information could be used to explain a remarkable number of personality failures. He didn't add that he, too, was from back east, originally.

"I know about that. I meet lots of types doing what I do. I'm a nanny."

"How come you're out here all the time, then?"

She blew more smoke. "I'm between jobs."

"Well," he said again.

"That's a deep subject." She laughed. "Get it?"

"Ho ho," said Landis.

"I just hope they're as normal as you."

"Who?"

"Whoever moves in next. Before you was a half-breed or a Mex, I never could tell. Spooky quiet. I believe he moved up to South Park someplace. I wouldn't be surprised if he killed someone, or was a terrorist, even. I keep waiting to see his face on the evening news." Her skinny, black-and-white cat pushed its way out the screen door behind her and started rubbing up against her leg. "Hey, Blaster," she said.

"Well, I can't say," said Landis. "It's not up to me." He'd rented the place through an ad in the paper, sent his checks to something called TNC Development at a PO box in Denver.

"You got any eight-track tapes in there?"

"No."

"I got a player, but I only got four tapes for it, and one of them doesn't work, and one of them is by Chicago and I can't stand it. Got it at a flea market—I figure it's a collector's item, or will be."

"Can I check that out?" Landis motioned to her copy of the *Gazette.*

She held it out to him. "Keep it," she said. "I already did the puzzle."

Landis took the paper back to his own stoop, sat down. There was a story about how the United States had accidentally bombed an

Afghan wedding party, another about the fire in Woodland Park. He turned to the Local section. Nothing, just more about the fire, which was mostly under control. A local teacher had published a children's book, which he'd illustrated, too. He paged further in, still expecting at any moment to find a photo of himself, or of Bernice, or of Emily. He didn't know how the paper could have gotten such a photo, but he felt it was inevitable.

When he was done looking, relieved that he still seemed to dwell in a temporary state of grace, he locked up and took the truck into town, dropping his trash into a Dumpster behind the Walmart on South Academy, where they'd bought the car seat. Bernice's apartment was downtown, near where the highway cut through, in a complex that looked like a Motel 6, complete with a battered swimming pool. Apparently she paid quite a bit for it, and it was unclear to Landis where her money came from. She'd quit her job at the coffee place back in April and begun working part time at a little gallery in Manitou that sold pottery and paintings and kachina dolls and other stuff to tourists and the occasional intrepid Broadmoor lady. She'd already cleaned the apartment out, more or less, and told the manager she was moving even though she had two more months on her lease, and she and Landis had stood one final time on her tiny balcony looking west toward Pikes Peak, improbably huge and wearing its barren top like some misshapen skullcap. On the horizon below it, attached to a building much closer, there was a red neon sign that read, simply, "Fish." Bernice had insisted it was a Christian thing, and while at first he'd argued with her, pointing out that it was a restaurant, and that he'd even been there, she was impossible on the subject—to the point of growing sarcastic with him—and he'd given in. "You think some restaurant is just going to put up a big Fish sign ?" she'd said. "It's the same thing as those symbols on everyone's cars."

"OK," he'd told her. "You're right. I'm just saying, it's a fish restaurant. That's what they serve."

"Anyone who orders seafood in Colorado ought to have his head examined," she'd said.

Landis parked down the block, walked to the complex, and checked Bernice's mail. There was quite a bit of it. He'd never been in her mailbox before, and it felt strangely personal. He told himself it was just a mailbox. And yet for a while she'd seen it as some kind of battleground, refusing to lock it, which resulted in the postman's refusing to deliver her mail. This went on for weeks until, eventually, the postman gave in.

He stuck the mail, none of which looked important, into the glove compartment of the truck, then walked three blocks to Tejon Street. Midnights was open for lunch these days, and he took a seat at the bar and ordered a Fat Tire and a burger special from a woman he didn't recognize, who didn't seem particularly friendly. She was probably around forty, pretty enough, with tattoos up and down her arms. There wasn't an ounce of fat on her. She had blue-black hair, and her T-shirt read "Don't Ask."

"What?" he said when she delivered his plate.

"Whatever it is you're thinking of," she said. "Unless it's more ketchup or another beer, it's off the table." She smiled at him. You could have slipped a quarter between her front teeth.

"Where's Reno?" he said.

"She's out sick. I'm Robin. You a regular?"

"Sort of. I work here sometimes. Tate calls me in when he can't do a show."

"Tate's an old friend of mine. What's your name?"

"Landis," he said.

"Nope," she said. "I never heard of you."

"Well, I do sound."

"So I figured." She maintained eye contact but didn't say anything else.

"Can you give me an example?" he asked, finally.

"A date. The time. Directions. To see my tits. You name it, I don't want to hear it." She leaned forward. "What don't *you* want to be asked?"

There was only one other person at the bar, a muscular young man with a military haircut and a newly sprouted goatee, reading a newspaper. "I don't have secrets," said Landis. "You can ask me anything you like."

"Hmm," she said. "I might just do that. Let me give it some thought."

"There a pay phone in this place?" asked Landis.

She held a finger up. "Uh uh uh."

"Just fooling with you," he said. "I know where it is."

She went back to work and he considered his position. There hadn't been a chance to call Bernice from the road, and today he'd continued to avoid doing it, so that now what he had was almost certainly a problem. The silence was a blister that was growing bigger and bigger, and when he finally did get in touch, the thing would burst and she'd use the opportunity to punish him and remind him how he was failing her, and possibly just failing in general.

He ate his burger and had another beer, occasionally casting his eyes on Robin, who, he had to admit, intrigued him. *We broke up*, he'd told his neighbor. It sounded so simple.

The military-looking guy asked him if he wanted to play pool, and he said sure. They didn't talk at all for the first game, and Landis beat him handily. The kid—because looking at him close, Landis saw that that's all he was, and possibly not even twenty-one yet—put in four more quarters and racked.

"You don't mess around," said Landis, gesturing to the kid's drink, which was straight whiskey. "Last time I drank that stuff in the afternoon, I ended up spending the night in jail. Drove off in someone else's truck, if you can believe it. Looked just like mine. Key worked, too, which has to be a one-in-a-thousand chance. The judge was understanding, but they suspended my license for six months in addition to the fine." He picked up some chalk and worked the end of his stick. "I'm Landis."

"Devon," said the kid, reaching out a hand.

They played two more games, and Landis won them both. Devon was intense, if not terribly good. He loped around the table like a highly focused dog.

"If you don't mind some criticism," Landis said, "you could stand to take a little off that stroke of yours. You look like you're trying to poke through a piece of drywall. You army?"

Devon stood straight up. "What makes you say that?"

"I don't know. The hair?"

"That's right. I am."

"I'm a patriot. Buy you another?"

Devon nodded and finished up his glass, then held it out for Landis to take.

At the bar, he got refills from Robin. He was beginning to feel what he'd hoped he'd feel, the community of strangers, the warm sense he often got in a bar.

"How'd you like jail?" Devon asked when Landis returned with his new drink.

"Not at all. You planning on giving it a try?"

"I might could. I'm AWOL right now." He shoved another round of quarters into the table, which rumbled and coughed out the balls. He racked with drunken attention to detail—it took three tries before he was satisfied none of the balls had rolled.

"From where?" Landis asked. "I mean, if it's not too personal."

"Well, I was in Bagram, three weeks ago. Migraine, I call it. Migraine, Migrainistan. Got sent to Baltimore for a couple weeks as a special treat. Decided I'd just as soon stick around, if you know what I mean."

"I don't get it. What are you doing here?"

"I got a girlfriend here. Well, she was my girlfriend in Georgia. Now she's here. Fort Carson, see? She likes army guys. Camp follower, you might say. We gonna play or what?"

Landis broke, sank one of each. "Guess I'll shoot stripes," he said, and put in three more before finding himself with nothing. He tried a three-cushion bank that appeared possible for a brief, prophetic instant, and scratched.

"Whoops," said Devon.

"Georgia?"

"I was stationed at Fort Benning. Rangers. I probably said enough already."

"They out looking for you, you figure?"

"Don't know. I was about to be RFSed, anyway." He grinned. "Disciplinary problems." He got down very low to the table, eyeing the distance to a group of his balls at the other end.

"You can't see the angles that way," said Landis. "You want to be looking down on things—that's how to see them."

Devon ignored the advice, shot, and missed, simply moving the balls around. "Ah, crap," he said.

"No, seriously," said Landis. "What happens when they find you?"

"I don't really know."

"But you must have thought about it. I mean, there you were in Baltimore, having a good time. Then what?"

"First of all, I wasn't having that good a time. My girlfriend never showed, although that was the plan. So I'm hanging around this strange city with nothing in particular to do and no place to do it. Good time. I went to a bunch of strip clubs, took a ride in a water taxi, got drunk. Finally, I just walked over to the bus station and got on a Greyhound."

"Just like that."

"More or less. You've got to understand. When you come back from over there, it's just different. You wonder what everyone's *thinking*. It's like, *What part of this shit is supposed to matter?*" He shot again, this time sinking a ball, though not the one he was after. "It's an education, though."

"You seem pretty calm."

"Hey, man, I jump out of airplanes. You know what? Fuck Afghanistan. See, I like to eat. In Baltimore, I went to restaurants. I ate crab cakes and pizza and steak and nice, fresh salads. I ate enough to last me another six months. And then I decided to come here." He drank some more of his whiskey, fumbled a cigarette out of his shirt pocket and lit it. "Who the hell are you?" he asked.

"What do you mean?" Landis tightened his grip on his pool cue.

Devon smiled, revealing a tiny set of discolored uppers. "I'm just fucking with you, Captain. I mean, who are you? You got a job or something?"

"I'm between things," said Landis. "But I'm a soundman when I'm working."

"What the hell is that?"

"Live sound, for bands, concerts—whatever. I always liked music, but I couldn't play anything. I figured this would be a good way to get to hang around it and get paid." In fact, he had yet to make any real money in his new career, but he had hopes, and it made sense to him in a way that most of his previous gigs never had. He'd always found work that involved using his hands and his body—lifting things, hauling things, fixing things. He'd had the idea that being a soundman would be substantively different—a chance to exercise his brain. Then he'd done his first job for Kevin at ProSound, helping set up for a fifties-sixties act called the Rockets who had a gig at one of the Cripple Creek casinos, and found himself wrestling speakers and equipment. It really wasn't all that different from the moving business. He'd managed to get some time at the blackjack tables, though, and had won two hundred dollars, which seemed a good omen.

Landis sank the rest of his balls, leaving only the eight, which was an easy shot for the corner, a little tougher for the side pocket, with some scratch potential as well. He decided to try that anyway, just for the challenge, and sure enough, although the eight dropped nicely, the cue ball headed straight for the corner, balanced momentarily on the rim, then fell.

"Well, son of a bitch," said Devon. "I win."

Landis shook hands with him. "If I were you," he said, "I'd seriously reconsider this. Tell them you lost track of time or something."

"Nah. It's OK. I'm going to get me some pussy, then turn myself in. I'd just as soon do it that way. But first off is the pussy. I figure even if she don't love me no more, she still owes me a little, returning soldier boy and all. Hey, you want to see something?" He fumbled in his pants pocket and brought out a small book. "It's a pocket Koran," he said. "I got it right off a dead one of theirs. They think the bullets will just swerve and go around them if they carry it, but I guess they're wrong about that." He checked his watch. "She gets off work just about now, I gotta bust on over there." Unsteadily, he made his way out the door.

"You hear any of that?" Landis asked Robin, after he'd taken his seat again at the bar.

"Not so much. I thought of something, though."

"What do you mean?"

"Something to ask you."

"OK, shoot."

"You want to go to a party later?"

"You serious?"

"Maybe, maybe not. You want to go?"

Landis thought about what he had to do later, which was to call Bernice and to finish up at the trailer. He figured it could all wait another day. He was liking being back in town, unencumbered by the weight of Bernice's plans. He looked again at Robin's blue-green arms. "Where at?"

"Manitou. Some friends of mine are having a barbecue."

"All right," he said.

She got a pen off the register and wrote down an address on a napkin for him. "The guy's name is Leroy—that's whose house it is. I'm heading over around eight or so."

Landis put the napkin in his pocket. Then he felt he was supposed to leave—if he didn't, he was going to have to talk to this woman more, and he already felt guilty. But he hadn't done anything, and he wasn't about to. *Bernice,* he reminded himself. *Bernice.*

"Tab?" Robin asked.

He nodded and got out his wallet.

»»»»»»

He knew it was a dumb idea, but when he got back to his truck, he decided to drive by the Hardings' house. They lived at the north edge of town, practically on the air force academy's grounds, in tight against the mountains. One afternoon, he and Bernice had gone up to spy on the house, parking a few streets away and entering the academy grounds though a rusty gate behind a water tower. They'd hiked up a good half hour before finding a trail that headed south and around the ridge to where they'd have a view, and eventually they'd found an enormous boulder from which they could see down onto much of the development housing that crept up in neat, curved streets lined with huge, expensive homes.

"There," she'd said. "That one."

"What now?" he'd asked. She wriggled out of her jeans and kissed him. He took a deep breath of the thin air and felt strangely disconnected, like a dirigible, floating. They arranged their clothes on the rock and lay on them, and he was on top of her and inside her within moments. She stared up at him and started to shiver uncontrollably, even though it was probably eighty in that sun. He tried not to think about why else they were there. Her eyes looked like they'd been painted onto her face.

Now, he directed his truck into the upper reaches of the city, felt the change in elevation as the housing around him grew nicer and more expensive. Three-car garages instead of two. Bigger decks. Bigger cathedral entranceways. They still all looked like they'd been put together out of kits, though, as if a toy train might come humming through at any moment. When he'd been with Cecil Wormsley, Movers, he'd seen the inside of lots of houses. He'd liked that job for just that reason—he'd gotten to see how other people lived, or at least a kind of reduction of how they lived, the boxed-up version. What had interested him about the process of moving was the uncovering: huge dust bunnies under the furniture, the lost items miraculously returned, and, if the people were smokers, the way the nicotine-yellowed paint on the walls suddenly became apparent when you took down the pictures. Once, they'd moved a man in his fifties out of a big modern house in an expensive development to an ugly bungalow downtown, where most of the nice stuff he had barely even fit. "Divorce," the guy had said, slipping Landis a twenty at the end of the day. "The great leveler." Landis had nodded in sympathy. Some years earlier, he has ducked out on his girlfriend Pam, after she'd messed herself up in a car crash, and stories of other people's breakups interested him. Landis had hurt his back moving a desk that day, and after some subsequent discussion about doctors' bills and lawyers, Cecil had given Landis a thousand bucks and told him he never wanted to see him again.

There were no signs of life at the Hardings' house—the garage doors were shut, the curtains in the windows drawn. He pulled up in front of the next house on the street and idled, thinking about what he might say to them, how he might undo this whole business. The house had an enormous driveway, a hedge along one side of it with yellow and purple flowers blooming. There were flowers, too, in the tiny front yard. If you went around the side, there was a back entrance, which was the one they'd used last week.

A police car cruised slowly over the crest of the hill and drove past him. Landis watched in his rearview mirror until it was gone, then pulled away from the curb and proceeded down the hill in the direction from which it had come, making sure to stay at twenty miles per hour. He was an idiot who made terrible choices. That's all there was to it. If they got him, it would be his own fault, pure and simple.

When he came to the next intersection, he wasn't sure which way to go, so he turned right. He passed a development called Stone Ridge, then another called Cragg's Landing. From behind a tall redwood fence, an invisible dog barked.

There was a church on the left, a big, glassy construction, sparkling in the late-day sun, the sky the color of wheat straw behind it, the lights of the city just starting to come on now. He pulled over here, too, and watched the traffic on I-25 as it crept along, ants in mindless procession, yet each car occupied by bona fide consumers, who bought Doritos and Cokes and Marlboros and televisions to watch crime shows on, their car trunks laden with things they'd probably picked up at the outlet mall in Castle Rock, their brains full of junk mail.

An alien spaceship sent a force field of light and sound through him and he shuddered right down to his balls. He turned as he heard the door of the police car open, heard the scrape of shoes on the gravel.

"What's up?" he said. "I couldn't have been speeding."

The officer, eyes obscured behind mirrored sunglasses, pursed his lips. "I was just kind of wondering what you're doing here."

"Looking at the view?"

"I saw you a few minutes ago, too, up there." He waved off to his left. "You lost?"

"No, sir."

"Got friends around here?"

"Nope. I'm just looking around, that's all." He tried hard to think of something that might explain his presence more adequately. "I'm checking out neighborhoods—my wife and I have a five-year-old. You know anything about the school district here?"

The officer looked at Landis, then at his truck, an F-150 with a fair bit of wear on it and a cracked windshield. "Not much. I live in Security. Got a five-year-old, myself."

"Girl?"

He shook his head. "Boy. Gonna play for the Broncos. Told me that just this morning."

"Hey, Security, that's pretty good," Landis said. "I mean, for a policeman."

"Yeah, we joke about it, me and the wife. Yours a girl?"

"That's right. We live up in Monument." He'd once gotten stuck in an ice storm in Monument. He hoped the cop wasn't going to ask for ID.

"How do you like that?"

"Not so bad."

"You get the weather, huh?"

"I like the weather."

"Not me." He was probably a year or two younger than Landis, and he looked hard, like a guy who spit-shined his shoes in the morning and shit in neat, identical cylinders. Landis realized that there was a secret fraternity of fathers out there in which he now held at least a temporary membership. "I don't need it. Weather is bad news for a cop. Accidents. That's all I know when I see on the news that a storm's coming."

"Any idea what one of these places might go for?" Landis asked.

"Nope. But I'm sure you'll be happy. Nice and quiet up here. You got the mountains, after all. There has been some trouble with bears getting into people's trash. That's something to think about. Well, all right then." He tipped his hat and got back into his cruiser.

As Landis watched him pull past, he wondered what Bernice was doing right now. *I'm lucky*, he'd told her more than once, and this was possibly true, if mostly in a bullet-dodging sense.

When he'd moved in with Pam, it had been a halfhearted decision, entered into under the influence of the better part of a bottle of Southern Comfort and the surprising news—whispered to him as he buried his face in a pillow to go to sleep—that she was pregnant. A lie, almost certainly, he now understood. He'd heard a few years ago that she was married, and he hoped it wasn't just the settlement from the accident that had made her attractive to someone. He hoped it was real love she'd found. They'd both been young then, just twenty-two and twenty-three. He could still see her face, the cross-stitching on it like train tracks, could still hear her slurred voice as she struggled, even weeks after waking from her three-week sleep, to wrap her tongue around the simplest, most familiar sounds. "Landish," she'd say, her grin now lopsided. "Landish, let's party." And he'd done that, watching her shaky hands roll huge, unwieldy joints that rained embers onto the cluttered coffee table in her apartment over a corner grocery in Trenton, *Born to Run* turned up so loud the dishes rattled in the kitchen sink. He did it for nearly a month—as well as the shopping, the cooking, the cleaning. He found her the lawyer, and dealt with her parents, who clearly suspected his motives, thought he was hanging around waiting for an insurance payday. He drove her to physical therapy, speech therapy.

He'd driven her down to see the car, which was at a wrecking yard near Toms River, a few miles from the spot on the parkway where she'd been hit by a stock trader who'd had three martinis and was heading back to his beach house.

"I don't remember it at all," she'd said.

"The accident?"

She shook her head, closed her eyes with concentration the way she did now when she was having trouble getting out a word or phrase, then brightened as it moved to her lips. "The car."

It was a Honda Accord, but it didn't look much like anything anymore. There was still a pair of plastic sunglasses tucked under what remained of the windshield. He took a photo for her.

That weekend while she was visiting her parents—he'd claimed a bad stomach—he packed his things. He had a distant cousin in

Denver who owned some commercial properties and had offered him work. In the note he left, he'd tried to make it sound like a sacrifice on his part, not simple abandonment—he was encouraging her to party, and it was messing up her recovery. Giving her space was the best thing he could do for her. He was even leaving her his stereo system.

Born to run.

The job in Denver hadn't panned out, but Landis had found other gigs—construction, handyman work, whatever people were willing to pay him for—and had eventually moved down to the Springs because he felt it was time for a change, and because it was closer to actual mountains.

From the strange-looking church, he heard the sound of someone practicing the organ, although he couldn't tell what the song was.

No one had ever said a word to him about a baby, not Pam's parents, who looked at him with obvious distaste when he'd shuffled into her hospital room to stare at her, not any of the various doctors he'd gotten to stop for a moment to talk, even though he had no family status. He wondered what she'd have done, eventually, had things gone differently. Invented a miscarriage, too? Contrived to actually get pregnant and hope he couldn't count up the months correctly? But that hadn't ended up mattering, because in the end there was nothing, not even the lie itself—her mind was wiped clean of it, too.

FOUR

She was supposed to fill out a bunch of forms. Emily lay on the floor playing with Legos, and a dog-faced woman with a little boy on her lap sat across from them, staring right at her. The boy's nose ran freely. Bernice thought of all the germs that must be floating around the room and shuddered. *What is the main reason for your visit today?* Carefully, she inked in the word "Fever." She read each of the following questions carefully before ticking off the "No" box, the accumulating weight of what she did not know about her own daughter growing like a tumor in her head. AIDS, no. German measles, no. Hepatitis, no. Allergies to medications, no. Major surgeries, no. The child was five—how much could have happened to her so far? Lots, of course. Lots.

Finally, when she felt she'd done her best, she turned in the clipboard. After another ten minutes or so, they were descended upon by an acned nurse in Minnie Mouse scrubs who singsonged "What a lovely little girly!" and led them to a room where she weighed Emily and took her *temperwemperture.* The child was not amused by the baby talk, and Bernice loved her for that. They looked at each other and shared something. The world is full of these people, she tried to say with her eyes. But not everyone. You have to remain hopeful. Then they were back out in the waiting area, with its vague scent of rubbing alcohol and throw-up, and flowery wallpapered walls. FastCare, the sign outside read—some corporate approach to medicine. Bernice hadn't been for a checkup herself since she was pregnant. She'd hated that doctor, Peregrine Stine, whom she'd suspected of being another born-again creep. She couldn't get over the idea that she'd accidentally walked into her own version of *Rosemary's Baby*. Emily went back to the Legos, and Bernice picked up an old copy of *Time* and looked at the ads.

Another nurse brought them to an examination room, where they had to wait again, which they both did quietly. The doctor knocked and entered. He was young, with a reddish nose and glasses, and looked like a third-rate comedian, but he didn't try to be funny. He listened to Emily's chest, poked a tongue depressor into her mouth, shined his light into her eyes, then peered into her ears.

"Well," he said.

"It's been like four days."

"How's her appetite?"

"What appetite?"

"I see. Aren't you hungry, Emily?"

She didn't answer.

"Emily?"

"Try calling her Pearl," said Bernice. "I know, it's weird."

"Aren't you hungry, um, Pearl?" he asked.

She shrugged. "Sometimes."

"Do you have any favorite foods?"

"Pop-Tarts," she said. "And spaghetti."

"But not together."

"No," she said. "That's not a good idea."

"Wise." He returned to Bernice. "It's an infection. Otitis media. You'll just want to keep an eye on her temperature, make sure she's well hydrated." He studied her forms for a moment, then looked up. "Do you have a regular pediatrician?"

"Oh, sure," said Bernice. "Back east. We're just out here visiting right now."

He wrote something on a pad. "Give her these, too."

"Give them to her where?"

"In the ear. It's an ear infection."

"It is?" Relief flooded her—just knowing something specific was so much better than the vague feeling of dread she'd been living with, the expectation of calamity and failure. "How did that happen?"

"Impossible to say. Kids get them. But she should be over it soon enough."

She wondered if the red spot on his nose embarrassed him. She wondered if maybe he wasn't such a good doctor, what with working at this Jack-in-the-Box clinic. "But other than that, she looks pretty good to you?"

He nodded. "Oh, yes, I'd say so."

"Nothing I should be, like, watching out for or anything?"

"Keep her oil changed and new tires on her and she'll run forever."

She examined the prescription he'd torn off. "And I just take this someplace?"

"That's right. I've got some samples I can give you, too." He dug around in a drawer and came up with two little cardboard boxes. "That'll start you up. She should be feeling better in a few days."

"Where would you suggest?"

"For what?"

"Where would you suggest I take this?"

"Any pharmacy will do. Albertsons."

He had a wedding ring on. She thought about his wife, his house, the life that she was only seeing the very tip of. "Do you like Eddie Murphy?" she asked.

His eyebrows lifted, little furry drawbridges.

"Not the later stuff," she said, "but back when he was funny. You can rent it on video. He did one skit where he pretended to be white for a day, and suddenly he found out that everyone else was in on something." Vasily had had a fascination with Eddie Murphy, in particular the movie *48 Hours*, but also compilations of old *Saturday Night Live* routines, and she'd sat next to him for repeated viewings, the two of them smoking cigarettes, he barking his hyena laugh. "Like, he gets on a bus and there's one black guy sitting reading a paper, and then at the next stop that guy gets off, and as soon as he does, the bus turns into this big party where they're serving drinks and there's balloons and confetti."

"Balloons?"

"Exactly. And when he buys a paper—this was before he got on the bus—the guy at the newsstand won't take his money. White people don't have to pay for things, it turns out."

"I don't watch that much television."

"Just once, I'd like to get on that party bus, that's all. But I guess if I want that to happen, I'll have to disguise myself like I'm white."

The doctor was now thoroughly confused. "But you are white."

"I know, I know." How to explain it to this person? It was impossible. He was a member of it, that other world they wouldn't let her be a part of. Or was it just that she'd chosen not to be? "Listen, I'm sorry. Thanks for these." She put the samples into her purse.

"Would she like a lollipop?" he asked.

"I don't know," said Bernice. "Maybe we should ask *her*."

He bent down in front of Emily. "Would you like a lollipop?"

"Yes, please," she said, and Bernice was filled with pride at how polite her child was, even if this had nothing to do with her at all.

The doctor stood back up. "They have a jar of them out by the desk," he said. He tore off a sheet of paper from his clipboard and held it out. "Give this to them, too. And remember, plenty of fluids!"

The bill came to an even one hundred dollars. She paid with her credit card. When she got herself situated, she'd have to contact Visa, let them know she'd moved. All those things she'd done to establish herself—cable, phone, her Pikes Peak district library card—all those things that made her *her*, she'd simply walked away from. Again. She wanted to be someplace. To be there, and to belong there. She signed the slip, handed it back to the receptionist.

"Thank you," she said to Emily as they exited the building into the hot sunlight. "You were really good with all that."

"You're welcome," said Emily, taking her hand. "Do you feel better now?"

»»»»»

The next day they all piled into Gillian's Neon and drove to Nogales. They parked on the U.S. side in a big lot for five dollars and then walked to the border. As they were waiting to go through the gate, a Mexican boy of about twelve came sprinting past them, pursued energetically by a border-patrol guard who managed to catch him halfway up the block. The guard picked the kid up under one arm and hauled him, laughing, back to the other side. It was clear this was a game for the kid, and Bernice found it reassuring that the patrols weren't under a shoot-to-kill order. Not yet.

"What are they doing?" asked Emily.

"Well, we're here, in the United States. Over there, where we're going, that's another country. It's a lot poorer in Mexico, so those folks want to be over here." They were moving along toward the entrance, shuffling with the crowd.

"Why?"

"Why, what?"

"Why is it poorer?"

"I don't know," she said. "Because life isn't fair. Some people, like us, get all kinds of nice stuff. Other people have to live on tortillas and work for fifty cents an hour."

"Mexico used to be part of Spain," Gillian explained. "And Spain is a very poor country. I've been there. The people who settled Mexico brought their way of life with them."

"Where are you getting your information?" said Bernice. She wondered if the Paxil Gillian was on—she'd seen a huge vial of it in the medicine cabinet—was making her stupid.

"I did a Eurail pass the summer after my junior year."

"I don't think Mexico is poor because of *Spain*. Jesus Christ."

"Don't," said Emily.

"Don't what?"

"Say that."

"Isn't she—you know?" Gillian gave her the kind of look that Bernice associated with sex talk, or perhaps money.

"I have no idea what you are trying to say."

"Technically, I mean. If your mother is, then isn't it sort of automatic?"

"Are you trying to say 'Jewish?'" Emily sucked more water from the bottle Bernice had given her. Her skin still looked ashy—almost green—but now that Bernice knew the problem, she felt far more in control about everything. An ear infection! Kids got them all the time!

"Sure," said Bernice. "Absolutely. She's exactly as Jewish as I am."

"Jesus loves me," said Emily, brightly.

"Antibiotics love you," said Bernice.

"It's pronounced differently over here," said Gillian, brightly. "It's *hay-zoose.*"

"Gesundheit," said Bernice.

They emerged into a very different scene from the one on the U.S. side. The streets were strewn with trash, and there were dogs everywhere, those yellow, lowest-common-denominator ones that were the product of mixing and mixing breeds until you had more or less reinvented the Ur-dog, the one that had first hung around some Stone Age campfire whining for bones and begun the long process of training mankind to take care of it.

They did what they were supposed to do in a border town choking with hand-painted pottery and cheap leather goods and wrought-iron knick knacks. Gillian wanted to go into all the shops, while Bernice was mostly interested in finding a bottle of tequila—the thing she'd agreed to in the first place—and going back. She didn't like being away from the apartment in case Landis might call. But on the other hand, if he did call, it occurred to her that she shouldn't answer anyway. This had been her advice to Gillian about Kirk, and another reason for the trip to Nogales—a way to get her mind off him and not to be there in case he called, which Bernice had assured Gillian he would.

Finally, they headed to a restaurant Gillian knew about and recommended. It was on the second story, above a courtyard, and one wall was built right into the rock of the adjacent hillside. Men with guitars wandered from table to table singing the "Ay yi yi yi" song and asking for tips, and Bernice wondered at what point it was that her life had turned into a bad play with no director.

They ordered off the English menu, a blackboard that the waiter brought over and held up for them. There was no pasta, but Emily liked corn chips and Bernice had discovered that she'd also eat guacamole, so they got some. When it came, Emily lowered her head.

"Stop doing that," said Bernice.

Emily's eyes were closed, her small face scrunched up with intensity.

"What do you pray for?" asked Gillian.

"That the cook washed his hands," said Bernice. "That the avocados were picked by union labor."

"No, seriously." Emily had finished and now picked a chip out of the bowl. "What?"

"I prayed for Mommy."

"Which Mommy is that?" asked Bernice. "Because this one doesn't need praying for, as I think I've mentioned to you before. I can't speak for that other lady you used to live with, though. She might be in all kinds of trouble."

Emily looked at her the same way Mrs. Charno had back in seventh-grade French class when Bernice had pretended not to be able to read the passage called "Dimanche en Famille," even though they both knew she was just doing it to be difficult and make points with her classmates.

"Both of you." She smiled. "In heaven, it's always sunny, and you don't have to eat asparagus."

"You don't like asparagus?"

"I like Archibald Asparagus. Do you know Archibald Asparagus?"

"Do you know what she's talking about?" asked Bernice. "Because I sure don't."

"I think it's something from a kids' show," said Gillian. "Is that right?"

"Emily," said Bernice. "Or Pearl. Listen to me. That could be Tucson you're describing. Do you understand? You don't have a demon in you, you have an ear infection. You don't have to eat anything you don't want to, ever. And sunny days—well, you'll have a lot of them. And then sometimes it will rain, but then that will just make you appreciate the sunny days even more when they come back. But most important of all is this: You are not a Christian. I know they told you Jesus wants you for a sunbeam, or whatever, but it isn't true. Say it after me, OK? I am not a Christian."

"Bernie?" said Gillian. "Maybe you're being a little hard on her."

"Later on, if she has to be something, she can go ahead and decide for herself, but this has to be stopped right now."

"I can't," said Emily.

"Can't what?"

"Can't say that."

"Sure you can. Just open your mouth and repeat after me: I am not a Christian." She pronounced each syllable individually. "See?"

Suddenly, Emily exploded. It was remarkable, really—zero to sixty in less than a second. A sound came out of her so anguished and high pitched, that for a moment Bernice thought the child must have been bitten by a snake. It repeated a few times, blasts on a factory whistle, before she moved on to something more recognizably like crying, her entire body heaving, wracked with sobs. Her nose had started to run, her face was red, and her little hands were clenched into frustrated fists, which she pounded against her own chest. It was as if for the past week the child had held on to every bit of her frustrations and emotions and was now letting them out in one great torrent.

Everyone in the restaurant turned to look at them. "Oh, boy," said Gillian. "You really pushed her button."

Bernice was alarmed. "Do you think she's OK?" She put an arm around Emily, who didn't acknowledge her and just continued crying, though now her wailing had turned to something almost like a whisper, in between short gasps. "Baby, are you OK?"

Gillian drank some of her water. "You know, in a way, this is the most normal I've seen her be. I mean, *this* I recognize. That other stuff, the junior Pat Robertson act, that's strange."

She was right. These were losing-your-favorite-doll hysterics, these were staying-up-way-past-your-bedtime hysterics.

"You can be anything you want," said Bernice. "I'm sorry. Mommy's sorry. Mommy's got her own problems, but they have nothing to do with you." She thought how, in fact, they had everything to do with her, but she didn't elaborate. Right now, the thing was to get the child back to her former, mini-adult state. "What about ice cream?" she said. "I'll bet they have ice cream here."

That seemed to help. Emily's sobs stopped, except for an occasional one that shook her like a hiccup.

"Perfectly normal little girl," said Gillian.

But what Bernice was thinking was that if normal meant this, she was going to need some help. "You ever go home anymore?" she asked.

"Christmas, usually," said Gillian. "And then back when my mom was getting chemo. But I don't like it there." Gillian was originally from Binghamton, New York, and both her parents were psychologists. "The place is horrible—no sun, ever. I want to blow it up."

"Shhh," said Bernice. "They'll hear you."

"Who?" asked Emily. "Who'll hear?"

"Them," said Bernice. "The government." She pointed her eyes upward, as if an FBI spy camera might be embedded in the stucco ceiling.

"Anyway," said Gillian, "you can't ever go home. Home isn't a real place. I mean, it is, but only partly. It's also connected to time and people and just the way the world was back when you were younger, and who you are inside, or who you were. There's nothing sadder than walking along a street that used to mean something to you and finding out it doesn't at all anymore, that you've moved on and it's just a street."

Bernice thought about a patch of sidewalk she'd always loved near the Walters Gallery, where there were two long, dark stains that looked like the stretched-out legs of a pair of pantyhose. Her mother had pointed them out to her.

"Anyone for dessert?" asked Gillian.

Bernice nodded. She noticed that Emily was still looking upward, trying to figure out who it was besides God keeping an eye on them.

FIVE

The address turned out to be a small house about a half mile up from the center of Manitou. Landis went there a little before ten, after treating himself to Vietnamese food at a place he liked out on Academy, then going to the mall and pumping quarters into the ski machine. He'd skied a few times growing up, but never really got the hang of it, and skiing in New Jersey was sort of a joke, anyway. The first time, his dad had taken him, back in the days of lace-up leather boots. In high school he'd gone on some midweek excursions to Vernon Valley, but those had been more about smoking dope than anything else. When he'd first come to Colorado, he'd had a vision of himself, a solo figure gliding expertly down vast fields of white, past half-buried aspen and spruce, but money had been an issue, and then he'd hurt his back. The machines they had at the mall made you feel as if you were in the Alps on a beautiful day. He liked how the image on the screen responded to the way he moved his feet, angling and carving through the imaginary powder. This was his secret, that he liked to do this. A virtual Franz Klammer.

The house smelled like must and fried fish, and there were people standing around in little clusters not saying much to each other, some who looked up briefly when he entered. It was a young crowd, and maybe an educated one—there were women with academic-looking eyeglasses, guys with beards. He sensed a certain desperation in the studied nonchalance around him. He searched the refrigerator, took the cheapest beer he could find, and headed out the back door to the yard.

Robin was standing looking at the fire, which seemed to have part of an old desk in it, along with a pair of skis and a bowling ball. "I told him it wouldn't do anything," she said.

"It might melt."

"You think so?"

"Seems a good bet."

"I figure it will just sit there. I don't even predict a glow. What's it made of?"

"Plastic," said Landis. "Or rubber, maybe."

"You came," she said. "I didn't think you would."

"I like parties."

They stood together in silence watching the bowling ball.

"We don't have to stay," said Robin. "We could go someplace. To tell you the truth, I hate these people. They're Magic Bussers. Street theater crap. Some of them are, anyhow. It's a cult. They plan public performances, and they all write the scripts together. Art isn't democracy, you know. Only nonartists—only people without the vaguest notion of what art is—would ever think it is. Art is the opposite. If anything, it's fascism. One person decides everything, and fuck you if you don't like it. That's art. What do you think?"

"Are you an artist?"

"Ha!" she said. "You're pretty funny."

Landis wondered what Bernice would think about any of this, or if she knew any of these people. She kept to herself. The time he'd suggested they could go to the museum up in Denver, she'd just shrugged and said, "Why?" But in the park one day, there had been a group of kids making a wall of paintings together—each of them worked his or her individual square, and then they were all assembled together into one huge canvas—and she'd wanted to join in, and had even made Landis paint a square, too. He'd tried doing his own work boot, but it hadn't ended up looking like much. Bernice had painted a pair of squinting eyes.

"I once knew this guy who worked for Bob Dylan," he said. "The guy would ask Dylan after a show if everything was OK. Dylan said things to him like, 'More green, man. Put in a little more green on the guitar.' Or he'd say, 'The drums are too red, man.' That's the kind of stuff you get to say if you're a genius."

"You married or something?" asked Robin.

"Oh, it's not like that."

"So what is it like?"

He took a sip from his beer. The bowling ball split in half with a sound like a popgun. "I really don't know much about art," said Landis.

"Here's what I'd like," said Robin. "The guy whose place this is, Leroy? We used to go out. Only now we don't, and he sees some Magic Bus skank. So what would be great is if you and I looked like we were together, and maybe even left together." She grabbed his arm and gave it a squeeze. "You wouldn't be required to put out, although we could see what developed. Mostly, this would be about making an asshole feel bad."

"I don't know," said Landis. "I'm supposed to make a phone call."

"You can make a phone call. I've got my cell—you want to use it?"

"No, that's OK." Telling Bernice he was at a party didn't seem wise.

"I hate my cell," she said. "It's a leash. It's like being on house arrest. When we were dating, he called all the time to check on me. 'What are you doing?' he'd say, all innocent. And I'd be, like, 'I'm taking a crap, if you want to know.' He was crazy jealous—it drove me nuts. But now, now he's got his skank. Of course, he invited me to his party, because we're still friends. Friends. Do you think you can be friends with someone you used to fuck but now don't anymore?"

"Never tried," said Landis. Robin wore a motorcycle jacket with the sleeves cut off, so you could still see the elaborate etchings on her arms. There was a dragon on one. He couldn't see the other.

"You have any tats?" she asked, noticing him noticing.

He shook his head. "Never got my ear pierced, either. All that started a couple years after me."

"So you weren't allowed?" She stepped right in front of him, close. Her jacket was open, and she pushed up against him, smashing her mouth against his, moving her tongue around. He could feel her ample breasts against his chest, and without really thinking about it, he put both hands behind her and squeezed her ass.

"Hey," she said, stepping back. "I didn't say you could do that."

"You didn't say I couldn't."

"Do you think he saw?"

"I don't even know who he is."

She gestured with her head toward a short guy with spiky hair and a Che Guevara T-shirt a few yards away, by the fence, backlit by a tiki torch. He had glasses and was laughing in a very fake way while holding forth on something to a group of three other people who seemed to hang on his words.

"He doesn't look like he saw."

"Hell, then. I'll just go tell him we're leaving."

She walked off, and Landis did not watch her. He felt embarrassed by this, and wasn't sure how exactly he'd agreed to whatever it was he'd agreed to.

They left his truck where it was and took her car, an old red Subaru. She wouldn't tell him where they were going. She had a six-pack on the floor of the passenger side, and he opened one for her, which she held between her thighs as she drove them down into Old Colorado City. She drove a little too fast, he thought, and he didn't care much for the death-metal tape she put in, but he tried to just relax.

She pulled over in front of a small, brick office building and led him around to a side entrance. "I work part-time for this guy," she said.

First, she showed him the back room, where there were various molds and casts out on a table, dentures that reminded Landis of joke-shop chattering teeth. There was an antiseptic smell to the place, vaguely sweet. She took him to the examination room and switched on the lights. "Go on, have a seat," she said.

He did, leaned back, stared up at a video monitor. "You sure this is OK?"

"Oh, yeah," she said. "It's fine." She was fumbling around in a cabinet. "There," she said. Music began to pump out of speakers hidden in the walls.

"I hate the Grateful Dead," said Landis. "And for some reason, I can't seem to get away from them."

"Resistance is futile," she said. "Anyway, different music for different activities." She had something in her hands.

He hopped up out of the chair. "How did you say you know this guy?"

"I work for him."

"Work how?"

"Office stuff, phones. He's a drummer, and we dated for a while."

"So you *can* be friends with someone you used to . . . you know."

"What makes you say 'used to'?" Her eyes seemed lit—it was a quality he recognized. He wondered why he kept finding himself with chemically unbalanced women. She turned around and adjusted a couple of dials on a little panel below the counter. Then she put a mask over her face and drew three deep breaths. She took it off. "That's the stuff."

"Whoa," said Landis. "You sure that's safe?"

"Come here." She stepped behind him, put the mask over his mouth and held it there with one hand, her other moving lightly over the front of his pants. "Feel anything?"

"I don't know," Landis said into the mask, his voice muffled. "You?"

"I think so. Yes, definitely."

Tentatively, he inhaled the sweet gas. He'd never had it before. Dentists had always just shot him up with Novocaine or used nothing.

She stepped away from him, settling herself into the chair and putting on the mask. Her expression had turned dreamy. She was old enough to be a mom, he thought, and then he realized he had no evidence she wasn't one. There were hollows around her eyes, and he wondered what she thought of them, or if she thought of them. He felt dizzy from the gas, although not particularly like laughing.

"You know what's sexy?" Robin said, leaning back, holding out the mask for him to have another whiff. "Dentists' chairs."

"Oh yeah?"

"Imagine if I were passed out in this one, for example. You could pretty much do anything you wanted to me and I wouldn't know. Have some more."

"What if someone comes? The police, for instance. Why would the lights be on in a dental clinic on a Saturday night?"

"Oh, he's in here working late all the time. Weekends, too. Here, have more."

He did. A lightness moved through his brain, circles and stars dancing in Hollywood musical choreography. He noticed she'd unbuttoned her jeans, the top two buttons, exposing the upper part of her purple satin underwear.

"But he's not coming tonight?"

"Who?"

"Your boss."

"These are the rules," she said, ignoring the question. "You can watch, but you can't touch." Taking another long hit from the mask, she let it dangle by her chin, reached down with both hands and pushed her pants and underwear down to her knees, revealing a shaved pubic area with labia that effloresced like the edges of an exotic mushroom. She licked her fingers and began to masturbate, slowly, eyes closed.

Landis wasn't sure what to do. He'd heard of things like this happening, but had never quite believed in them.

"Oh," she said. "Mmmm."

"Um," he said.

"Shhhh," she said, peering out at him through one eye, just for a moment, then closing it again.

The "Ode to Joy" beeped out in asynchronous contrast to "Friend of the Devil," and without any noticeable shift in rhythm, Robin reached into her pocket and removed a phone, which she flipped open with one hand, the other continuing to massage herself. "Hey," she said.

Landis helpfully went to the stereo and turned down the volume, then began to make leaving movements.

"No." She waved at him to stay. "It's all right. I'm with him now." She smiled, listening, her left hand paused for a moment. "That's right. No. At the office. I'm in the chair." She winked at Landis. "Uh-huh." She began to move her hand again, this time quite dramatically, and she groaned a bit into the phone. Then she held the phone out for Landis to take, which he did. He held it up to his ear as she worked herself with a new intensity, one hand holding her lips apart, the other rubbing up and down vigorously.

"Buddy?" said a voice.

"Yeah?" Landis answered.

"Tell me what's going on over there, really."

"Well, I can't say. Nothing for you to be concerned about, at any rate."

"What did she tell you about us? Never mind. It's probably not important." Landis heard the sound on the other end go muffled, as if the guy had his hand over the receiver. He'd turned away from Robin, who was now making sounds like a singer warming up for choir practice. The guy's voice came back, clear, deep, and nasal. Landis was glad for having something, anything, to occupy himself. "Tell me what she's doing."

"Nah," said Landis.

"Why not?"

"Wouldn't be right."

"I can hear her."

Robin's legs were spread out over the arms of the dentist's chair now, her pants kicked off and on the floor.

"OK, then, if you won't tell me what she's doing, will you at least tell her something for me?"

Landis retrieved his beer from the counter where he'd left it next to a poster about gum disease. "What?"

"Tell her Summer Adelman is giving me head, right now."

Landis held the phone away from his ear. "You tell her." He held it out to Robin, who took it without stopping what she was doing.

"Oh," she said into the phone. "Oh, God."

"That's it," said Landis. "Thanks for everything." He pushed his way out of the room and went back through the hallway, letting himself out by the side door, the way they'd come in.

He was outside by the curb trying to figure out how he was going to get back to his truck when Robin emerged from the building, fully dressed.

"Don't do anything on account of me," said Landis. "I don't want to break up a party."

"I'm sorry." She poked at him with an outstretched finger. "I didn't know he was going to call. Well, maybe I did." They stood in silence for a while, Landis feeling embarrassed and a little perplexed at how the events of the past few days had deposited him here, on this particular patch of concrete, staring at traffic. Finally, she asked, "You want to get coffee?"

At the Waffle Barn, they both had the Big Breakfast. It was 2:00 AM. The old couple opposite them—a scowling woman and her blank-faced husband—reminded him of a painting in a book Bernice had once shown him where all the people in it had distorted features and smeary eyes. That, she had said, was the real world. Our brains and eyes just compensated for it so we wouldn't be too scared.

"How about telling me what's up with you?" she asked.

"What do you mean?"

"I mean something's up. It's pretty obvious. You rob a bank?"

He was tempted to explain, but thought it would probably be a mistake. He put a third cream into his coffee. "How's Tate doing, anyway?"

She stared at him hard. "If you know that sonofabitch, you also know that no one who knows him gives a shit how he's doing."

"The last gig he called me for was some college kids who didn't think they even had to pay—they just figured the sound guy came free. I had to have a long talk with one of them, if you know what I mean."

"You're dodging the subject. That's OK, though. Dodge away. You don't have to tell me."

He poked at his eggs. "Say you had a locking mailbox, and you didn't feel like locking it," he said. "But the mailman, he won't deliver to an unlocked box. Regulations, or something. What would you do?"

"Lock the box," she said. "You thinking about becoming a postman?"

"I'm with this woman."

"We already established that. I guess that's why you don't feel like playing dentist, huh?"

"She's got a kid. Only she gave it up for adoption. And then she changed her mind. Kid's five now, lives here in town. Except we sort of boosted her the other morning."

"You boosted someone else's kid?"

"Yeah."

"There's another word for that."

"Not someone else's. My girlfriend's. I told her this was the wrong way to go about it, but she wouldn't listen. I think she'd had this plan for a while, but I don't know if she'd have done it without help."

"Which has *what* to do with mailboxes?"

"That's this chick. She wouldn't lock her mailbox, and she'd rather not get her mail than lose a stupid fight with the postman. Do you see? I didn't have much choice. This was going to happen, and I had to either go along or get out. I didn't want to get out." He thought about how Bernice would sometimes disappear into her apartment for days at a time, turning out the lights, refusing to answer the phone, spending hours in bed under the covers. He'd attributed this to her not having Emily—to the frustration of being so close to her.

"What happened with the mail?"

"Eventually, the postman gave up and just started sticking it in the box anyway."

"So, she won. She got her way."

"She did. She's all about proving things, and she doesn't like being told what to do."

"This is serious," said Robin, laying down her fork. "Where did you boost the kid to?"

"I can't say."

"OK. Do you have someone you can talk to?"

"I just talked to you."

"I mean, like a friend or something?"

"You think I'm making a mistake?"

"Probably. But it seems like you've already made it."

"I don't want to go to jail."

"Yeah." She put out a hand and touched his briefly, then withdrew it. "I think you're a nice guy. Maybe too nice. What's the kid like?"

"Weird," he said. He thought about how she'd smelled vaguely of talcum powder and chewing gum, how she'd slept quietly most of the trip to Tucson, her mouth partway open. "A little on the religious side."

She wrote something on a napkin. "Here's my cell. I'm going to take you back to your car now. We've had enough fun for one night. But you can call me, OK? I hope you do. Maybe things won't work out with this crazy chick, or maybe they will. I like you. And in spite of what you may think after tonight, I'm real normal. Honest. I hope you'll call me."

Landis took the napkin. To the *o* in her name, Robin had added two eyes with a little smile underneath. He folded it and put it in his wallet.

"You know," said Robin, "that whole mailbox business? You say it was about proving something, but did it ever occur to you she might just have lost her key and didn't want to admit it?"

SIX

Tessa Harding almost never went into her husband's home office, but she wanted to see the photos again, and they were on his computer. David was out on his bike—he'd be gone for hours. After calling in sick the past three days, she'd gone downtown today to meet her Saturday students, only allowing herself to cry a little in between lessons—sweet Ashley Jackson, who was working on *Mikrokosmos*, dead-eyed James McMullen, who robotically pounded his way through the first *Invention*, falling apart at exactly the place where he always fell apart—and afterward she'd gone for coffee and a cookie because she hadn't been eating at all lately. She'd gotten through half the cookie before growing nauseated. Then she'd gone out and stood by the playground in the park and watched the children jumping in and out of the fountain, laughing, shouting. She'd never brought Emily here, but she found it calming to stand at the edge of all this hubbub and imagine that she was in fact a part of it, that one of these children in shorts and a T-shirt, or a little pink bathing suit, was hers. She saw a man who looked like the man in the photos cutting through the park. He was big, with an earnest, unremarkable face. He wore jeans and a black T-shirt, and he moved with the sort of lope she associated with stray dogs. What if they were still here? It seemed possible. There was that girl in the news who had been abducted, and it turned out later that she'd been living right in the same town for nearly a year and no one noticed. The man crossed the street and she lost sight of him.

David had wanted to call the police immediately, but Tessa had told him they should wait. "We know who it is, and we know why she did it," she'd said. "At some point, soon, we'll hear from her."

"She's just a common criminal," he shouted "I don't know why you would even want to consider her side."

She didn't explain that for five years she'd lived with the certainty that something like this was coming, that the happiness she was supposedly enjoying—she *was* happy, wasn't she?—was illusory, the brightly lit, glistening sunscape at the center of a hurricane, and that eventually God would reveal to her the true, darker nature of his plan.

She had her own computer—a laptop—but the cameras were hooked up to David's. There was one on the front of the house, another around the side. She hadn't wanted them, originally, but now she was glad he'd put them in.

Taped to the bottom of the monitor was a printed-out strip of paper that read "I believe in the bodily resurrection of the Just, and the everlasting punishment of the Lost."

Lost. She hated that word.

She went to Pictures and located the folder marked Webcam. In it, she found the images he'd captured of Bernice and the man. They weren't terribly clear, and the light was poor, but there was no mistaking the girl. The camera only went off at thirty-second intervals, and there was nothing of Emily. But the man was there. Tall, with dark, shoulder-length hair parted in the middle to reveal a high forehead, a nose that seemed just slightly off kilter, possibly even broken. He looked relatively strong. There was no real way to tell if it was the same person she'd seen this afternoon, she realized. Perhaps it was just that she'd *wanted* to see him so much.

Tessa hadn't known anything was wrong. David had already left for work, and she'd made herself a new pot of coffee rather than drink the sour-tasting stuff he'd left her. She'd gotten out the cereal for Emily, and also the milk. Usually, Emily came upstairs and they ate together. She'd listened to the radio, waited. It was going to be hot and dry again. The fires up in Pikes National Forest were under control, but not out. KCME was playing Glenn Gould, and she thought how it was probably going to be a reasonably good day. But Emily didn't come up for breakfast, and the sense that something was wrong began to creep over her, and eventually she walked downstairs—she purposely didn't hurry, because that would be admitting there was a reason for worry, and she couldn't see one—and opened the door to the empty bedroom.

In that one moment, her every fear came true. Even as she ran through the house, the alarm in her head giving way to panic, even as she shouted her daughter's name to the empty rooms, then started shouting nothing coherent at all, just sounds of anguish, like those some wounded animal might make, even then, she knew it was pointless. Returning to Emily's bedroom, breathing deeply to calm herself, she became aware of a faint scent that was almost pheromonal: Bernice. She realized, too, that she had been smelling it for some time—on the sofa where she watched TV, possibly even in her own bed. And so Tessa did not call the police, had called only David, who hurried home and confirmed, with the photographs, what she already understood to be true. Bernice, who knew the alarm code. Bernice, who might easily have kept a key. Bernice, about whom Tessa had wondered and worried constantly all this time, now come back, prodigal child, thief.

She peered through the blinds out into the sunny landscape of their neighborhood. The garbage men were coming, and she watched them stop at the house below with the noisy dog. Then the truck started up and groaned its way to their driveway, where David had put the cans out before leaving—he was incredibly reliable in this and other domestic ways—and the men emptied them. How could they do these normal things? How could life go on oblivious of what had happened?

Bernice had come to them in the summertime, left in the winter. Tessa had hoped they might be friends, and early on it had seemed possible, but the girl had turned resentful and just grown more so. Tessa tried everything she could think of to get through to her, suggesting shopping trips together, asking her what she would like to eat, trying to draw her out with questions about her family and interests. Almost everything she said was met with narrowed eyes, one-word answers. Tessa watched in envy as Bernice's body changed, her hair thickening, her stomach filling out. But it was like having a sullen teenager, or perhaps a delinquent under house arrest, living with them. In the seventh month, Tessa took her to the mall to buy new clothes. Afterward, they ate hamburgers at Red Robin, and out of nowhere Bernice broke the silence and said that one strange thing that Tessa still remembered: "You're better than him."

She pointed the cursor so it hovered over a folder marked Dental. Business records, probably, and none of her business anyway. Except why would he be keeping records at home when there were computers at the office? She hesitated. She should not look. They both understood what a good family was, and what the hierarchy was within it. David was in charge. Tessa considered herself a liberated woman in all the ways that counted. She thought for herself, she wasn't afraid of her husband, she had a job. But a marriage was like any other organization—there had to be an acknowledged leader or there would never be a clear direction and the whole enterprise would founder.

She clicked anyway. At first, she wasn't sure what she was seeing. She stood up and took off her glasses to rub her eyes. She put them back on and sat down again.

In front of her was a photo of a person hanging upside down from what appeared to be a clothes rack. She wore a blindfold and a black garter belt and nothing else. She was not particularly pretty or thin, and her makeup and heavily rouged lips added to the unreality of the scene.

Tessa shut her eyes and held her hands together and tried to summon some of the casual ease with which her husband was able to converse with the Almighty. "God," she said, "I just want to thank you so much for letting me find this picture, and giving me a window into what David is doing and thinking." She hesitated, unsure what else to say. Should she pray for his soul? She was and always had been thoroughly convinced of the essential goodness in David, and even in light of this evidence that he had—what should she call them? tastes?—so antithetical to anything godly, she still didn't think of him as tainted, particularly. She tried to imagine for a moment what it might feel like to be naked and suspended upside down from the ankles.

On the other hand, if you believed in a cause-and-effect world—and she and David did—then perhaps this was the explanation, the key. Sin brought punishment, just as inevitably as too much pie led to porky thighs and smoking led to cancer. She thought again of the man she'd seen today. An unwitting angel of the Lord? This was not the first time it had crossed Tessa Harding's mind that motherhood had never been her true destiny, but it was the first time she'd thought that the reason might be her husband.

"Please watch out for Emily," she said, "although I'm sure you are already. Keep her from harm and return her safely to us as soon as you possibly can." She stood and closed the photograph, the screen returning to the Rush album cover David used as wallpaper, an image of men in red suits moving paintings up the steps of a stone building with arched doorways, one of the paintings apparently on fire.

She walked down the carpeted stairs to the lower level, the second living room they'd more or less turned into Emily's playroom. The fireplace was ready to be lit, with wood stacked carefully, the glass doors she cleaned every Saturday so perfectly you almost couldn't tell they were there. Arranged on the stone ledge in front of it was the crèche scene from last Christmas that they'd left in place because Emily enjoyed playing with it, talking to the baby Jesus as if he were her own child, sometimes making up dialogue for the cow and the donkey. They had another nativity for the upstairs mantelpiece, but this one was Tessa's favorite—she'd found it in a shop downtown. It had been made someplace in South America, and all the figures were brown-skinned and lumpy, their painted faces like something a child would make.

Her baby was gone. Her husband was leading a secret life (or so it suddenly seemed to her—she had already moved on to imagining him in the strange scene, too, perhaps just off camera). She hadn't eaten more than the occasional bite of food for days now, and she was weak and light headed. She'd planned to take Emily clothes shopping tomorrow, after church and Bible class. In a few weeks, school would be starting up—Emily's first year at New Jerusalem, the school she and David had picked out for her. She felt helpless in just about every way—what was she supposed to tell those people? What was she supposed to tell anyone?

She wandered down the hall, past the photos of David's mother and father, of his grandparents and hers, of David with his long hair, playing his drums, and, of course, the ones of serious-faced Emily, those strange eyes that looked right at you and seemed to know so much more than she let on. As she had been doing nearly every day, Tessa went into the child's room and lay down on her tiny bed, closed her eyes, and wept. Then, when there was nothing left in her, when she had once again returned to the state she spent most of her time in these days—a combination of uncertainty and exhaustion—she went back upstairs to look at the rest of the pictures on her husband's computer.

SEVEN

Bernice found herself standing in her underwear on the balcony of Gillian's apartment, with no idea how she'd arrived there. Moreover, she was smoking a cigarette, which, if she'd really lit it while asleep, seemed more than a little dangerous. It was early morning; her watch read 4:31. Below her, a car door slammed shut, the engine fired, and the car pulled out, its tires squealing on the asphalt. Some couple had been fighting, and the sound of their voices, she realized, was what had brought her to her senses. She had no memory of going to sleep, only of sitting in the living room flipping through channels on Gillian's TV. It was quiet out now, although she was aware of a low hum, as if from a huge electric motor buried miles deep in the earth. She ground the cigarette out against the concrete wall. She had the sensation that it was she who had been arguing, with Landis, and she was full of anger. She paced, went inside and got herself a glass of water, considered, paced some more. Bastard. She hated him. He was an asshole, an abandoner, a person who strung together odd jobs, incapable of making a success of himself because he didn't want to. He did everything slowly, even sex, to which he had the same methodical approach he had to setting up the sound equipment at that dive club. Tweak a knob here, push a button there. He'd taken an eight-week course at some school up in Denver four years ago. Loser. She'd never, never have done this thing about Emily, never in a million years, if she hadn't thought she had his one-hundred-percent help on it. She was convinced that what she must do now was leave Gillian's and head back east. It humiliated her to sit waiting for a phone call that might never come; it humiliated her to stay in this town where she'd thought they might have a future. Tucson was ruined, and when she imagined the mountains that surrounded it, she was simply reminded of the Springs, which didn't help matters—if she and Emily were truly after a new life, they needed a new landscape.

Emily was sound asleep, her body radiating heat, her faint breathing regular and just slightly wheezy, like a squeeze toy.

"Pssst," Bernice said to her. "Hey."

No reaction. What did Emily dream about? Her old life? Her future? Jesus doing party tricks for her next birthday? (Water into wine, or chocolate milk? Bernice pictured a bearded man dressed up sort of like Mr. Peanut doing amazing things with colorful handkerchiefs.)

She took her jeans off the back of the chair where she'd draped them, stepped into the legs as quietly as she could. Emily's breathing had changed and was now even quieter, though still very regular.

Bernice packed her clothes into her duffel bag and put Emily's back into the Macy's bag they'd been using for them, then made her way as quietly as she could out the apartment door, down the concrete steps, and out to the parking lot and the car. The air was cool, but she knew what was coming—yesterday the temperature had reached 103. No wonder the plants around here looked like space creatures, hunkered down and covered in spikes. When the darkness faded, so would this pleasantness, and the heat would return.

She went back in and picked Emily up. Her head smelled salty and warm, and Bernice was astonished that this body, or a version of it, had been inside her once. She took her into the bathroom and shut the door. "You need to pee," she said, helping Emily onto the toilet. "Come on, now. We're going on another trip."

Still more or less asleep, Emily did what she was told, Bernice turning away to give her privacy, listening to the sound of it, thinking, *This is what it's like—you're so close to another person you might as well be them, and then one day they peel away from you, shuck you off like a snake does its old skin.*

"Where are we going now?" asked Emily.

"Hush," said Bernice. "You'll see. Trust me—we'll have fun."

She left no note, just shut the apartment door softly behind them. She didn't want Gillian to have any responsibility here, should the police somehow find their way to her, which struck Bernice as completely possible, given Landis's defection. Who knew what else he had done? She had to think of all the angles. She had to not be stupid.

They made their way to the car. The morning air smelled like flowers. With Emily securely fastened into the booster seat, Bernice turned the key in the ignition. The engine made a weak, hesitant noise, then coughed to life. Piece-of-crap car—she'd get rid of it as soon as she could. Another thing to hate about Landis—he'd ruined *her* car, then traded down for this embarrassing death trap. Nova. No-va. It had to be Spanish, she figured, for "won't go." This car was what he thought she was worth.

Going cautiously over the speed bumps, she drove them through the six different parking areas that defined the perimeter of the complex and out to the main entrance, where the balloons were just visible against the advancing light of the sky. The eight bays of the U-Do-It car wash across the street were dark mouths. She made a right and felt a certain excitement, a sense that once again her life was starting afresh, and that this time was going to be the one that counted.

After a few wrong turns she managed to get them onto I-10 heading east and was soon squinting into the direct sun, driving nearly blind. The car smelled old, and it was an unfamiliar kind of old—who knew who and what might have been in this thing over the years. Couples having sex, dogs licking the windows (she liked that idea), drug dealers transporting dope—maybe even murder victims—fast food from strange places that Bernice would never stop at. It should have felt like wearing someone else's clothes, which she did all the time—she'd picked up her favorite T-shirt, the one that said "Beech Boys Tree Experts" on it, in the women's locker room at the Y—but it didn't, it was more like living in someone else's house, and she'd done enough of that.

At a gas station outside of Wilcox, she filled up even though she still had a quarter tank. Her head hurt. She bought herself a coffee that tasted like tar, and a Mountain Dew and Fritos for Emily, who had been drifting in and out of sleep. She laid out Landis's Rand McNally road atlas on the hood and stared at the map of the United States, a medical diagram of a body in which they were a couple of insignificant cells floating in one extremity. It seemed to Bernice that the multiplicity of possible wrong choices she might make was overwhelming. Red roads or purple roads? Lubbock or Amarillo? Lubbock sounded stupid, and possibly full of cows. Amarillo might be worse—she pictured armored rodents wandering the highways stopping traffic.

"What do you think?" she asked Emily, who was tracing the loose trim on the car door with her index finger. "Amarillo or Lubbock?"

Emily said nothing.

"Sodom or Gomorrah?"

"Where is he?" she asked.

"Who, honey? Where is who?"

She continued to poke at the trim. "Daddy."

Bernice tried to think about what to say to this. There were a number of answers, depending on what the child thought. Bernice didn't even know what *she* thought anymore. "You're going to have to be more specific," she said. "Do you mean your Colorado Springs daddy, who you know was not your real daddy?"

She shook her head. "The other one. Your one."

"Oh, him." Of course—she meant Landis. She stared out across the highway, which was more or less deserted. The rising hills were sandy, harsh, seemingly devoid of life. "Gone," she said.

"I liked him," she said. "He was nice."

Bernice wanted to tell her no, he was not nice, but then she thought about how she'd made her cry yesterday and thought better of it. What was the point? You lied to children, that's just what you did. You lied to them, and at the same time you tried to teach them *not* to lie, and as they grew older they figured out that there was this whole double-standard thing with the world, and then they either grew hopelessly cynical or they stuck to their guns and believed what they believed, in spite of all the evidence to the contrary.

"Sure, he was nice," she said. "Maybe he'll come see us when we're back east."

"Are we going to your house?" she asked.

It occurred to Bernice that Emily saw her less as a mother than as a friend, someone she might have met on the playground—hell, they *had* met on the playground—and that the reason the dislocation and transience hadn't bothered her was that all along she'd figured there was something tangible and solid in her future: She'd be going over to Bernice's house. They were on a kind of extended play date, and maybe when they got to her house, Bernice's mother would be there with cookies and games to play and sleeping bags set out on the floor and videos rented.

"Yup," she said. "We're going to my house."

At which news, Emily's face lit up with a smile Bernice hadn't known the girl had in her. She wanted to frame it.

»»»»»»

Bernice made the call from a truck stop, Emily standing a few feet away staring through the glass of a vending machine with the fascination a normal child would have for a video game. "Dad," she said, "it's me."

"Hello," he said. He'd accepted the charges, which was a good sign, but now they were both silent, and she figured he was probably counting the seconds, watching them add up like taxi fare.

"I'm coming there," she said.

"When?"

"I don't know. In a couple of days. I'm driving, and I don't like to go too fast, or for too long."

"You should take regular rest stops and drink plenty of coffee," he said.

"Don't you want to know where I am?"

There was a fairly long silence before he spoke again. "I suppose you're somewhere between Colorado and Maryland."

Emily was still staring at the vending machine, which had in it things like Alka Seltzer, a pocket comb, playing cards, and tiny binoculars. The air smelled of French fries, with an undercurrent of bathroom deodorizer. They were in the hallway between the store area, where you also paid for your gas, and the restaurant, which was full of men with hats and sideburns who reeked of cigarettes. Bernice wanted one badly, herself.

"So, I want to stay at the house."

"I'm sorry. I'm afraid you can't."

It was what she'd expected. The hell with him. But she took a breath and tried again. "Please?" she said. "You're not there—someone ought to be around to keep an eye on it. And I need a place."

"What did you do?"

"What do you mean? I didn't do anything."

"I think you did. You need a place? Why? What happened to your place?"

"I left. Personal reasons, OK? Look, I'll pay you rent, if you want."

"The market rent for that house is considerable. I doubt you could afford it. And besides, I'm selling the house."

"I know you're selling the house. But you've been selling the house for two years now. Couldn't you just let me use it for a little while, at least until you really sell it? When that happens, I promise, I'll get out."

"I told you my answer."

"Well, where should I stay?"

There was a long pause. "You can stay on my sofa for a while. A couple of nights."

"You think I'm going to burn the house down?" When he didn't answer, she just said, "How's everything else?"

"Everything is a mess. Don't you read the papers?"

"I meant with you."

"I'm not complaining."

"You could if you wanted to. I wouldn't mind."

"Is it raining there?"

She looked over her shoulder through the exit door to the parking lot, where the asphalt was soft with the heat, the sunlight a relentless assault. "Not really," she said. "Kind of the opposite. Everything is on fire."

"It is here."

She waited for something, anything, but she knew it wouldn't come. He'd always been more interested in his art than in the people around him. "I'm bringing someone," she said.

"That's good," he told her. "You can share the driving. But two is too many for the sofa. You should probably stay with friends."

"OK," she said. "I'll just call up some of my friends."

»»»»»»

She'd bought Emily the comb, then showed her how to play it using a piece of paper between her lips and the plastic teeth, and now the girl wouldn't shut up. Bernice had the radio on, but they'd entered an all-country zone, and she hated everything that came through the buzzing aftermarket speakers some former owner had set badly into the doors. The engine made a droning noise, too, the dashboard rattled like a loose window in a storm, and, in general, it was as if she were surrounded by bees. Turning the radio dial hard to the left—was it coincidence that the more radical stuff on FM radio was all on the *left*?—she found something that came in clearly and sounded interesting. It seemed to be Native American chanting, and it sounded exactly the way white people did when they made fun of Native American chanting, a kind of hey-ya, ho-ya, hey-ya, ho-ya refrain. She pictured Hollywood Indians parading around a campfire, rhythmically slapping their mouths. In the back, Emily was humming through her comb what seemed to be a kazoo version of "Angels We Have Heard on High."

"Hey," Bernice said, "listen to this music. It's Navajo or something."

Emily stopped making noise.

"Do you know about Indians?" asked Bernice.

"Not really," she said. "Maybe."

"Well, before white people came to this country and discovered it, there were already people here, and those people were the Indians. They'd been here pretty much forever, and this was their country. Only we sort of took it from them." She was starting to wish she hadn't begun, since the truth was, she didn't have much in the way of facts about Indians to offer, nor was there a way to make this a story a child would want to hear.

"Why did we do that?" asked Emily.

"Actually, *we* didn't do anything. It was the Europeans. It was . . ." she stopped herself from saying Christians, even though she had a feeling the word was probably accurate. What else? There it was, that sense of entitlement, of knowing so absolutely and certainly that you were right and everyone else was wrong, to the point that you didn't even care if you wiped out entire villages, entire cultures. "Indians are very spiritual," she said. "Listen to this song they're singing."

On the radio, the voices continued to chant. After a few moments, Bernice realized that they were not chanting in Navajo at all, at least not all the time. Some of the words were clearly in English. It sounded as if they were saying, "Mickey Mouse and Minnie Mouse," and then something about how they lived down in Disneyland.

"Disneyland!" said Emily, excitedly.

"I guess you know about that, huh?" She looked up into the rearview mirror. "You feeling all right? You're not going to get carsick on me, are you?"

There was no response. She'd been good about giving the child her ear drops every four hours, and she didn't seem as sick anymore, but Bernice assumed that the next bad thing was just around the corner. She'd never been able to keep even a house plant alive.

"Mickey Mouse and Minnie Mouse," chanted the radio Indians.

"OK, that's enough of that." Bernice turned it off and they were left with only the high-speed rattlings of the ancient car. She tried not to think about how stressed the rusty metal probably was, how it wasn't unreasonable to imagine the whole thing coming apart like a low-tech version of the space shuttle, wheels heading off in all directions, she and Emily skidding along the asphalt on whatever remained of the undercarriage like tobogganers.

"Is it much farther?" Emily asked.

"Oh, yeah. A lot. I just hope we can make it in this piece of junk. Remember my car? That was a great car."

Emily blew a few notes on the comb.

"You know, I lived with those people, too—your other parents. I didn't spend as much time with them as you did, but we had the same room. Did you know that? I'll bet they never even told you. It looked different when I was in it, though."

"I know," she said. Then, after a moment, she asked, "How did it look?"

Bernice tried to remember. "Well, for one thing, it wasn't all pink on the walls the way they did it up for you. That happened about a week before you came. They had painters all ready to go, and then presto, change-o! We took down all of the postcards I had up of artists I like. Stanley Spencer. You'll like him—he was religious, too, but in a weird way. And Philip Guston. His work is funny. Let's see. I had my CD player, and my VCR. I watched a lot of movies with you, even if you don't remember them. Ate a lot of popcorn, too. Do you like popcorn?"

"I love popcorn," said Emily.

"Who likes popcorn?" Bernice said enthusiastically. When there was no response, she answered the question herself. "We like popcorn! Now, once again, who likes popcorn?"

"We like popcorn!" shouted Emily.

"That's what I'm talking about," said Bernice. "You probably like Preston Sturges, too, even though you don't know it yet. I went through a whole thing with his movies. *Palm Beach Story*, *Christmas in July*. They're in black and white. In the old days, everything was in black and white. Anyway, you asked about the room. There was a desk, and a desk chair, and I had an easel, but I had to promise not to use any oil paints because I was pregnant and we didn't want you coming out with two heads, so I tried doing watercolors. Which I incidentally suck at. Sorry, I shouldn't say 'suck,' I guess. I did some charcoal drawings. I wonder where those are?" When she thought back on those long months, mostly what she remembered was the intense isolation, the anger that threatened to blow her apart. A couple of times, just to scare them, she'd gone out to the bars, but pregnancy had erased any desire in her for drinking, and without that, the scene had seemed dumb. That last week, she'd slept in a nursery, her bags packed and ready both for the hospital and for her return to Florida—a former coworker of hers had a sister in Miami with whom she would crash temporarily—and the rest of her life. The last thing she'd seen before closing her eyes each night was the brand-new crib, empty and waiting.

"Yeah, I really hate watercolor," she said. "Do you like to make art?"

"Of course," said Emily. "I like to draw. And I like crayons."

"Maybe later we can try drawing together some, huh?"

"OK," she said.

"What else can you do? You can read, I guess. You know your alphabet."

Emily demonstrated that she did, and Bernice sang along with her.

"Well, we'll have to find you a nice school to go to."

"I'm going to New Jerusalem."

"How about numbers? Can you add or anything? What's two and two?"

"Four."

A truck that had been tailgating her for some time suddenly pulled out and passed, its slipstream making Bernice almost lose control of the car, just for a moment. She gasped and tightened both hands around the wheel. "I hate this," she said. She felt despair growing in her, despite her determination to be cheery and forward looking.

"And four and four is eight. And eight and eight is sixteen."

"That's great. That is amazing, actually. What else can you do?"

"'For God so loved the world, that he gave his only begotten Son, that whosoever believeth in him should not perish, but have everlasting life.' John 3:16."

"'Believeth'? What do you think that means?"

"I don't know," she said.

"And who was John?"

She was silent.

"Do you even know what death is?"

"Of course."

"Explain, then, smarty-pants. Tell me someone who's dead, for instance."

She was quiet, thinking.

"Dead people go away," said Bernice. "They just go away, and they never come back, period. And at first you're sad, and then you might be angry for a while, and then you just do your best not to think about them anymore." She watched the truck that had passed them get smaller as it accelerated toward the horizon, the legend "England" across its back doors brightly lit by the afternoon sun.

"I want french fries," said Emily.

"You do?" She felt suddenly hopeful. It was such a normal, such an un-Emily thing to say. "OK, then. Let's find some." They were in the middle of no place, but how far could it be to the next french fry? This was America, after all.

"With mustard," she said.

"That's weird," said Bernice. "I'm not criticizing you, but I want you to know, that's weird. Most people go for ketchup, though back where I'm from, you'll find people ordering them with gravy. I don't know why—it just makes the fries all soggy. But mustard? That's a new one on me." She was silent for a bit, thinking of various french fries she'd known and loved. The Sip 'n' Bite had good ones, particularly at three in the morning after you'd been out drinking hard. There had been a place in Atlanta, right near the campus, and she'd often had a whole basket for dinner, nothing else.

"I'll pray for them."

"For what?"

"French fries."

Bernice nodded. "OK, I will, too." In the rearview mirror, she could see Emily grin at this news.

"Hey, Emily," she said. "I just want to ask you something. Are you, like, OK with all of this? I mean, I know I never checked it out with you officially. Because here's the thing—if you hate it, there's always a way out, you know? It would be difficult at this point, and I'm not sure exactly what I'd do, but I could do something. Do you understand what I'm saying? You don't hate it, do you? I'm mean, you're not, are you? Just tell me you're not and I'll shut up."

"Not what?" said Emily.

"Not angry at me," said Bernice.

EIGHT

On Sunday, Landis went to the movies and took a hike on Section 16. Monday, he closed out his checking account, which still had a little over four thousand dollars left in it. He stopped by ProSound, but Kevin's truck wasn't there and the building was locked up tight. Landis felt disconnected, as if he were spinning in space, living outside of time. He'd eaten almost nothing but Mexican food, and his stomach was starting to hurt. It crossed his mind a couple of times to call Robin and ask her if she wanted to meet and talk some more. He wanted to tell her that he wasn't a criminal, and he wasn't dumb either, even if he had gotten into something a little over his head. It was just that he was changing himself, or trying to, at any rate. He'd abandoned one woman, years ago, when things got rough, and he didn't know if his karma could stand up to doing the same thing again. But it seemed a lot to explain, and he doubted she was the person to tell it to, anyhow. At Kaw-Lija's, a Mexican restaurant with a huge Indian's head atop it in the north part of town, he saw Devon having dinner with a pretty girl with makeup and big hair. Devon grinned at him as if he'd just won the lotto. Later, he drank beer at the Copper Dollar across the street, a tiny tavern with an oval bar that he'd always kind of liked, until the same songs had cycled around on the jukebox one too many times.

Tuesday morning, he left his nearly empty trailer, got himself eggs at the Purple Castle Diner, then drove to a 7-Eleven, went inside and got set up with a lot of quarters. He came back out to the pay phone and called.

"They're gone," said Gillian. "You missed them. She left."

"She did what?" Landis said, holding his free hand to his other ear to block out the street noise. His head hurt and his eyes felt as if they'd been dipped in candle wax and hung out to dry.

"Took her and left," said Gillian. "I've been looking around for a note or something, but I haven't found one. She just got up early and went. Yesterday."

"Did she say anything about where she might be going?"

"Not really."

"Think hard, OK? This is important."

"I know it's important. Do you think I don't know it's important? You're the one who ought to think. Where have you been? She's been waiting to hear from you. She probably thought she never would again."

"This is not my fault," he said. "Maybe she just went someplace for a few hours, like on a picnic or something. Maybe she'll be back soon."

"Picnic? Her stuff is gone, and she stripped the mattress and folded up the sheets."

A voice told him to deposit another dollar fifty, so he did, taking the quarters from the stack he'd placed on top of the phone box. A low-rider sixties Buick with gold roulette wheels for hubcaps pulled up to one of the gas pumps, its engine revving before falling silent.

"I'm coming there," he said.

"Why?" she said. "I'm telling you, she left. You should have called before. What happened to you?"

"I was busy," said Landis. "There was a lot to do."

"Maybe you should leave well enough alone," said Gillian.

"What's that supposed to mean?"

"She told me all about it. When that kid's parents find her, at least Bernice will have some kind of excuse. She is the mother. But you—you're not even related. I think what you did is kidnapping, no matter how you try to slice it, and if they press charges, you're going to jail. Actually, they may not even have to press charges—it's probably just automatic."

Landis didn't like being lectured, and he didn't like standing at a public phone while someone told him he'd be going to jail. "Where's she from?" he asked.

"Where's she *from*? What, are you serious?"

"She never said. I know it's back east someplace. I know about Atlanta, I know about Florida after she had the baby. She just—" he closed his eyes in frustration at all the games he'd let her play—"she never said where she was from. New York? Washington?"

"I find this hard to believe," said Gillian.

"I don't care how you find it," said Landis. "Philadelphia? New Haven? Why don't you just fucking tell me."

"Baltimore," she said. "But I doubt she'd go there. She's not on good terms with her dad."

"What about her mom?"

There was silence on the other end, and Landis fingered the diminished pile of quarters. He wondered if he shouldn't hang up soon—everything was monitored these days. You typed *Islam* into an Internet search engine and some light went off at FBI headquarters. You said *kidnapped* on a pay phone, and before you knew it, the cops were pulling up with sirens wailing.

"You don't know anything, do you?" said Gillian. "Her mother's dead."

"I didn't know. How'd that happen?"

"She told me she killed her."

"She what?"

"Well, that's Bernice. She speaks in code. I doubt she *actually* killed her, although I am pretty sure her mother is dead."

"Do you have an address?"

"Someplace. Maybe. You could probably find it yourself. Her dad's name is Don. I'm sure he's listed."

"Could you go look for it? Please?"

There was a pause. "Now that I think about it, she did ask me about going home."

"When?"

"In Mexico."

"You went to *Mexico*? Whose bright idea was that? I'm going to call you back later, is that all right? You look for the address, and I'll call you back."

He went into the 7-Eleven and scanned the front page of the paper for an abducted-child article, but found none. His breakfast was moving around in his stomach, and he thought he ought to find a bathroom. There was a deli across the street, Spooners, next to a running-shoe store.

Spooners held only a scattering of customers—a man in a

business suit reading the paper, two middle-aged women talking and laughing. A short guy with Down syndrome and a reedy voice greeted him like an old friend. "Hey!" he said. "Where you been?"

"Oh, all over," said Landis, who felt certain that if he'd ever met this person before, he'd remember him. "You know."

"Yeah," said the guy, his eyes tiny and set at angles in his face, like pinball flippers. "I know." He had a rag in his hand, and Landis realized that he must be working here. "All right, then."

"You bet," said Landis. And then he was left alone. A transaction had occurred between them, but he couldn't say what it was, exactly. The kid had glowed with good feeling, proud to be at his job. Landis inhaled the warm smell of the blueberry-and-almond muffins arrayed on the counter, and of the three flavors of coffee sitting hot in their brushed-steel urns.

He used the bathroom, then bought a coffee, brought it to a booth and stared at it. This was his fault. Why hadn't he just called? He took out the portrait Bernice had done of him one night on the back of a bar-tab receipt and unfolded it. It was remarkable—somehow, she'd captured everything about him with only a cheap ballpoint pen. His eyes, in particular, surprised him—he saw they looked like his father's. Bernice had entrusted herself to him, difficult parts and all. She'd put herself in his arms and he'd dropped her.

There had been problem moments before with Bernice. A week after they'd met, she'd shown up unannounced at his trailer when he was on the phone talking to Junebug, a waitress he'd been dating, and he'd held his hand up in a "wait-a-minute" gesture because the conversation was at a critical juncture, as he was explaining to Junebug that she wouldn't be seeing him again for a while, possibly ever. He was happy to see Bernice, happy that she felt free to come over without calling. A new relationship was like a new shirt or shoes, and he still had the excitement of unfamiliarity, that pride that he'd managed to find something so great for himself. But then he heard the angry, consumptive sound of the Hyundai's engine, followed by her tires spitting gravel, and she was gone, headed back up the drive toward the access road and, ultimately, the highway. He called her for an hour, but she wouldn't pick up. And when he drove over, she wouldn't answer the door. He stood there on the concrete walkway outside her door in the cold pressing her buzzer. Finally, she opened it. She had changed into a nightgown—a very old-fashioned-looking thing—and the look she gave him was withering. "What?" he asked. "What was all that about?"

"You can't do that," she told him. "You can't treat me that way."

"I was on the phone."

"With *her*?"

He had not, up to that point, made it clear that there *was* a her, but he found himself unsurprised that Bernice had intuited the circumstances of his life.

She allowed him in, but wouldn't speak, though he tried to make conversation with her, even after she buried herself back inside her bedclothes and put a pillow over her head. So he sat in the dark beside her for over an hour. Then she put a hand out toward him. Without saying a word, they made love until they were both sweating like marathoners.

He paged though the free paper's classifieds in the ridiculous hope that she might have left him a message there.

She could have found herself a place in Tucson. Possibly. Except Landis knew her well enough to know that if she'd left, she'd really *left*—gone someplace far away.

Where exactly was Baltimore? South of DC? North of it? He'd been past it before, he knew that, knew it was someplace along I-95, but he'd just never paid any real attention.

He went back to the 7-Eleven and dug his remaining quarters out of the pocket of his jeans, then dialed Gillian Cooper's number. She answered on the first ring.

"Did you find it?"

"Yes. It's old, though. It's off a sketchbook of hers she gave me." She read him the address and telephone number. "If she calls here, should I tell her anything?"

"Tell her what you like." He hung up the phone. "Damn," he said. He said it again and kicked at a rock on the ground, sending it skittering into a parking meter. Then he went to check the oil level in the truck.

NINE

"See that?" Bernice said to Emily, pointing up, as they walked from the illegal spot where she'd left the car. Baltimore's Washington Monument stood fifty yards away, its base like an emperor's tomb, the high column sticking up into the soupy evening, George himself atop it dressed in a toga and holding what appeared to be a lightning rod. "That's the father of our country. He never told a lie, and he had wooden teeth."

"If I had wooden teeth, I wouldn't have to brush them," said Emily.

"That's right. You just slap on another coat of paint. It's very convenient."

"Or buy more at the store."

"Exactly."

She found his new place easily enough, although she was surprised to see it had a steep set of marble steps, since the whole point of his moving out two years ago and taking this apartment had been to get *away* from steps. He'd written her a letter at the time, and she remembered how formal it was—no questions about her, only the single statement, "I hope you are well." Just news of the move and his knees. She'd been living in a musty apartment on the corner of West and Ninth in Miami Beach, a concrete box on the eighth floor of a building called the Sun Palace. The letter had made her cry. She hadn't wanted him to move.

Calling these things houses was ridiculous—they were mansions. People wouldn't have lived in them without a full staff, and all of them would originally have had their own coach houses. Her father's had a Greek revival front complete with massive Ionic columns. Looking up the front steps, through the glass of the front door with its elaborate wrought-iron decoration and heavy security bars, Bernice could see into the entrance hall, where a newel-post nymph held aloft a lit torch, an imposing staircase rising above and behind her.

She climbed the steps and pored over the brass mailboxes. Beneath the bottommost one, a piece of paper taped to the metal read, "Click—Terr. Rownaside." She stared at this for a while, wondering whether it was in some way about killing. Insecticide, parricide, homicide. Then she pronounced it in her head. *Around the side.* Humor.

She was fried. Her legs felt like noodles, and her entire body was buzzing. Her eyes were so sore and dry from staring out at the highway that she thought she might have done permanent damage to her brain and would for the rest of her life see everything with superimposed little white lines running toward her. They'd stayed in Amarillo at a Motel 6, then gotten up early and driven all day and well into the night, until they reached Nashville (another Motel 6); today had been more of the same. Only when they'd hit the mountains of Virginia and started seeing signs for Baltimore had it become real to her that she'd done this, that there would be an end to the traveling. The last challenge had been swinging around Washington, and the beltway traffic had nearly made her scream. But she hadn't. She hadn't. Instead she'd tried to keep up a stream of happy chatter for Emily, telling her about Dulles Airport and the National Gallery and the Mormon temple, the spire-topped towers of which rose up windowless and white like something from a science-fiction novel.

She walked with Emily around the side and downhill, past two sets of low, barred windows, to what she guessed was the side entrance of the house, a simple white wooden door in a brick wall with an unmarked buzzer. A few feet away at the curb there was a cast-iron post in the shape of a horse's head for travelers to tie up to and an oval lozenge of white marble for their descent. Across the street on the stoop of a crumbling brownstone, a fat man with a long beard sat watching her, drinking soda from a liter bottle. She ignored him and pressed firmly on the bell. There was no sound, so she pressed again.

Eventually she heard noises. There was a peephole, and she figured he was behind it, checking them out. He opened the door.

"You made good time," he said. He wore jeans and a white oxford shirt, flip-flops. His white hair rode his head like a wave. He looked down at Emily with surprise. "Well," he said, and opened the door wider. "What do you know?" He stuck out his hand toward Emily. "Don Click," he said. "Who are you?"

"Pearl," she said.

He gestured toward Bernice. "You go with her, do you?"

"Yes, I do."

"Pearl, do you like buttermilk?"

"I don't know," she said. "I don't think so."

"Well, we'll just have to find out. Come in."

On the other side of the wall there was a small courtyard accommodating a fire escape, two concrete planters with flowers in them, a couple of pieces of plastic lawn furniture, and a yellow Weber grill with a picture of Homer Simpson on it. They passed these things and entered the back of the house through another door that led them into a dim hallway.

"Kitchen's that way," he said, gesturing. "Rest of the place is over here."

"*The Simpsons*?" she said.

"You don't like *The Simpsons*?"

The next room was enormous—perhaps thirty feet across and at least twenty wide. The floors were polished hardwood, and the inner wall was brick painted white. The street-side wall bulged outward where the windows were. Peering out through the dusty blinds, Bernice could see the sidewalk, which was more or less at eye level.

"Welcome to the Bunker," he said.

"Great place." Bernice looked around. One end of the room had been arranged as a living area, with chairs and a sofa and a television set, all of which she recognized from the old house. There was a massive fireplace in the south wall, complete with fake logs and a set of fire tools. The other end of the room had been fitted out as a work space, with his easel and a desk with a computer.

"It used to be the kitchen for the whole house. I know the owner. Taught one of his sons, years ago. His brother lived down here, after he had a hip replacement. They made it nice, installed grab bars in the bathroom, rehabbed all the fixtures. But the brother got worse. Now he's at a nursing home, and I get his apartment. I call it the Bunker, but sometimes I think of it more as the Waiting Room. You know, like Florida is God's waiting room? Anyway, I get a very good deal." He looked down at Emily. "Buttermilk, right? I'll get you a glass."

"But I don't want it."

"Never know if you don't try."

"I'd take a beer," Bernice called out.

"I'll get you one," he said.

She pointed at the sofa, its weathered brown leather so familiar to her. It had been on the second floor, in front of the television. "Why don't you sit down?" she said. Emily made a face at her, raising her eyebrows dramatically.

"Where's your bathroom?" she called out, as she started opening doors. "Never mind."

Emily went first, with Bernice standing outside waiting for her, as she had done at every rest stop for the past three days. She didn't like to let her out of her sight—there were too many crazy people out there who wanted to kidnap little girls.

When she was done, they took seats in the living room area. Emily wore blue shorts and a flower-print top that had ketchup and grease stains plainly visible on it. Bernice needed to do laundry soon, maybe take her shopping. The child had a smudge of something on her cheek that looked like chocolate, and Bernice licked her thumb and rubbed at it to get it off.

Her father joined them and handed out the drinks, and they sat facing each other. She sipped her beer, which was so cold it hurt her teeth. "Any shows coming up?" she asked cheerfully.

"Nope."

"New work?"

"Some. I was at the studio today." He held up his hands, which had dried paint on them.

There was a long silence, and she felt a combination of embarrassment and impatience. Even his eyes, which flickered behind the lenses of his rimless glasses, seemed to lack any real interest.

"We saw a fire," offered Emily, pushing her untouched drink away from her on the coffee table.

"Really," he said. "Where was that?"

"On the side of the road."

"In Oklahoma," said Bernice. "This truck was just burning up. Black smoke everywhere, cops." She remembered how the scene had taken so long to unfold in that flat, lifeless landscape: first the distant smudge against the sky, the way it grew as they approached, finally the small line of traffic that proceeded past the truck itself at a respectful twenty miles per hour, waved on by a highway patrolman in a storm-trooper uniform. It had remained in the rearview mirror for miles. "She won't shut up about it. Have you thought over the house question a little more?"

He took a drink of his buttermilk, then put the glass down. "I didn't think there was anything to think about."

"So you're saying no?"

"No, I didn't think about it, or no to the question?"

"What do you think?"

"I don't know what I think. I was asking you."

"No to the question."

"Ah." He leaned back and pressed his hands together. "Pearl," he said. "It is a pretty name. You are, what, about five?"

She nodded.

"I envy you. Five is such a good age. What kind of an artist do you plan to be? Painter? Sculptor? Performance?"

"Come on, Dad. You think she has any idea what she wants to do when she grows up?"

His eyes widened in mock surprise and he sat up straighter on the sofa. "I did."

"Well, you're different. She doesn't know, and she shouldn't know. She's a freaking *kid*."

"I'm going to be a missionary," said Emily.

Bernice looked at her. "Not anytime soon, I hope."

Don Click smiled. His teeth were the yellow ivory color of aged piano keys, or Bakelite radios, and Bernice was surprised to sense in him some relationship to death, not necessarily his own imminent death—in fact, he seemed quite healthy and vigorous, as he had all his life—but death as a subject of study, like the Italian he'd taken up years ago, when she used to hear him sometimes in his office repeating the phrases spoken by the recorded voices on the tapes: *Buongiorno. Come stai? Bene, grazie.* He got up and went into the kitchen, leaving them alone again.

Bernice picked up Emily's buttermilk and gave it a sniff. "Don't drink this—it's gross."

He returned with a box in his hand. "Tastykake, anyone?" he asked.

Bernice shook her head. Emily accepted the chocolate cupcake with such obvious enthusiasm she wanted to give her a poke. *Don't trust him,* she wished she could say. *Don't. Don't.*

"They're my vice," he said. "And for some reason, they always seem to be on sale." He smiled again, a bit of cake stuck in the corner of his mouth.

"It won't be for long, Dad," she said. "I promise."

He tossed a key onto the coffee table. "When I told you no, I didn't realize your situation. Obviously, this is different. There's no furniture in the master bedroom, so you'll both have to stay in your old room. Those beds are still there. Nothing to eat, either, and the whole place could probably stand a good cleaning. You'll find plenty of supplies in the basement."

She stared at the key. "You're sure?" she asked. "We could just do the sofa thing."

"Oh, no. You go on."

"I appreciate it."

"Don't make me sorry. Don't make this go wrong some way."

"I won't."

"And no smoking there, all right?" he said, catching sight of the pack in her purse. "You really ought not to, particularly now. What do you think, Pearl? What do you think of your mother's smoking?"

"I don't know," she said. She'd finished her cupcake and her eyes were half closed.

Bernice picked up the key and stood. "We're both pretty pooped, so maybe we should get moving. You don't have anything to worry about, I promise. And I'll call you tomorrow."

"It's unnecessary. I like to know where you are, but I don't need to hear from you. I assume you're capable of taking care of yourself."

"Sorry."

"Nothing to be sorry about. You'll find the phone still works, but there's no long-distance service. I had it turned off. You might want to look into that."

She felt as if the air were draining from the room. She wanted something from him, some acknowledgment—she was here, after all. She'd come all this way, piloting a tin can of a car with his own granddaughter in it. They hadn't died; they hadn't even had a flat tire.

"Question," he said. It was something he used to say to her, not only to find out about her life, to which she had decided to deny him admission, but also to spot-check her on things he was sure she wouldn't know. *Question*: Are those clothes what everyone is wearing at your school, or just you? *Question*: What are the Antipodes?

"All right."

"What are *you* working on?"

"Working on?"

"That's right."

"I don't know."

"You should always be working on something."

"I'm just hoping for a shower, Dad."

"What about a mural? You should consider a mural."

"Sure," she said. "I'll consider one."

"People want murals. I never did one myself, but I think maybe that was a mistake. There's money in murals." Don Click saw them out as far as the courtyard. "It was a pleasure," he said, stooping to shake Emily's hand. "I see great things in your future."

»»»»»

The neighbors were having a noisy barbecue in front of their stoop, and the smell of grilling hot dogs hung in the thick evening. They were a black family she'd never seen before, and they seemed to have at least ten kids, all different ages, some chasing each other around the sidewalk, others sitting on the steps. The green van in front of their house was adorned with American flag stickers on every available surface.

Rather than go in the front, Bernice led Emily along the breezeway, to the back alley. A tall, bony-looking man with an oversized head was checking the doors of the car parked in the space behind the neighboring house. She didn't think he was a thief—she didn't know what he was.

"Hello," he said, eyeing them suspiciously.

"Hello," said Bernice.

"It's not supposed to be here," he said.

"Is that your parking place?"

"No. But it doesn't matter. This car doesn't belong here."

"Well, what do you care then?"

He gave her a peculiar look, his head tilted to one side. "I care because I live here. Serve this guy right if something happened to his car, you know what I mean? Parking where he's not supposed to."

She didn't remember this person, either. He seemed like a nut. She'd only really paid attention to the kids: perpetually snot-nosed Ginny Lester up the block, two years younger, or Stefan Kurkowski, who'd shown her his penis one day in the crawl space underneath his parents' rotting back porch; for the most part, the other residents of the surrounding houses had remained anonymous, adult, and mysterious.

"You thinking of buying?" the man asked.

"I live here," she said.

He stared at her hard, then suddenly smiled in a fake way. "My mistake!" he said. "I know the old guy moved out. I keep thinking there'll be a For Sale sign one of these days. Probably worth a few bucks, this house. Well, none of my business, right? You have a good one!" He made a little gun out of his thumb and forefinger and pointed it at Emily. "Pow," he said.

"Pow," she said back.

They climbed the back steps that led to the kitchen door. Bernice had forgotten what Baltimore was like in summer, so airless and humid. There would be another two weeks of this to get through, at least.

The air inside the house smelled stale and mousy. Three phone books lay stacked on the radiator just inside the door. She locked the door behind them, stood for a moment taking in the strange feeling of being here again. The refrigerator was off, and she opened its door; it contained only a small, ancient box of baking soda. She found the switch and brought the appliance shuddering to life.

"We need to go shopping," Emily observed.

"Tomorrow. You ready to brush and go to bed?"

Emily nodded and yawned.

"Come on, then. It's up a bunch of steps."

She moved through the dining room to the center of the house, where the front stairs rose three stories, a small glass skylight overhead at the top. Emily looked practically drugged, so Bernice lifted her and carried her up to the first landing, then put her down.

"Whose house is this?" asked Emily.

"Yours," said Bernice. "For a while, anyway. One more flight. You hike this one, OK? I'm tired, too."

Her old bedroom was more or less as she'd last seen it, which at first she found surprising, but when she thought it through, she decided that this was not sentimentality on her father's part but the opposite—he'd simply been too lazy to change anything. And so there were the children's books she'd read, lined up on the shelves he'd built for her and painted himself. There were her stuffed animals, Ucello the horse and Bobo the dog. A clear plastic drop cloth had been thrown over the twin beds, which were made up and ready to be slept in. It was a good thing, too, because, everything in the house was coated with about a quarter inch of dust.

"Here it is," she said. "Our own private suite. Bathroom just outside the door. Nice view of the neighbors' back porches."

Emily took a step and tripped over an untied shoelace, going down on one knee.

"Ouch," said Bernice, helping her up. "You OK?"

The child nodded. She looked so tired. Bernice wondered how long she'd gone without noticing the shoelaces. There were so many things to worry about. What else was she overlooking? She opened the windows and turned on the ceiling fan, which helped a bit, but it was still pretty awful. The air outside felt as stale as the air inside.

She found an old green T-shirt of hers in the dresser and helped Emily get undressed and into it.

"It smells funny," Emily said. The hem was around her knees.

"You smell funny. It smells clean. You've just been on the road so long you don't know the difference." But it did smell funny, like fifty-year-old toast. "Hey," she said. "Why did you say that about being a missionary? Do you even know what a missionary is?"

"You go places and help people and bring them clothes to wear. Then you teach them about Jesus."

"OK," Bernice said. "I guess you know more than I do. That doesn't sound so bad. I mean the clothes part. People need clothes."

They brushed her teeth, then Bernice removed the drop cloth from the beds and tucked Emily into one. She arranged stuffed animals to either side of her for company, then gave her her ear drops. As she left to go downstairs, she heard the familiar murmuring sound of Emily's prayers.

She went straight to the dining room and the liquor cabinet. There were still a few bottles in it, and she found a fifth of Black Bush that was half full. She wondered why her dad would have left this behind. He enjoyed fancy booze. They had always lived like people with money—it was all part of the big lie. She took the bottle into the kitchen and found a glass. In general, the house was as she remembered it, with the occasional gap where a table was missing, or a picture removed from the wall. It looked as if the people who lived here were simply away.

When she was little there had been moments—while getting out of the third-floor shower, or searching for a toy in her closet—when her mind would suddenly open like a door onto the past, and she was sure she could see back in time. She never saw people, just rooms. Her bathroom was no longer the peach color her mother had painted it, but an unpleasant green, and the steamed mirror held no image, even though she should have seen her blurry self in it. These glimpses never lasted long, and she'd shake herself from the daydream and be back in the unremarkable present, but they had left her with a certain persistent distrust of reality, the sense that if you didn't pay attention to it, it could simply slip away from you.

She finished her whiskey and got a glass of water, letting the tap run while the ancient pipes clanked and complained. A car alarm went off somewhere outside, followed by an ambulance siren. All that time driving, listening to the radio, and there hadn't been one mention of an abducted Colorado child and her distraught parents. Why not? What were they waiting for? Where was the Amber Alert?

She'd thought maybe being back here would feel comforting, normal even. But mostly what she felt was afraid.

TEN

Landis drove across the dry, flat expanse of eastern Colorado as it tipped ever so slowly down toward Kansas. His remaining belongings were in the back of the truck: a duffel bag full of clothes, some shoes and sneakers, a box of books, another of CDs, his tools, a pair of good cowboy boots, a sleeping bag, an Ovation guitar he'd accepted from a guy in lieu of the two hundred dollars he was supposed to get paid for fixing a hole in a wall. He had nothing from his childhood, with the exception of an old collegiate dictionary he sometimes enjoyed paging through, looking for curious words. *Ameliorate. Feckless.* His parents had retired and moved to Florida a few years earlier, after his father finally gave up on the insurance business, which he claimed was giving him ulcers, and within a year he was dead of pancreatic cancer. His mother had an apartment in Tampa where she smoked cigarettes and watched television. She called Landis once a year on his birthday, but never had anything to ask him, talking instead about herself and her elaborate social life, the details of which Landis was convinced she made up out of bits of movies and TV shows. She had at one time been a catalog model for Sears, and Landis owed his generic good looks to her. His father had had large ears, sad downward-sloping eyebrows (Landis had inherited these), and a way of carrying himself that implied he was uncomfortable in his own skin. Landis was an only child.

Some country singer he'd vaguely heard of was on the radio being interviewed about the self-help book he'd written after surviving his own bout with cancer. Testicular. Landis shifted in his seat as he rolled the word around in his mind. The singer, whose name was Hoyt Crudup, claimed that after first becoming depressed about his diagnosis, he had a talk with God, then decided to take matters into his own hands and be positive about his life. "I embraced it," he said. "Every day, in every way." Landis snorted. He had no doubt that embracing life was a good idea, but it was no substitute for chemotherapy, which old Hoyt had gone through, too.

He'd eaten a big lunch at the McDonald's in Limon, where he'd hopped on the interstate, and was now making good time, having passed Arriba and Flagler, with Burlington perhaps an hour away. The Ford's big V-8 engine hummed powerfully in front of him; occasionally a crosswind forced him to correct course. The sun was high and behind him, and the world looked pretty. Flat and lifeless, but still pretty in its own stark way. Every now and then he'd see a distant cluster of buildings with a few cottonwoods planted around them. He passed a cattle yard that stunk of ammonia and manure, the mottled browns and blacks of the steers a complicated patchwork spread over a vast number of muddy lots.

Besides his truck, Landis owned one thing of real value, a Neumann U47 condenser mic from the early sixties that had been used at Motown, though he wasn't sure exactly which stars might have actually breathed into it. Smokey Robinson? Diana Ross? Sometimes he told himself it was likely to have encountered them all at one time or another. The mic had left the studio with an assistant engineer in the early seventies, after Motown moved to Los Angeles. That man, Russell Braithewaite, ended up in Denver years later, teaching at the Denver Sound Institute, where Landis earned his certificate in recording and live sound technology. Landis substituted a reproduction U47—it had cost him six hundred dollars—for the original, which Russell kept displayed on the bookshelf above his enormous mixing console. It was not a premeditated theft. He'd bought the new mic after hearing Russell go on and on about how wonderful his was. It was just the two of them that afternoon, and Russell left him alone for a few minutes to go to the bathroom, and Landis took the mic down just to hold it. His own was in his knapsack—he'd been planning to show it to Russell, but then suddenly felt embarrassed, because what did he think, that owning a fine mic was going to automatically make him an engineer? And then the thing in him that was given to snap decisions, almost always the wrong ones, the genetic predisposition to larceny he'd inherited from his grandfather on his mother's side, who'd embezzled from a bank in Camden, New Jersey, back in the twenties, kicked in. He saw what he *could* do, if he wanted to. And he did.

In five years he hadn't used the mic once. He was afraid of it. All the work he'd done in the Springs was live stuff, and the U47 was a condenser mic. He hoped to make it the centerpiece of a studio someday, but he knew that was unlikely. Recording was all about computers now, and he was no good with them—at DSI they'd worked with ProTools, and while he'd done a lot of nodding, it was like being back in high school chemistry class, that sense of drowning while trying to appear that he wasn't. His lab partner had helped get him through the computer mixing and editing. What Landis was good at was live sound. He liked the physicality of the equipment, the weight of the speakers, the questions of placement and power, amperage, ohms, crossovers. When he looked at the mic, all he saw was a physical manifestation of his own bad judgment. More than once, he'd thought to mail it back to the man, but that would be admitting what he'd done, and he wasn't sure he could.

Russell Braithewaite had worked with Marvin Gaye. And yet, there he was in Denver, part owner of a recording studio that was just scraping by. And here was this Hoyt Crudup, trying to sell books since no one listened to his songs anymore. You were never really safe. You thought you had it made, but then time came along and put cracks in the foundations you'd laid, and before you knew it the walls were coming down around you. People built little houses for themselves—Bernice going to stay with the Hardings, he with his relationship to Bernice, which he'd burrowed right into without ever thinking hard about it—but none of these shelters were permanent, and it was just arrogance to assume otherwise. Or willful ignorance.

At some point in this reverie, he'd fallen almost totally asleep while still moving at slightly over seventy miles per hour, and it was only the sound of his tires that brought him back to consciousness. He'd drifted onto the gravel shoulder, and now the truck was rocking back and forth. He braked and tried to keep himself going straight as well as he could, and after another twenty-five yards or so he managed to bring the truck to a safe stop. A tractor trailer flew past him with a warning blast on its horn.

"Fuck you!" he shouted. His heart banged in his chest like a windup monkey. He tried to remember the last thing he'd been awake for, but could not. There had just been a warm cozy feeling, then this. He'd been inches from dead.

The radio was still going. "That's what you got to understand," said Hoyt Crudup. "We're not human beings who occasionally have spiritual experiences. We're spiritual beings having a human experience."

Landis breathed more slowly. The sky had grown dark and a wind was kicking up, and then within seconds hail pounded down on him in a deafening rush of ice on metal, the white balls hitting the ground with such force that they hopped up two feet into the air. A few more moments and then the sun returned, illuminating a strange, steaming landscape that appeared to be covered in wet aspirin.

»»»»»

In Burlington, he got more quarters and fed a gas station pay phone, then dialed the number Gillian had given him. When no one answered, he called information and asked for Donald Click. The number was different, but he tried anyway.

"Yes?" said a man's voice.

Landis hesitated. "Have you got, that is—can I speak to Bernice, please?"

There was a long pause. "Who is calling?"

"Landis."

"What an interesting name."

He didn't know what to say to that. He didn't find his name interesting at all. He'd had an uncle with that name, although he'd never met him. "Have I reached her father?"

"That's right."

"Listen, I really have to talk to her." He didn't know why this guy was being so cagey, but it was starting to make him nervous, because he'd seen enough TV shows to know that when they tried to keep you on the line, it was usually for the benefit of the geeks huddled a few feet away, triangulating your position with their laptop computers.

"What about?"

"I just need to, that's all."

"Are you the father?"

"Yes, yes," he said. "I'm the father."

"Well, she's not here."

"Can you give me another number?"

"No, I'm afraid I can't."

Landis wasn't sure what to say next. He could smell the bathrooms, which were around the side of the building, not far from where he stood. "Can you tell her I called?"

"I don't know. Is that something she'll want to hear?"

"Absolutely. We had a misunderstanding."

"I see."

Landis had the sense that this was not going well. It was odd to think of Bernice as having a father at all—he'd sort of imagined her arriving on a shore in a clamshell like the naked woman in the poster she'd had taped up to her bedroom wall. "Are they all right?" he asked.

"Landis," said Don Click, "is there a reason why they would not be all right? Is there something you want to tell me?"

"No," said Landis.

"Well, then."

Landis could feel him getting ready to hang up. "Wait," he said.

"Yes?"

He felt peculiar—it was as if his body were a loudspeaker's copper voice coil, heated now, gathering resistance. "Nothing," he said, as the operator broke in to suggest he buy more time. He looked out past the highway where a bunch of cranes had landed in a field, wings held momentarily aloft like maestros preparing to conduct a symphony. Hoyt Crudup was right—he *was* a spiritual being, parked at this particular moment in the body of one Landis James Ford, standing in the late-day heat in eastern Colorado at a pestilent gas station, but no less connected for that to the higher meanings and purposes of life on earth.

ELEVEN

Tessa Harding sat behind the wheel of her Jimmy and watched the windows of the small house on San Rafael, imagining what was going on behind those drawn shades. It was a pleasant little house, with a garden alongside that had tomato vines and pretty purple flowers. This was a house for a single woman to live in, and from her position—elevated, curbside—she mentally roamed the interior, imagining a small refrigerator with a few diet items in it, yogurt, apples, bottled water from Italy or France. Perhaps there were postcards on the refrigerator door of some niece or nephew in a Halloween costume, or fluffed and combed and decked out for Christmas. Thinking of this brought back the knot in her chest that had been there almost continuously this past week, and she thought of all the photos she'd dressed Emily for. She kept the albums by her bed now, looked through them each night before going to sleep.

That her husband was cheating on her explained a lot. It made sense—his withdrawal, his moodiness. But she'd had Emily to focus on, and so she'd deluded herself, constructed a little space that wasn't real, or wasn't realistic, anyway. What she couldn't understand was how, in the face of the current crisis, he could still be inside this cute little house, having sex. If she got up the nerve to ring the doorbell, which was her intent, that was what she wanted to ask him. She wanted to shake him and say, "What are you thinking?"

Amid the various pornography on David's computer there had been a series of shots taken at the office of a girl in a dental chair, a girl with dark hair and elaborate tattoos. She knew who it was—the part-timer David had taken on last year, after laying off Esmeralda Ortiz. The practice wasn't doing well, though David didn't share much in the way of details. There were three other dentists in the Springs who advertised their offices as being specifically Christian, and that was a lot of competition. What about non-Christians who needed work on their teeth? Wasn't his business plan excluding them? Of course not, he'd said, they're welcome, but she doubted they felt it. Did Hindu people go to their own dentists, she'd asked? Muslims? Jews? Teeth were teeth.

She pushed open the car door and stepped down onto the curb. A light rain was starting to materialize the way it always did late in the day in summer. In a couple of hours, it would be clear again, but for the next little while the winds would kick up and the skies would turn the color of pencil lead.

She mounted the front steps, doing her best to ignore the huge fact of David's Jimmy parked in the driveway to her right. *Working late,* he'd said. *I'll get some Chinese.*

In response to her quick press of the bell, there came a sound of footsteps. She imagined she heard whispering, too, but it might just have been the wind in the trees. The door opened with a jangle and there was the woman from the photograph, though this time fully dressed. White T-shirt, tight jeans. Robin. A birdy name. Her arms were blue with drawing, but her face seemed nice enough. "Yes?" she said.

"I'd like to speak with my husband," said Tessa.

The woman's expression remained unchanged.

"Can I come in? Is he naked or something? It's all right if he is. I've seen him that way, too."

She opened the door wider. "Well, I guess if you want to." She had a gap between her front teeth, and Tessa wondered if this was attractive to David, somehow, from a professional point of view.

Tessa entered. From somewhere beyond the living room, which was small and decorated with lots of little art objects—pottery and framed things that looked like they came from craft fairs—she heard the toilet flush. "I hope I interrupted something."

The woman gestured toward the kitchen table, which had a Scrabble board set out on it. "What do you think? Is *calzone* a fair word? I say it's Italian, but he says that doesn't matter."

David entered the room. He wore jeans and a yellow short-sleeve shirt, a white T-shirt showing underneath the collar. "What the hell are you doing here?" he said.

"Aren't I supposed to be asking that?" She felt suddenly less sure of herself. Perhaps this could be innocent? The air smelled of coffee.

"I can leave you two alone, if you'd like," said the woman.

"Robin, right?" said Tessa. "Robin Zierler. It's easy to find an address these days, once you have a telephone number. Yours was on David's desk. I don't think you need to go anyplace."

"This isn't what it looks like," said David, blushing visibly. "We're playing a game."

Tessa bit her lip. She was doing her best to keep up a front, to be tough, to not care. But she felt she had no breath. "How?" she said. "How can you be playing a game at a time like this?"

"Don't you think this has been hard on me, too?" he said. He came toward her, but she stepped back. With his unruly sun-bleached hair, he still looked young—younger than she did. He looked like a surfer. He'd done drugs in college back in Indiana, where he was from, had been born again while playing in some heavy-metal band there. She'd met him after he moved to Colorado. She'd liked it that he had a past, liked how his smile was so full of confidence and good cheer, how nothing ever seemed to get him down.

"Excuse me," said Robin, "and I know it's probably none of my business, but what are you talking about?"

"Nothing," said David, keeping Tessa in his gaze. "It's nothing."

"Are you crazy?" said Tessa. "Nothing? This means so little to you that you haven't even mentioned it to your mistress?"

"Hey, wait a minute," said Robin.

"Our daughter," said Tessa. She started to tremble.

Robin went over to the Scrabble board and began to put the pieces away. "Listen," she said. "This is really nothing to do with me. I think maybe you guys need to go someplace and talk. Obviously, you've got stuff to work out. A little talk never hurt anything." She paused, then looked up. "I still say *calzone* is illegal."

"Our daughter was kidnapped," Tessa said. "Or abducted. Taken away."

Robin put the bag of tiles down onto the table.

"We don't know where she is."

"Is it about money? Do you think it was about money?"

"No," said Tessa. "It's not."

"That's enough," said David.

"Was there, like, a note?"

"You see, we know who took her. We just don't know where." She looked at David, who had shoved his hands deep into the pockets of his jeans, ones she had washed for him just last night. She peered down the hall toward where she figured the bedroom was. Had they done it already? Were they getting ready to do it? Was Scrabble some sort of turn-on for them? She didn't know anything. The energy she'd felt moments ago was draining from her like water. She had the idea that she must be hungry, and she thought about asking for a sandwich. Nothing seemed real anymore.

"You're not going to faint, are you?" asked Robin.

"I'm fine," she said.

David came toward her again and put his arms out in a gesture that indicated he was going to hug her. At the last moment, she suddenly brought her hands up to cover her face—she didn't want his hug—and her right hand came in sharp contact with his nose, her finger actually traveling some distance up his nostril.

"Ow!" he said, jumping back. "What the hell?"

"Are you OK?" She tried to see past his hand, which he held tight against his face. There was blood coming out from underneath it. "You should lie down. We need a paper towel. Can he lie down someplace?"

"There," Robin said. "Why don't you use the sofa? But try not to get a mess all over, huh? I'll get the paper towels."

David found his way to the sofa and lay back. Tessa arranged an embroidered pillow—she liked Robin's things—under his head. "Serves you right," she said.

"You hit me." His voice was muffled by his hand.

Robin brought over the towels, which she'd dampened under the faucet. Tessa took them and put them in David's hand, tearing one off and using it to clean some of the blood off his cheek. "Noses can really gush if you bump them right," she said. "You just keep applying pressure and don't change position."

"I'm going out for a cigarette," said Robin. "You want to come?"

"I don't smoke," said Tessa, looking with concern at the figure of her husband clutching a wad of bloody towels to his face.

"I didn't think you did. You could still come out."

She stood and followed Robin into the evening air.

Robin closed the door behind them and lit her cigarette. Tessa's parents had smoked, and she'd always loved the toasty, fresh smell of her dad's Camels or her mom's Marlboros right after they lit them. She had this thought, and then wondered at the way her mind was wandering these days. She might be going crazy.

"Do you think you broke it?" asked Robin, after a while.

"Nope. Though maybe I should have."

Robin took another long drag on her cigarette. Her fingers, Tessa noticed, were long and bony. She could hear the sounds of a baseball game on someone's television coming from across the street. "I'm really sorry about this," said Robin.

"Thanks."

"There's Chinese food coming in a little while."

"Ah," said Tessa.

She took another drag and exhaled. "Did you know that your husband doesn't pay income taxes?"

"No, I didn't. What do you mean?"

"I mean that he thinks he's exempt."

"How do you know this?"

"I'm the office wife, right? IRS sends stuff all the time. He ignores it, mostly. We talked about it one time and he launched into this whole explanation about taxes being illegal, anyway. I think he believes it, and maybe he's right, but so what? The U.S. government believes we're supposed to pay them, and when you get right down to it, they're the ones with the guns and badges."

Tessa listened to the baseball game, thought how calm it sounded, how much like summer. "I don't get involved in the finances."

"I didn't figure you did. That's why I'm telling you. I mean, I've been thinking about it for a while, and it really does bother me. It's you he's hurting, too."

"I have other worries."

"I'm sorry to hear about your daughter. Really. I can't even imagine. I had a cat that ran off once, and I was busted up about it for two weeks. Made me swear off pets, actually. But, look, there's another thing. Sort of bigger." She paused. "I met the guy who took her."

"What?" said Tessa. "How?"

Robin pushed her hair back from her forehead. "I bartend part-time, and he came in. We got to talking and I invited him to a party."

"How many boyfriends do you *have*?" asked Tessa.

"None. Zero. I have no boyfriends. I'm currently playing the field."

"I don't understand that."

"Well, I'm not sure I can explain it to you, then. I think maybe I don't even like men that much. Sometimes I think that, anyway. But this guy was pretty nice. Name's Landis."

Tessa watched the ember of Robin's cigarette write script in the air. A gust of wind brought with it some pinpricks of rain. She thought again of the man she'd seen downtown. "Did you sleep with him, too?"

She shook her head. "Uh-uh. But we did talk a bit."

"About Bernice?" said Tessa. "About Emily?"

"Yeah. I didn't realize it was your kid."

Tessa closed her eyes for a second, then opened them. "Did he tell you anything about where they took her? Is she still here in town?"

"No."

"Well, where are they?"

Robin stared at her. "I don't know." Tessa felt as if everything about her betrayed her weaknesses. Her outfit, tan pants and a matching top she'd ordered from J. Crew, and her necklace, three pieces of amber on a leather strap she'd bought at a boutique downtown, all of it spoke to the fact that she was a big phony. She'd actually dressed up to go meet her husband's lover. What a loser.

"Please?"

"Honestly," said Robin. "I don't. If I did, I'd tell you. I didn't even know you guys had adopted. Hey, was that about him or you? I mean, if you don't mind me asking."

"I was—I had problems. I'm barren."

She took another drag and exhaled. "That sounds kind of biblical."

"I don't see why. It's just a word."

"What kind of problems? Do you want to say?"

"Does it really matter?"

Robin flicked her ash and peered in through the front window. "He's still on the sofa," she said. "I can see his feet sticking out."

"I need her back. Do you know what this is like? It's like my heart was taken from me."

"Me, I'd be angry," said Robin. "I'd want to kick some ass."

"I'm not like that," said Tessa.

"I guess I'd want to kick my ass, too. We didn't do anything, incidentally. We were just waiting for the food."

"Thank you," said Tessa.

Robin nodded. "This Landis, he's no criminal. I've known plenty of criminals. It would be a shame for him to end up in jail just because he tried to help his girlfriend do something she was convinced was right."

"She could have come and talked to us," said Tessa. "For some reason, she hates us. She made sure we knew it from the moment she moved in. Living with her was like living with a piece of radioactive material. I never did anything to her, never said an unkind word—nothing. In the beginning, I tried to think of it as my own pregnancy, but I gave up on that—I suppose it wasn't fair to try. But she could have shared. One time, I found her eating ice cream in the kitchen at 2:00 AM, right out of the carton. I just stood, watching. She pretended she didn't know I was there, which of course she did. She stood with her back to me, eating, taking her time. I kept thinking of things I could say, little conversation starters, but I heard them in my head and they sounded foolish, and so I kept quiet. After a while, she put the carton back in the freezer and tossed the spoon in the sink. Real loud. I wish now I'd said something. I wasn't mad. I wanted her to eat ice cream. If only she'd given me a chance, I'd have liked to eat it out of the carton with her."

"The old fuck-you spoon toss."

"That's right."

"I don't know where they are," said Robin, "or where they went. He was careful not to tell me actual details, because then I'd be involved." She bit her lip. "And yet here I am, involved. But I gave him my number. He might call." She stubbed out her cigarette. "You can come stay with me if you want to. I have a spare room. I hate to see someone so beaten up like you are."

Tessa just looked at her.

"Dumb idea?"

They were joined on the porch by David, still holding a paper towel to his nose. "We should go," he said.

"You could have told me about this stuff," said Robin. "I can't believe you didn't."

"It's none of your business," he said.

"Oh, right, because I'm just your employee."

He took Tessa's arm and steered her off the porch, and Tessa did not resist. It was raining harder now, and she could taste it, and there was a hard, mineral smell in the air. "I could use you Friday," he said to Robin.

"Use me how?" she shouted.

David walked Tessa to the door of her car. "She doesn't mean anything to me," he said, leaning close.

"Is that supposed to make it better? That makes it worse."

"Hey." His voice was soft—flirty, even. "Let's not go home. Let's do Bear Canyon."

"Why? Why would we do a thing like that?"

"Shhh," he said. "I think we should go." He touched her cheek. "I think we need to."

"It's late." She heard how the word hung in the air. Late in lots of ways. Possibly too late.

"Please?" He had a plug of paper towel up one nostril. In spite of everything, she found herself listening to him. *Who are you?* she'd have said, if this were a romance, or a made-for-TV crime movie. *Who are you, David Harding?* But she knew. She knew exactly who he was. She'd watched him struggle into his socks in the morning. She'd prayed with him before morning coffee and Krispy Kreme doughnuts, and before take-out fried chicken. Even as the eye behind the camera that had taken those pictures of Robin, she knew him.

One of God's children.

»»»»»»

She followed his taillights through town, down Tejon, west on Boulder. Eventually they worked their way out of the densely populated areas, and the bungalows gave way to development housing, some of it military, and that gave way to rocky, open terrain as they headed up into the mountains. They finally parked just short of the trailhead, her car nosed right up behind his bumper. Bear Canyon was a one-mile hike, nothing too strenuous, that culminated in a summit with good views and a few big rocks suitable for a picnic, something they'd done back in the days when they were still dating, before they'd bought the house.

"It's kind of dark for this, don't you think?" she said when they were both out of their cars.

He flicked on a small flashlight, then flicked it off. "You'll be fine," he said. "Just remember to pick up your feet." Then he began hiking up the trail at a fast clip. Within moments, his white shirt disappeared ahead of her. He was an athlete—on weekends he ran the abandoned Incline Railway in Manitou, climbing the old ties like steps. She wasn't wearing the right shoes for this sort of thing, but at least she hadn't worn heels.

A couple of times she managed to catch up, but then she lost sight of him again. After a while, it was hopeless. She didn't know where he was. She could no longer hear his breathing up ahead, and the path had a thick covering of dead leaves on it, so his footfalls were inaudible. It even occurred to her that he might be playing some sort of trick—that he had circled around and was now actually behind her and planning to sneak up and surprise her. For a moment she felt panicked and wondered why she was doing this. She could only see a few feet in front of her. And yet, she was closer to the top than the bottom at this point, and she'd certainly been up the trail enough times in the light, so it wasn't particularly scary. Her own breathing sounded deep and labored as she hurried upward, sweat pooling on her brow and dampening her underarms. It was unusually humid out, and the chill air emanated from both sides of the path, as if the trees were refrigerated.

Finally, she emerged at the summit. David was seated on a rock, playing the beam of the flashlight around on the boulders and trees. "Come on," he said, holding out his hand. She went to him and took it. He stood and together they walked over to the edge. Tessa had never liked heights much. She didn't even particularly like looking down a flight of stairs. Below and across from them, Seven Falls was lit by a series of colored floodlights. In the dark, it almost seemed like something she could reach out and touch with her hand, though she knew what was in front of her was a deep canyon.

"You haven't been fair to me," he said. "This hasn't been right."

"What are you talking about?"

"I'm the one in charge. I'm the head of the family, I make our decisions. You know that. Understand that we are always under his watchful eye." He moved behind her and grasped both her arms tightly. "I'm going to do something now, all right?"

"What?" She tensed, suddenly afraid.

"A test. For both of us. You need to trust me. That's your job. Even now, knowing that I've been unfaithful to you, you need to trust me. Can you do that?" His hands were squeezing her so hard that her arms hurt.

"What are you talking about?"

"Can you *do* that?"

"Yeah," she whispered. "OK."

She closed her eyes and waited for him to throw her off the cliff—she felt certain that that was what was coming. Trembling, she anticipated the weightlessness, the initial collision with something—would it be a tree first? a boulder?—the few moments of confusion mixed with pain, and then the surrender of thought. That part might be just the ticket. She was tired of thinking so hard. The past week had eaten away at her until she barely knew what she was anymore, or who. Perhaps the problem was her pride, her inability to surrender. If God was truly in charge, who was she to argue? She'd been keeping Emily in her mind constantly, feeling that somehow this gave her control, but wasn't that just vanity? What control did she have over anything?

She should never have hit him in the nose.

She was being lifted up, and she took a deep breath. She closed her eyes and heard the crunching of gravel, felt the world turn, smelled piñon pine. *Every wise woman buildeth her house, but the foolish plucketh it down with her own hands.*

"Here," said her husband. He had lowered her to the ground, away from the precipice. She wasn't falling, she wasn't dead. This was the thing she'd needed to be reminded of, that only in giving herself completely to Jesus could she ever truly find salvation. She was on her knees, and David was in front of her. When she opened her eyes, she saw that he was pulling down his zipper. She shook her head. He took a handful of her hair and it was suddenly not her decision. "You want to," he said. "Right here, where anyone could see us. Where *he* can see us. Say it." He had his other hand in there, moving around. The one gripping her hair tightened.

She was silent.

"Say it," he whispered.

"I want to."

"I am your master," he said. "You can never forget that."

She felt as if she'd opened a broom closet only to find a desert inside. As hard as she'd been clutching the past, she now understood that there was no going back, no regaining the state of innocence they'd been living in for the past five years. It hadn't been real anyway, at least she didn't think so. It was a holographic garden, all smoke and mirrors and piped-in scents.

There was another insistent tug. She leaned forward and did as she was told.

TWELVE

They had been talking about naked people. *You don't see them like that,* she'd told him. *You look at lines and curves, light and dark.*

But isn't it, like, distracting? Even a little bit?

Not if you don't let it be. Everything in the world isn't about sex, dumbass.

It was Christmas week, and Bernice had dropped in with her gift for her mother, a book of poems by the writer-in-residence at her school that she'd started to read, but found just made her squirmy. The school was private, in a northwest suburb, paid for by her grandmother. Bernice understood that she was seen as troubled—possibly even dangerous—by her classmates there, most of them rich kids who smoked and drank at least as much as she did, and this was fine with her because it meant that, for the most part, they left her alone.

She didn't know how people wrote poems like that, ones that admitted to things like longing and loneliness. Plus, it seemed so easy to fake. The book had been a gift to her, and she didn't want it because she didn't like the way the poet had looked at her when he'd said, *Here, have this*, as if she were something good to eat, after she'd come to his office to talk about the paper she was supposed to be writing on *A Farewell to Arms* but wasn't. She had in fact thought about cutting the book up into pieces to use in a collage.

Her mother was out—shopping, CC said. He'd only gotten up recently himself. His eyes were still puffy, and he needed a shave, and the denim shirt he wore was unbuttoned. He was feline, of the big-cat variety, mysterious, dark, sudden. Did she want coffee? He'd just made some. She said no, just some water. They sat at the kitchen table. She'd never been there before. When she and her mother got together, generally on weekends, and only about once a month, her mother always picked her up and took her out somewhere. It was dim inside the house, even though outside there was a cold, sunny day going on just a few feet away. Ballpoint-pen drawings of CC holding his guitar were tacked up on the wall and they made Bernice feel depressed—this was high-school-girl-crush stuff, not art. She saw cobwebs over the refrigerator, a blackened banana in a blue bowl next to the sink. *I'll bet you've got some boyfriends*, he said. *I'll bet they're all over you at that school of yours.*

And then, somehow, they were kissing. She didn't know for sure if she'd made it happen, or if he had. When she was nine, in Wyman Park ravine, a skinny Hampden boy had filled a paper cup with gasoline and put it in the stream, let her light it with a match. She'd fumbled, had to go through three before getting one to strike. The ignition came as she held it out toward the acrid cup, somewhere in the space between, as the vapors sucked in the tiny flame and exhaled a silent bloom of fire.

She felt about this something of what she had about that—and now that it was happening, there was nothing she could do but watch as the cup tipped over and spilled its contents onto the surface of the water, an island of fire floating downstream and away from them, where it would undoubtedly set fire to half the city.

They made out, but she wouldn't do more. She wanted to, or at least she thought she did, but she wouldn't. *Too weird*, she said to him. *Don't you think?* He looked at her through eyes that were ridiculously pretty—all lashes and nearly black, like Greek olives—and she pushed him away and laughed, and then grabbed him and pulled him back to her, hard. This was similar to sex, only better, and she wouldn't, no matter how much she wanted to, even though the ache was moving through her, hot as steam, making her want to burst out of herself, but still she wouldn't, though his knee was between her legs and they were back on the sofa and his hands were under her blouse.

Uh-uh, she said about her panties, after her jeans were off and on the floor, curled up like some stranger's clothes. He was attempting to remove them with his mouth. How had this happened, how had they come this far? A blur of lips, and grabbing, urgent motions, though she'd certainly been complicit with the difficult bit when her pants had snagged at the ankles. *Why?* he wanted to know. She almost didn't know how to answer that. Why? Why, indeed? Once you've stolen a car, what's the difference if you then break the speed limit? From the couch, her view of the kitchen was limited, but she could just make out the spout of a teakettle. He climbed on top of her, sucked at her ear. *Tea!* she nearly shouted. He was unconvinced. But she insisted that tea was next. In her Jockey for Hers, if that was how it was going to happen, but definitely tea. And so, after some more fumbling, he'd grudgingly gotten up and made them cups of

Darjeeling, her mother's favorite, and she'd thought better of the underwear and slipped clumsily back into her jeans.

Kiss me more, she said, after she had some tea. They were back at the table.

You're as nutty as she is, he said. *I don't think so.*

Didn't you like it?

I liked it.

That was close, wasn't it?

What do you mean?

You know. She closed her eyes, and when he reached out for her hand, a shiver of longing ran the length of her body like a tremor down a saw blade.

You want to, he said. *You know you do. We could just go upstairs. There's a roof deck. I could show you that.*

Too cold, she said. *You got any cookies?*

He brought out a bag of Chips Ahoy and tossed them onto the table. She saw for the first time that lust and hostility were within shouting distance of each other, at least in men. His arms were long and hard with muscle, his fingers thick at the knuckles. She took pride in being a person who noticed things.

You shouldn't start what you don't want to finish, he said.

I want to finish.

Well, then.

But she wouldn't. Instead, she just sat there, sipping tea, waiting for whatever was to happen next, trying to decide if she was a chickenshit for not going all the way. When it began to feel embarrassing, she stood up and left.

THIRTEEN

The Harborview was in Fell's Point, a few blocks up from the water, just north of the gentrified part of the neighborhood, a converted row house staring out darkly through plate glass front windows, its immediate neighbors a tattoo parlor and an antiques store that was open only two afternoons a week. It didn't have a view of much of anything. Bernice pushed open the door. Afternoon, and the place was empty. The front area contained the bar, and it didn't look too bad: a chalkboard listing beer specials, and a large mirror behind the bar itself that created the illusion of a bigger space. The opposite wall was exposed brick, hung with dusty, black-and-white publicity photographs of blues performers, some of them signed. She examined one at random: Luther "Slideman" James. The picture was of a smiling older black man, seated with an impressive-looking guitar, squinting through the smoke from the cigarette in his mouth.

"It stinks," said Emily. She wore a new outfit Bernice had purchased for her this morning on sale at the mall in Towson after driving around the parking garage for so long they'd both felt ill. Looking at her, Bernice wasn't sure anymore. The shorts seemed too large, and the shirt—white with pink trim—seemed too small. She hadn't known what size to get, and Emily had been no help at all.

"That's the smell of beer," she told her. "Stale beer." She peered around for any sign of a human being. "I promise we won't stay long."

The door opened and a short guy with a shaved head came in, carrying a guitar case and a colorful cloth bag. "Hey," he said. He seemed a few years younger than she was—maybe twenty-three or so—and had a hint of a harelip.

"Hey, yourself," said Bernice.

"I'm Max."

She nodded. "Good for you."

"Max Lucca."

"I suppose you play that thing?" She gestured toward the case.

He grinned, his lip lifting awkwardly over his small teeth. "That's what I'm here about." He looked around, saw that they were alone, then looked over at Emily, who was on a bar stool, watching a videogame screen.

"Well, go on then, play us a song."

"OK," he said. He looked around again. "Where do you want me?"

"Any place you feel like." She pointed to a stool by the front window. "There."

Max Lucca opened his case and took out an acoustic guitar. From his bag, he brought out an aluminum contraption, which he hung around his neck. He inserted a harmonica into this, then adjusted a couple of wing nuts, bringing the instrument into position a few inches from his lips. He put a purple strap onto the guitar and slung it around his neck. "You got any requests?"

"I don't know," she said. "What are my choices?" She noticed that at least one of the games Emily was looking at the previews for was pornographic. She considered pulling her away from the screen, but thought perhaps it could be considered educational.

"I've got blues. I've got originals."

"How about original blues?"

"I can do that, too."

"Max," she said. "Max."

"What?"

"Before you even start, let me give you some advice. You do not want to do original blues. No one wants to hear your white-boy original blues. Original blues is *such* a bad idea."

Max checked the tuning on his guitar. The sound was sour and flat in the big room. "Are you the manager?" he asked. "They told me the manager would be here this afternoon."

"Does that matter, Max? I'm trying to help you here. You are not Blind Lemon Lucca. You are just Max, from—wherever you're from. Glen Burnie? Harford County? Dundalk? Now let's hear some music, OK? Why don't you just pick something. Impress us."

Max Lucca began strumming minor chords, his eyes closed, his head lowered toward the body of his guitar as if he were communicating with it in some way besides the tactile and the auditory. Bernice was reminded of the attitude of Mary in certain Renaissance annunciations. He began singing, and she thought she recognized the song, but she couldn't be sure, because in addition to being quiet, he mumbled.

"Max, Max," she said. "Hold it."

Max stopped and looked up.

"You're mumbling."

"That's my style," he said.

"Was that 'Light My Fire'?"

He grinned again. "Yeah."

"The Doors, or José Feliciano?"

"José who?"

"Or Brasil '66? Max! Was that Brasil '66?"

But Max Lucca wasn't looking at her anymore, he was looking past her, over her right shoulder, and when she turned she saw CC Devereaux holding an enormous burlap sack.

"Damn," he said, "I thought I locked that door."

"We didn't steal anything," said Bernice. "I promise. We didn't even drink anything. Max here was just auditioning."

"'Light My Fire,'" said Max.

"Well," said CC, putting down the sack, recognition dawning on his face. "Whoa." He looked over at Emily, who had given up on the video game and was now trying to make animals out of plastic straws. "Sorry, I didn't see her."

"Oh, she's heard worse."

"Yours?"

"Can't you tell? Emily, this is CC." Bernice watched Emily's liquid eyes acknowledge him momentarily, then return to the straws. Nothing. She was doing pretty well, all things considered. New places and people every day. The kid had inner reserves.

"Should I keep going?" asked Max.

"Should he?"

"Long as you're all set up, sure," said CC. The impression he gave was still one of lean muscle and shady dealings. There was no gray in his hair and she wondered if he dyed it. He still had the soul patch he'd had when he lived with her mother, and he wore small, round glasses with silver frames. His T-shirt read *Natty Boh* in faded letters.

"What's in the bag?" Bernice asked.

"Peanuts."

Max began again, and they all listened politely. Bernice thought he was bad, but bad in a good enough way—she could imagine someone, somewhere, liking it.

"So?" he said, when he was done. "What do you think?"

"I don't know," said CC. "It's not what we usually have in here."

"What?" said Bernice. "Oh, come on. Give him a shot. How about tomorrow? Can you come in tomorrow? Around eight?"

"Seven," said CC. "You can have the seven-to-ten slot. We'll see what happens."

"Seriously?" said Max.

"Woo-hoo!" said Bernice. "You go, man. You got a gig."

"Any pay involved in this?" Max asked.

CC moved behind the bar and filled a cup with ice, then squirted soda into it and pushed it toward Emily. "Pay? You want to get paid?"

"I was hoping."

"Ten percent of the bar while you're on, plus whatever you pick up in tips."

"That's good, Max," said Bernice. "You could make out."

"Bring your friends. Bring your friends' friends."

CC chatted with him a bit and the two exchanged business cards, and then Max left, the heavy glass door sighing shut, and it was just the three of them.

"So, Bernice," he said. "You look good."

"I want a job."

He leaned forward, his hands pressed palms down on the shiny bar top. "A job doing what?"

She shrugged. "Waitress? That's my experience. But I could bartend, too."

"Yeah? What's in a martini?"

"Gin. And a little vermouth."

"A Harvey Wallbanger?"

"Galliano."

"A boxcar?"

"I don't know. Rock and Rye?" She threw her hands up in defeat. "I don't even know what Rock and Rye is. I'm good with rum drinks."

"That's OK, no one ever orders a boxcar. Or a Harvey Wallbanger, or a martini, for that matter. Well, maybe a martini. We might serve a couple of martinis a week. Basically, bartending here means selling beer and the occasional whiskey drink. Jack on the rocks, Jack and Coke, Jack and 7UP, etc."

"Jack-in-the-box. Jack-in-the-pulpit. Jack up the price."

He squinted. "What do you want, really?"

"I told you. Pearl and I are on the lam, hiding out from the law. I figured I could work here, off the books."

"How'd you even find me?"

"Your name is in the paper. Don't you read the paper? 'Blues Jam night with CC Devereaux. Bring your ax.' Anyone ever show up here with a real one?"

"What?"

"Ax. Or is that just not funny?"

"This place is going under. The owner didn't pay his water bill for a year and a half because he broke up with his old lady and she didn't forward the bills, and then the city took the building and sold it out from under him. He's got a lawyer, but I don't see how it can work out. Mike bought the bar for, like, fifty thousand. The new owners won't sell it back to him for less than about three hundred. So, you see, we're kind of in limbo here."

She looked around. "What's with the paint?"

"You don't like black?"

"It's what teenaged boys paint their bedroom. Pearl?" she said. "What do you think of the colors in here?"

Emily appraised the wall. "I think orange would be better."

"Orange?" said CC. "That might work for a sports bar. You an Os fan?"

"She doesn't follow baseball," said Bernice. "She hates baseball."

"I like the Rockies," said Emily.

"National League?" he said. "You need to rethink your affiliation."

Bernice pointed to the back wall, where there was an enormous, poorly painted mural of a drum set. "You're not proud of that, are you?"

"No," said CC. She saw there was a T-shirt with the same image hanging on the wall to the left of the cash register. A handwritten label pinned to it read $13.

"It's pretty lame," she said. "Actually, lame is being nice."

"I can't argue. Mike did it himself."

"Do you think Emily and I could have some of those peanuts? We skipped lunch."

He took a switchblade out of his pocket and sliced open the burlap. Bernice took a handful over to the bar and deposited them in front of Emily. "Throw your shells on the floor, sweetie." She cracked one open herself. It was delicious and salty.

"I get 'em over by Lexington Market. Best peanuts anywhere."

Bernice had another. "Mmm. That one tasted like wet dog."

"Mine tasted like clouds," said Emily.

"No way," said Bernice. She ate another. "That one tasted like England."

CC got himself a glass of water. "Those there are American peanuts. You might find one that tastes like Cincinnati or something, I don't know. But they shouldn't taste like England."

"We could paint the place for you," said Bernice. "Help you get a bit more business. You pay us what's fair."

"Did you hear what I said? We're on the downslide here. You don't polish the silver on the Hindenburg. If you need money, you should look into other avenues. Get a real job someplace."

"I just told you, I don't want to be on the books."

"Hell, I don't know anyone who works on the books." He took a long drink of water, stared at her with obvious interest, then put the glass down gently on the polished bar. "Anyway, I'd have to check with the boss."

"I just saw you hire someone. Seems like you could do the same for me."

"There a father?"

"CC. What kind of question is that?"

"You know what I mean. In the picture. I don't see you wearing a ring."

"You interested in applying for the position?" CC was probably closing in on fifty. Landis was forty-two. The bastard. Last night she'd had a dream in which they were making love and he wouldn't look at her but instead kept his eyes closed. *Hey!* she'd shouted at him as he thrust away, imagining God-knows-what, or who. *Hey!*

"Probably not."

"It comes with benefits," she said. "You should consider it. Anyway, what about me? Can I work here?"

"Let me think about it," he said.

"You mean no. 'Let me think about it,' means 'Go away, and once you're gone, I'll forget you came by and I won't feel too bad about never calling you back.' If you mean no, say no, but don't wimp out with that 'Let me think about it' crap."

"All right, then. Yes."

"Really?" She was surprised he'd been this easy to turn, and she wondered if he weren't perhaps smarter than she'd been giving him credit for.

"Yes," he said. "I don't know about the wall part. I'll have to check. You can start tomorrow. Jimmy's on, and he can show you the ropes. After that, I'll see what the schedule looks like. We had one bartender quit last week, as it happens. Everyone knows what's coming, so everyone's looking for work. Also, they opened a Red, White, and Blues three blocks from here, and it's a lot more tourist-friendly. Clean bathrooms and all."

The peanuts were making her hungry, and she'd promised Emily pizza. "We gotta go," she said. "What time tomorrow?"

"Seven?"

"All right. Seven."

"What are you going to do with her?" He nodded toward Emily.

"Don't you think that's my business? Come on," she said, holding out her hand. Together, they left the bar and headed out into the bright, muggy day.

At a parlor nearby, they each had a slice of plain pizza, Emily eating only half of hers. Then Bernice told her to use the bathroom, even though Emily claimed she didn't need to, and as she waited by the door, Bernice looked past the customers chewing away to the street. A kid was riding a unicycle on the cobblestones. She'd held it together pretty well, she thought, but now she suddenly felt as if she were going to burst into tears, and it was only by biting her teeth that she was able not to.

FOURTEEN

Landis had been on the front porch for about an hour when he heard the voice. He had fallen asleep with his head against the brick footing of one of the columns that held up the porch roof, and he was dreaming about fishing. Someplace in western Maryland he'd picked up a radio program on the subject, and now, in the thick afternoon, speckled trout leapt about the dark streams of his subconscious.

He opened his eyes to a female police officer standing a few feet below him at the bottom of the steps. "Excuse me?" she said. "Hello?"

"Yeah?" Still groggy, he saw the glint of sunlight off her badge and thought again of his dream fish. The river in his dream had been in Colorado, out near Divide. He was not himself much of a fisherman, but once a few years ago he'd gone with another guy who worked for Cecil Wormsley. He sat up, tried to get himself in order. Her police cruiser was double-parked a few yards away, lights flashing.

"Is this your house?"

"No."

"Then can I ask you what you're doing sitting on the porch?"

"I'm waiting for someone."

"Who are you waiting for?"

He didn't want to say Bernice's name. He wasn't sure how dangerous this conversation was, but it struck him as meaningful that police seemed to latch on to him these days like dogs on to a bad smell. "Is it illegal now to sit on someone's porch and wait for them?" he said.

"Not necessarily. But you could be trespassing."

"I promise you, I'm not." The cruiser was disrupting traffic on the two-lane, one-way street. His own truck was parked on the next block north. "This house belongs to Donald Click. Go ahead and check."

"And you know him?"

"Of course I know him. Do you think I'm a burglar who just felt like catching some *z*'s before making off with the TV and stereo?"

She took a step forward and he was suddenly sorry for being a smart ass. He needed to control that. She had heavy-lidded eyes, and her cornrowed hair was pulled back tight against her scalp. He liked the idea of a black woman doing this job—you'd never see it in the Springs. Maybe in Denver. He figured she probably had to be plenty tough. "We got a call about a suspicious person."

"I'm not suspicious," he promised. "Honest."

"Someone thought you were."

"Someone was wrong." He watched as two more cruisers pulled up. The police here didn't mess around, it seemed. He wondered how many other, real crimes were going unattended to right now.

"I'm still going to need to see some ID."

He dug out his wallet and handed her his license.

"Colorado?" she said. "Long way from home."

"That's right."

"Here for business?"

"I'm visiting friends. I might stay."

"Depending on?"

"I don't know. Can't say I like the weather much. But the people seem friendly." He smiled.

She left him and went to confer with her fellow officers, all of whom had gotten out of their cars. There were five of them now, all discussing the fact that a man was sitting on a front porch. She began writing something up, then returned and handed it to him. "You have a good afternoon."

"This something I have to pay?" He scrutinized the yellow paper, searching for numbers.

"No sir. It's a citizen-contact form, that's all."

"Thanks," he said. Landis watched her and the others leave, the stalled line of traffic behind them finally freeing up and flowing again, like backed-up detritus behind a snagged bit of branch in a river. Out of the corner of his eye, he caught a movement of blinds in the basement window of the apartment across the alleyway that ran alongside the house. Some subterranean busybody. The world was full of control freaks. He waved, then resumed his position on the steps.

A few minutes later, he heard the door behind him rattle heavily, then open. It was a big door, probably swollen in its frame from the weather, certainly original to the house, which seemed about a hundred years old. Emily came out, dressed in blue shorts and a green T-shirt with the Road Runner on it. They must have come in through the back. He stood.

"She says you can come and sit in the parlor," she said.

"She does? All right, then. That sounds great. I've been kind of hot out here."

"There isn't any air-conditioning," she said. "But there are fans."

He followed her in. The house was grand, but also broken down. It listed noticeably, and he could see cracks running along the plaster at the top of the walls, close to what must have been ten-foot ceilings. The parlor was to the left of the entrance hall, through pocket doors, its parquet floor made of geometric shapes in contrasting shades of oak. He settled himself onto the small sofa, with its back to the shuttered windows, and his weight displaced a noticeable amount of dust. In the corner opposite him, there was an old piano.

"Lemonade?" she asked. "We have Country Time. It's pink."

"That sounds great. I can get it."

"No, you sit here."

"Where is she?"

"Upstairs." She left and Landis sat, waiting. He picked up a magazine off the table, a *National Geographic* from 1996, with a farm scene on the cover. It felt dusty, and he ran a hand over it, then wiped it on his pants. Bernice's apartment in the Springs had always had clothes and newspapers strewn everywhere. A month after meeting her, he'd spent a day cleaning her refrigerator. It had been stuffed with unrecognizable and rotting things, and on the floor, under the drawers, was a congealed soup of mysterious, leaked fluids covered in a fur of mold. This dust was not hers, of course, though perhaps mixed in were bits of her childhood. He sniffed the air, which seemed like the inside of a long-unopened closet. He heard stairs creaking and felt, in spite of himself, like a teenager waiting to pick up his prom date.

"Well," said Bernice when she entered the parlor. "Thanks for the subtle entrance."

"Someone called the cops."

"It wasn't me." She cast her eyes over him. She had on oversized chinos and a tight green T-shirt with a big white soft-serve ice-cream cone depicted on it. The ice cream had eyes and a smile. "You look like hell."

He had slept in the truck, and hadn't bothered to shave, and he suddenly wished he had. He'd been running hypothetical versions of this conversation through his mind for some time, but now that the actual moment had arrived, he found himself stumped for a good opening line. "What's wrong with you?" he said.

"Is that really how you want to start this?"

"I was coming back. You needed to trust me."

"You dumped us. Tell the truth."

"I didn't dump anybody."

"Sure you did. It's all right. Go ahead and say it. The truth will set you free."

"Is she OK?" he asked. Emily was standing behind Bernice outside the parlor, in front of the central staircase, whispering quietly to a small doll.

"She's fine. Thank you for your concern."

"She forgot my lemonade."

"Don't change the subject. Do you want to tell me about it?"

"What do you want to know?" He did not believe he was technically guilty of anything, but with Bernice he always had the sense that he was accountable on other levels as well. Sometimes you hesitated about things, sometimes you had thoughts—that was just human nature.

"Did you go see *her*?" she asked. "Is that what happened?"

"I don't know what you mean," he said. "Who?"

"Her."

"Her, who?" He wondered if she meant Robin, and then he wondered how she could even know about Robin, though it somehow didn't surprise him.

"You know who. Cricket. Cockroach."

"*Junebug*?" he said. "Hell, no. I haven't talked to her in months."

"I'll bet."

He was sort of relieved that this was what she'd thought, but it also worried him that she'd gotten him so wrong. "Come on. You have nothing to worry about on that count. That's ancient history."

"I think you still love her."

"That's just not true."

"Admit that you were planning to get out of this whole thing, and that's why you didn't call. You were going to go back to your old life and forget about us, right? Maybe you didn't go see *Junebug*"—she puckered her mouth in saying it, as if she'd just eaten a cranberry—"but you were leaving us. I know you were. If you said it, if you just admitted it, think how much better you'd feel."

He didn't know what to do, admit to something that wasn't true, or continue with a denial she wouldn't accept. "What is your problem?" he said, finally.

"It's not my problem we're talking about here. It's yours. You have a problem."

"I drove all this way. Doesn't that tell you something? I'm in this. I'm with you."

She stared at him, trembling. "Do you know how you made me feel?" she asked, quietly.

"I'm sorry."

"Sorry doesn't fix it. Sorry doesn't even get the tools out of the trunk to *start* fixing it. You abandoned me. You abandoned *us*. Both of us. This was going to be everything, our new family, our big do-over. And now it's all ruined and instead of being out west where we're supposed to be, we're here."

He wished for some perfect thing to say, knew it wouldn't come, because it never did. Usually, if he waited long enough, it didn't matter, and Bernice would just continue.

"You look pretty," he offered. "Motherhood agrees with you."

"I don't want to hear that. I want to hear the truth."

"All right," he said.

"All right, what?"

He stood up. "What you said."

"I want *you* to say it. You'll feel better."

He'd had an easier time with the cop outside. "OK. Sure, I thought about things."

She blushed with anger. "I knew it."

"Hey, hey. I'm sorry." His eyes strayed to the bookcase behind her, which was full of art books. "I didn't mean it." He didn't even know what he meant by this and had basically lost sight of the thing he was supposed to be guilty of. All he knew for sure was that he had betrayed her, or had considered betraying her, and that was enough. He was beginning to think he should have stuck to his guns and denied everything. "Anyway," he said, "I'm here. How about I start unpacking?"

She shook her head. "How can I trust you?" she said. "After what you just admitted."

"Oh, come on," he said. "I didn't do anything."

"Everything's different now. It's Emily and me. We live here. All the plans have changed."

"What plans? You never let me in on what the plans were to begin with, not really. And I'd like to point out that if the plans are different, it's because you changed them! I call up Gillian and you're gone. Just vanished, no forwarding address, nothing. What am I supposed to think?"

"What am I supposed to think? You didn't call!"

"I did. Just not . . . immediately."

"Did it take you three days to find a phone? You left me. That's what it is. It's sitting right here in the room with us like a stinking pile of shit. I need someone I can count on. Someone who will fight for me, not run away."

There was a pounding of feet and a high-pitched moaning sound as Emily ran up the stairs.

"We upset her," said Landis.

"She's tired, that's all. Tired and hot. I have to go talk to her."

"I'm coming."

She didn't try to stop him. He followed her up, noticing the scabs around her ankles where she must have been picking at mosquito bites.

Emily had shut and locked the door to the room at the back of the house on the third floor. "What's in there?" Landis asked.

"Bedroom." She knocked. "Honey, can we come in? It's OK. I'm sorry about the shouting just now. Don't be upset."

There was no answer. "What should we do?" asked Landis.

"I don't know." She tried the door again. "I guess nothing."

"She'll come out on her own," he said, thinking it through. "She just needs a time-out. This can't have been easy on her."

"What do you know about anything? A time-out is a punishment. Jesus."

"You know what I meant." He knocked on the door. "Hey, Emily? I brought you a present." From his shirt pocket, he took out the small windup crab he'd bought at a gas-station gift shop. It was red, with a smiling face and black-and-white eyes. He gave the knob on the back a couple of cranks and set the crab on the floor, where it began to walk sideways, buzzing quietly.

"A present?" said Bernice.

"It's just a little something."

They heard the sound of the lock turning. Then the door opened, and Emily came out into the hall. She watched the crab slow down, and when it had stopped, she picked it up and examined the mechanism. She wound it up and put it back down, where it began to move again.

"Say thank you to Mr. Landis," said Bernice.

"Thank you," said Emily.

"What do you think of this big old house?" he asked her. "Really something, huh?"

"I like it," she said.

"What do you like most about it?"

She poked at the crab.

"Don't put her on the spot," said Bernice. "Maybe she doesn't like anything about it. I never did."

He looked around, then up at the skylight, with its dangling metal chain. "Why not?"

"Bad parents," she said. "The usual story. You hungry or something?"

"I could eat."

"Well, then come on downstairs. We've been to the store. Emily, baby, you want a snack? Fig Newtons? Goldfish?"

She shook her head. "Pearl," she said.

"Right. You just go ahead and play, then. Though he wants lemonade," Bernice said, pointing at Landis.

"I'm sorry," said Emily. "I completely forgot."

"Pearl?" said Landis, as they headed down the stairs. "Who's Pearl?"

»»»»»»

He sat at the dining table and ate what Bernice had made for him—salami and cheese on rye bread with a pickle and some potato chips on the side, and a Coke, which he'd opted for when he learned that the can of lemonade mix had yet to be opened. She sat opposite, eating potato chips straight from the bag, staring at him.

"What?" he said finally.

"I'm just thinking about it all."

"And what do you think?"

"Well, I'm impressed. You tracked me down, you came all the way here. That means something."

"We're in this together."

"You say that. But on the other hand, how can I trust you after what you admitted in the parlor?"

He closed his eyes momentarily with frustration, then took a breath. "I didn't say anything in the parlor."

"You may not think you did, but you did." She popped a few potato chips into her mouth and chewed them noisily, then sucked the grease from her forefinger. "It's like on airplanes, when they explain the safety procedures to you. You know? The flight attendant tells you that in the event of an emergency, oxygen masks will descend from the overhead compartment. If you're traveling with young children, you should put on your own mask first, then put on theirs. Do you see what I'm saying?"

"No," said Landis. "Are you planning to fly someplace with Emily?"

"I have to put on my own mask first."

"What mask? What are you talking about?" He still had half a sandwich, but it was starting to stick in his throat. She hadn't put anything on it, and it was very dry. "You got any mustard?"

"It's not good?" She looked alarmed.

"No, no, it's great." He drank some more Coke. "I just thought it would be better with mustard."

"See? Now I'm all upset because I made you a bad sandwich. I'm emotionally shaky these days, in case you hadn't noticed. So what I need is to be left alone to adjust my own mask and just breathe oxygen for a while."

He thought about Hoyt Crudup. "I nearly died on the way here," he said. "Ran right off the road. I had a kind of revelation."

"Please," said Bernice. "Spare me. I've got enough trouble with her." She raised her eyes ceilingward.

"All that time alone, you get to thinking about things."

"You should be careful. Thinking isn't your big strength, is it? Anyway, you can't stay here," she said. "I can't run the risk of you abandoning me again. You understand that, right?"

"I would if it made any sense," he said. "But I *didn't* abandon you. It's the opposite—I drove clear across the country to find you and be with you. I think it's crazy that you don't see that."

"Well, maybe I think you're crazy to have come all this way."

"That's what your friend said. She said I should stay out of it. She said if we get caught eventually, I'm the one that's really got a problem, my not being related to the kid at all." He took another swallow of Coke. He was conscious of sweat all over his face. "So, I've been thinking, and it seems to me that we ought to get out of the country. Maybe up to Canada."

"I'm staying here," she said. "For a while anyway."

"Why?"

"I'm from here. I've got a place to stay. I got a job."

"We'll need a birth certificate for her, even for Canada, but we could say something happened to it, like there was a fire."

"I doubt that would work."

"Then we'll get a fake one. We could go to Canada."

"Except then there'd be a record. I don't think that would be so smart."

"Bernice, I found you. You haven't exactly disappeared off the grid. You're findable. You know what else? What is your money situation, anyway? You can't raise a kid on nothing. What kind of job did you get? Are you sitting on some trust fund, or what? I look at this house, I don't know what to think."

"The house is my dad's, and he is not rich. When he bought this place, it was dirt cheap. Everything in this neighborhood was. As for money, I got some insurance money when my mother died, all right? Not much, but some."

"I thought the whole thing with giving up Emily was because you needed money."

"Well, that just shows how little you know, doesn't it? You think I sold my own baby? Is that what you think?"

"No, but you said they bought her. You said it, not me."

"This is none of your business," she said. "*We* are none of your business."

He finished his sandwich, chewing slowly. "You won't leave with me, and you won't let me stay with you." The lower halves of the big dining-room windows were pebbled glass, but through the upper part he could see the fire escapes on the next building, black against the painted red brick. Dust motes hung in the air, and there were cobwebs up against the crown molding in the corner. "Is that what I'm hearing?"

"That's the size of it. I'm sorry you came all this way."

He closed his eyes. "Goddamn it," he said. He brought his fist down on the table hard, the contact rattling everything on it, his plate, his glass, the tarnished brass candelabra.

"Don't," she said. "You made it happen. You weren't reliable. I need reliable."

"You can't do this alone. I know you. You don't even *want* to do this alone."

"I'm putting on my mask," she said. "You should see about yours."

FIFTEEN

A little after midnight, Landis drained his fifth beer, asked the bartender to change a five for quarters, pushed back from the bar, and headed out to the street. If he was going to sleep another night in the truck, he figured he might as well do it drunk. But he wasn't tired yet, so he went walking around the neighborhood, peering at his reflection in the window of the dry cleaner's, reading the lost-dog and yard-sale notices taped to the streetlight outside Neon, the coffee bar. There was a pay phone across the street, and he went over to it.

Robin picked up on the second ring. "Hey," he said. "Remember me?"

"I was just thinking about you," she said.

"Yeah? Anything interesting?"

"Very. Where are you?"

He looked around. At the bus stop at the end of the block, a big, Nordic-looking man in a stained tracksuit was muttering to himself angrily. Seventies rock rasped out into the street through a tinny speaker above the door of a burgers-and-beer place. The night air felt like something pressed out of a steam iron. "Hard to say. Between a rock and a hard place, maybe."

"I quit the dentist's office."

"No kidding?"

"Yeah. I'm going back to school, I've decided. This way, I get to buy school supplies. I love that, you know? Getting pens and notebooks and stuff—you just feel this sense of possibility. Of course, it never lasts. But I'm looking forward, I really am."

"School for what?"

"Nothing in particular. Just school."

A bus pulled up, but the Nordic-looking man did not get on. Moths swam and fluttered in the light of the streetlamp above him. "I'm in Baltimore," he said. "First time."

"What's it like?"

"Not so great. Like it went a few rounds with a much bigger, meaner city. Like it could use a vacation someplace nicer. But I guess it'll do."

She didn't say anything for a moment. He listened to a saxophone tracing a thin, vertical melody into the air. "I have to go," she said.

"You do?"

"Yeah. But I'm glad you called. I hope you will again. You take care of yourself, and you take care of them, too."

"I don't know. How do you take care of someone who doesn't want it? Who won't let you?"

"Just go ahead and do it anyway," she said. "Don't be so damn polite."

»»»»»»

He awoke early the next morning to the sound of birds. His back felt like someone had kicked it with a steel-toed boot, and he badly needed to piss. He kept some foam in the back of the truck, but it hardly constituted a mattress, and he'd had to sleep tucked awkwardly in among his belongings, aware the whole time of the odor of gasoline. Clearly, he was getting too old for this. After climbing out, he took his toothbrush and walked back to the little commercial district to get some breakfast and clean up. There were plenty of signs posted in the neighborhood, and he figured it wouldn't be too hard to find himself a cheap flop for the short term. The long term, well, he'd have to see.

At a place called Joe Mama's, just off the main drag, he met a college girl who let him use her cell phone. "Go ahead," she said. "I never get near to using up my minutes." She was typing things into a computer. He told her thanks and tried some numbers from the *City Paper*, but it was still early and no one was picking up.

"You'll find something," the girl told him. "This neighborhood is full of ratholes. I lived in one last year. I woke up one night and there was a kid in the next room walking around talking to himself. I screamed and he went back out the window he'd come in. This year I found someplace a lot nicer. Anyhow, you just have to look around a bit."

»»»»»»

The linoleum-covered stairs sagged noticeably to the right, and as Landis followed the fat man up them, he imagined the whole thing giving way, and the two of them in free fall toward the cat-piss-covered floor. It was going to happen to someone, someday. The row houses in this neighborhood were like old teeth—you'd get a couple of strong healthy ones, but then one like this, decayed and rotten and stinking and soft. The fat man wheezed with the effort, the back of his white nylon shirt soaked through with sweat. On the third floor, in the back, was apartment five. The number was glued on and crooked. Some previous tenant had left stickers with the names of what Landis figured were local bands plastered on the cheap door: Skull Divers, Rainbow Pest, Enigma. He could imagine these bands and the bars you'd have to go in to hear them, and it made him feel old. And yet, if he wanted eventually to work sound here, these were some of the people he'd be getting to know.

"No drugs," the fat man said, as Landis handed over the cash. "Got me?"

"OK," said Landis. "Don't worry."

"I'm serious about that."

"So am I."

"Refrigerator's new. I hadda throw the old one out."

"Nice," Landis said, admiring it. It was so undersized he doubted you could stand a carton of milk inside.

"I ordinarily wouldn't do this, you understand, but my last tenant died. Usually, I like a commitment of at least nine months. You are paying well below market rates."

Landis nodded. "I appreciate that."

"That's a new mattress on that bed, too."

"Excellent."

"You're not a student?"

"Nope."

"Not a talker, either, huh? That's all right. I respect a person's privacy. Just make sure you respect my building and we'll get along fine." He summoned something like a smile. "Know what was in that refrigerator?"

"Do I want to?"

"Eggs. The guy kept buying eggs, then not throwing them out when they expired. Must have been two hundred of them in there." He put out a hand. Landis counted two hundred and fifty dollars and gave it to him. He handed Landis a key and heaved himself back out the door.

When Landis was alone, he used the tiny bathroom, which looked clean enough, though he detected a hint of old urine smell. He hated to think about what was under the layers of cracked linoleum. The apartment had been a bedroom at some point in the building's past, before someone started carving it up. Wood paneling hid what were probably crumbling plaster walls, the laths showing through like ribs. The paneling was warped and bulged oddly in places, and Landis thought you'd want to avoid staring too hard at it if you were drunk.

He sat on the bed and looked out the window. He was surprised to discover that he could just see the back of Bernice's father's house across the alley and a few houses up—the wooden balcony that was built on to the second floor, the broken shutter that hung askew at one side of the back window beside it. The guy was letting the place go to shit. Houses needed to be lived in. Getting down onto the floor, he did a couple of push-ups, holding his breath as he did so against the foreign, slightly sick aroma of the gray carpeting. He wasn't used to this weather, not after nearly twenty years in the West. His skin felt clammy and he was aware of a ripe smell rising out of his work boots. It had taken all day to find this place, and he was tired, tired.

After two trips to the truck, he'd moved in what he needed. For now, this would do. He'd never cared much about his surroundings, really, and he figured if you took actual square feet, this place probably wasn't much worse than his old trailer. But there he'd had the outside. Many evenings he'd sat out staring down on the lights of the sprawling city, drinking a beer, pretending he owned the world. It hadn't been happiness, exactly, not in the sense that he'd always assumed people were supposed to be happy, either with a lot of money or a big loving family, or maybe pursuing some dream like photographing bears at the South Pole or having sex with movie stars, which he assumed was probably the ultimate happiness, judging from magazine covers. But there had been a stillness, the sky over him a great inverted bowl full of stars, and some nights that was exactly what he wanted.

He had a quick nap, then took a shower and put on clean clothes, walked to the same bar he'd been in last night and ordered a burger and fries, ate in the smoke and friendly noise of the place. When he stepped back out into the early evening an hour later, it was with the pleasant sensation of a full stomach and of having had a couple of beers among men. He could get along here. He could get along anywhere. He walked to the big house and rang the bell.

This time Bernice answered. She had on tight jeans and a shiny blue top that exposed her shoulders and emphasized her breasts. She looked good, going-out good, and he hoped it was for him.

"It isn't the Jehovah's Witnesses," he said. "And I'm not running for office. I'm just letting you know I'm still here."

"Where did you stay?" She bit at her thumbnail nervously.

"What's the difference?"

"I worried about you."

"I slept in the truck. I've done it before. But today I rented a room, one street over, on Frederick."

"Why did you do that?"

"I just walked around. There are signs all over advertising rooms. I saw one of these old houses with eight mailboxes out front. How the hell do they get eight apartments out of three floors?" He leaned his hand up against the door frame. "Do I have to stand out here all night?"

She let him in. They sat again in the parlor. "Don't you think this is all a little ridiculous?" he said. "We love each other. Let's move on from there."

"What did you say?"

"You heard me."

"You're drunk."

"Not even close. A few beers. Should have seen me last night, though." He could see there was something wrong. "What?"

"They called today."

"Who did?"

"*They* did."

"Bernice, you have to say things in a way that makes sense. Who called?"

She pointed up toward the ceiling. Her face seemed pale to him, and her eyes, though bright, looked tired and shadowed.

"Emily? Is she OK?"

"She's upstairs talking to Jesus. Listen, they know where we are. Worse, they know *who* we are. I don't know why I ever thought they wouldn't."

"Tell me exactly what happened, all right? Who called?"

"Tessa Harding."

"And how did she get the number?" But even as he said it, he was pretty sure he knew. "What did you tell her?"

"I didn't tell her anything. When I heard her voice, I hung up the phone."

He stood and went to the front window, peering out over the top of the shutters. There was nothing unusual, just parked cars and the green exuberance of the trees, a stylish-looking woman in a short skirt and heels walking a small, brown dog.

"This is bad, right?"

"Let's get Emily," he said. "We bring her downstairs and we talk to her. Ask her what she wants. That's what they did with me when my parents split. My old man had this woman he used to see a couple times a week, and then my mom started up with the neighbor. So Dad moved out and rented this dump on Route 1 that came with a broken-down MG in the yard. Told me if I came with him, he'd teach me about cars and we'd fix it up together. That was going to be the big prize."

"And?" she asked. "What did you choose?"

"I picked her."

"Because you already knew he was a liar, and that stuff about the MG wasn't true?"

"No, he did give me the MG. We got it running, just like he said. I crashed it a couple of years later, wrapped it right around a phone pole. Lucky again—I just walked away. I chose her because I thought that of the two of them, she was the one who was going to need the most help." He belched, tasted onions, pictured the small house in West Windsor, the green living room with the RCA color TV on its wheelable metal stand, the neat rows of *Reader's Digest* and Condensed Books by the mantel. "A lady came, with a briefcase and greasy brown hair pulled back. She said she was from the court, and I figured I was going to jail—that someone had found out about the LSD I kept hidden in the toe of my old basketball sneaker. Then I realized it wasn't about me at all, it was about my parents."

"You were how old?"

"Fifteen, I guess. It didn't stick, though. They got back together two years later."

"Well, Emily is five. She can't make a decision."

"Even so," he said. "I think we should find out. What if she wants to go home? It makes a difference."

"I'm her real mother," said Bernice.

"What do you think that even means to her? She doesn't know about sex, does she? She probably thinks when God wants there to be another person on earth, he just beams them down with a big laser transporter."

"It's not your problem what she does or doesn't know."

But then she materialized in the doorway. "Hi," she said.

"Hi, honey," said Bernice. "You surprised us. What's going on upstairs?"

"We're having a tea party." She came in and sat beside Bernice, leaning her head against her shoulder.

"Oh, good. Tea."

"Emily," said Landis, trying to sound upbeat. "Do you ever miss your other house?"

"Hey," said Bernice.

"I'm just asking."

Emily looked right at him. "Where do you go when you're not here?"

"I go around the corner. Just one street away. I'm renting a very nice room. You can come see it sometime, if you want."

"Can I have a Fig Newton?" she asked Bernice.

Bernice touched the side of Emily's face. "Still a little warm. Anyway, of course you can. But first, answer Mr. Landis's question. Do you sometimes, ever, even a tiny bit, wish you were back at your other house, your Colorado house?"

She nodded.

"But you like it here, too, right?"

"Uh huh," she said.

"See?" said Bernice. "She knows what's what." She stared down at her hands for a moment. Outside, a light rain had begun, the tapping on the roof over the front porch reminding Landis of the way rain had sounded from inside his trailer. "OK," she said. "Let's get cookies. Then in about a half hour or so, we'll have dinner."

All three of them went into the kitchen, and Bernice found the package and handed two cookies to Emily, who ran off with them, back toward the entrance hall and the front stairs. The kitchen counters were a mess, with plates and pots left out, and blue plastic Safeway bags strewn around from where Bernice had unpacked groceries and simply left them.

"I know," she said. "I'm getting around to it. Stop judging me."

"The way I see it," said Landis, "we have two choices. We can either run, or we can stay here and get a lawyer. Because that's where this is going, eventually."

"You mean I have choices. You are just some person who followed me from Colorado."

The phone rang and they both looked at it. "It's her," said Bernice. "I know it." When she made no move to answer, Landis picked it up.

"Hello?" said a woman's voice.

"Hello," he replied.

"Oh," said the voice. "I didn't expect—please, can I just talk to her?"

"Depends," said Landis. "Talk to who?"

"Emily."

"Hold on." He held his hand over the receiver. "She wants to talk to Emily."

"She can't." Bernice spoke in a hot whisper. "I told you not to answer."

"No, you didn't. You just said it was her."

"Well, now what?"

"I don't know. What's the difference, really?"

"Are you serious? What's the difference?"

Landis put the phone to his ear again. "Listen," he said, politely, "do you think you could call back? This isn't the best time." Then he hung up.

They stood staring at each other. Outside, the rain was picking up, as was the wind, and the old glass rattled in the window frames. The phone rang again, and they let it go for a while, but after the sixth ring, Landis picked up again. "Yes?" he said.

"When?" asked the voice. "When should I call back?"

"I don't know," he said. "How about later on? Around nine?"

"She goes to bed at eight thirty. Do you put her to bed at eight thirty?"

"I don't know. Right around then."

"And give her a bath?"

"Of course. All right, 8:30."

"Can I read her something?"

He covered the mouthpiece again. "She wants to read her something."

Bernice's cheeks had flushed an angry pink. "No, she can't read her anything. And she can't call back. What the hell are you doing?"

He spoke into the phone. "Maybe not the reading part." From the other end, he heard what sounded like a hiccup. "Please don't worry," he said. "Everything is fine here." He hung up.

"Look," said Bernice, "will you babysit? I have to go out to this bar. I'm training to bartend. Some guy I used to know runs it."

"What the hell?"

"You heard me."

"How, exactly, were you planning to do this? What if I hadn't come over?"

"I'd have brought her with me, or maybe left her with my dad for a few hours. Forget it, it was just an idea. She's not your responsibility.

You don't have to worry." On tiptoes, she reached into the cabinet and brought down a box of spaghetti, which turned out to be open, and its contents cascaded over the top of the ancient gas range.

"You weren't going to leave her alone, were you?"

"No," she said. "Of course not."

Landis helped her pick up the spaghetti. "I'll stay," he said.

"You sure?"

"Oh, yeah."

"I won't be out too late. Midnight or earlier."

"Do you figure on these being your regular hours?"

She ran a hand through her hair. Her dark roots were getting more apparent. "I'm going to see if there's an afternoon shift I could do. This will just be training. I'm going to paint something in there, too."

"Paint what?"

"I don't know yet. A mural. Like Giotto."

"Like what?"

She brought an aluminum pot out from a cabinet below the counter and went to the sink to fill it. "Giotto. I'm going to paint the walls."

"Why?"

"Do I have to have a reason?"

"I guess not." Landis watched her work, conscious, suddenly, of how pretty she was. "Who is he, this Giotto?"

"Giotto isn't the guy. Giotto is a famous painter. Was. He painted a lot of walls." She turned on the flame and adjusted it. "Are you eating with us or not?"

"I already had something."

"That's not what I asked you."

"No," he said. "I'll just watch you."

She got out a jar of tomato sauce, tried to open it, then handed it to him. He popped the lid and handed it back.

"You're going to paint this guy's walls?"

"Jesus, Landis. I don't know. Now that we're found out, I don't know what's going to happen. But I'm not running. I'm staking out this little patch of ground."

He picked up a saltine from the counter and bit off the corner, put it back down. "What is he, an old boyfriend?"

"Not even close. Actually, he used to go out with my mom."

Stepping up behind her, he slipped his hands around her waist and rested his chin on the top of her head. "I missed you," he said.

"You did?"

He pressed against her, moved his hands up, stroked her shoulder. It had been a long time since they'd touched. Her head smelled familiar to him, salty and shampooed, the skin almost unnaturally hot, as if a few centimeters farther in, her brain was working too hard. She backed into him and made a quiet, sighing sound. The pot in front of them came to a boil, foam climbing toward the edges. He moved his head and kissed her where she liked it, on her neck, running his lips back and forth lightly there. He wanted her badly, and he could tell she wanted him, too. He undid the top button of her jeans and she didn't stop him, but instead gasped in a way that made him hard with desire.

"Hey," she said, abruptly, pulling away and removing his hands. "What do you think you're doing?"

"Just making sure you remember who I am," he said. "Who we are."

She buttoned her pants back up, turned, and squinted at him. "I know who you are," she said.

»»»»»

In the parlor, Emily took Landis's order. "Woof?" she asked. She held a pencil and an invisible notepad.

"I'd like a nice, juicy steak," said Landis. "Medium rare."

"Woof."

"And a side of french fries, and some coleslaw, and some Mallomars."

"Woof woof."

"You don't have Mallomars?"

"Woof."

"Well, then just substitute asparagus, OK?"

"Grrrrrr . . ."

"Never mind then. I'll take whatever the chef recommends."

Emily yipped, then danced off toward the kitchen, and Landis paged through a book he'd pulled off the built-in bookcase, a history of Western art, and tried not to think about how he was probably being played for a first-class chump right now. He thought maybe he'd look up Giotto. He opened to an interesting-looking page, but was interrupted by Emily skipping back in.

"Rowr rowr rowr," she said.

"Don't tell me, let me guess—you're out of steak?"

"Rowr."

"What about chicken? You do have chicken, don't you?"

She gave this one some careful thought. "Woof," she said, at length. "Woof woof woof, rowr."

"Well, you go check then."

He paged though some pictures of statues and plates. Then he turned to the index, first tried the *J*s, then had success with the *G*s. He found the chapter on Giotto and looked over the pictures in it, and the main thing he felt was confused. After all her complaining about religion, why was Bernice interested in pictures of Jesus? He liked the faces of the women looking down at the dying man. Their eyes were strangely wide, like the slits in the sides of helmets, or as if they were wearing masks.

"Woof," said Emily, returning. "Woof woof."

"No chicken, either? What kind of a restaurant are you running here? All right, I'll just have soup."

She made a whining noise.

"Peanut butter and jelly?"

This set off some enthusiastic yipping and growling, and she was gone again. He reconsidered the painting and wondered whether Bernice was really planning to put religious pictures on the wall of a bar.

The restaurant game showed no signs of running out of steam, so he eventually got them both some ice cream out of the freezer; they ate it out of coffee cups since he couldn't locate any bowls.

At eight, the phone rang. They were in the living room on the second floor, a large open space that Landis could see from the repairs to the floorboards had been converted from a hallway with separate rooms, going through Donald Click's old LPs. Most of them were jazz: Monk and Mingus and Parker and Getz. Landis was more of a rock-and-roll guy, but he wasn't totally ignorant about jazz. He liked to listen to it on the radio—it always seemed to sound best that way, as if it were being beamed forward in time from the deep past. There was a Clancy Brothers album, too, which Landis remembered his own father owning, and which the old man had sung along to on nights when he was particularly drunk.

He thought about letting it ring, then decided there wasn't much point. The phone was near the stairs. It was old, with push buttons and a cord, and the receiver felt heavy in his hand. "Yes?" he said.

"It's me," said Bernice. "Everything OK?"

"We're fine," he said. "What are you doing?"

"Nothing. Literally, nothing. There's nobody here, and the band doesn't start until ten. I already told him I couldn't stay all night. Did she call?"

"No one called."

"What are you doing?"

He looked at Emily, who was trying to draw the cover of Thelonius Monk's *Underground*, using a ballpoint pen. "Just hanging out. Don't worry about us."

"I'm thinking maybe you're right. Maybe we should keep moving."

"We'll talk about it when you get back," he said.

"You still can't stay over. You know that."

"I have my own place," he said, suddenly fed up with her, with her ridiculous changes. He put down the phone without saying goodbye. A second later it rang again, and he picked it up. "What?"

It wasn't Bernice this time. "Can I talk to her?" He heard the tension and desperation in the woman's voice, the careful attention she was paying to her words for fear of letting this thing she wanted so much slip through her grasp.

"Let me ask." He cupped the receiver with his hand. "Hey, Emily," he said.

"Pearl," she said.

"Whoever you are. There's a phone call."

She put down her pen and came to where he was standing. "Go on," he said. She put the phone to her ear. It looked big there.

"Hello?" she said. "Mommy!"

Landis stood watching her for a moment, then returned to the albums. He thought she might like some privacy.

Lying on his back, he looked up at the slowly spinning ceiling fan. The cross-country drive hadn't helped his back. He shifted and stretched, aware of the dusty floor around him, but happy to have his spine in this new position. Emily wasn't saying much, just an occasional obedient child's *yes*, and Landis supplied the questions in his own mind. *Are they feeding you? Are you OK? Do you miss me?* But inevitably there would be another question: *Do you want to come home now?*

"All right," he heard her say. He got up and went back to where she stood. "She wants to talk to you."

"Yes," said Landis.

"Listen," said the woman, "I don't want this to sound the wrong way, but can you tell me a little about yourself?"

"I don't know. I'm not sure I can."

"It's important to me. You've stolen my child. That's a criminal offense. Are you a criminal?"

He thought guiltily about the microphone currently under the bed in his rented room. "No. I'm not a criminal. Seriously. Not in the sense you mean. I'm just a regular person. I'm real sorry about all of this, if that means anything. It wasn't supposed—"

"What way was it supposed to be? What way? Were you thinking there would be no consequences? Did you think that you could just walk off with the most important thing in someone else's life and that would be it? That a mother wouldn't fight for her own daughter? That there aren't laws in this country? Go ahead, please, tell me—I want to know. What did you think? Why did you think this was a good thing to do?"

"I don't know." He looked down at his feet and wished he'd never picked up the phone. It had been a lot easier when Tessa Harding was just an abstract idea, a Bible-toting, SUV-driving yuppie who wore coordinated pastel outfits. The person on the phone didn't sound at all like what he'd imagined.

There was a long silence. "That's it? You don't know?"

"Not really." It occurred to Landis that he might be experiencing his last few minutes of freedom. At any moment, police would burst in, guns drawn. "You can see she's fine. She loves her mother, and she's adjusting very well."

"I'm her mother!"

"Hey," he said, "it's OK. Everything's OK."

"I'm sorry," she said. "I'm trying to be understanding. But it's not OK."

"How do you know Robin?" he asked.

"That's none of your business."

"Well, can I ask you something else?" he said. "Have you called anyone?"

"Just let her come back," said Tessa Harding. "I'll fly out there and get her. You won't have to go to jail. There will be no consequences. We can solve this whole thing easily, don't you see? Nothing has happened, not really."

"That's not up to me. But I can suggest it to Bernice."

"Please do. I can get her more money, if that's an issue. I just want my daughter back."

"This isn't about money. But I'll talk to her. It might not do any good, but I'll talk to her."

He put Emily to bed a little after nine, deciding to skip the bath since the idea of giving it to her alone made him uncomfortable. There was a ceiling fan in the room, and he turned it on low. The temperature outside had dropped somewhat after the rain, and a suggestion of a breeze came in through the window screen. Looking out, Landis could see rooftops jammed together, a jumble of chimneys and roof antennas and, lower, the stretched-out spiderweb of phone and power lines and the rickety wooden porches clinging to the backs of their brick houses.

"You want a story?" he offered. There was a whole bookcase full of things to choose from.

"Can you make one up?"

"I don't think so," he said. "But I read pretty well."

"No," she said. "It's all right."

"Got your own thoughts to occupy you, huh?"

She didn't answer. He was pretty sure she was gifted in ways he was unequipped to understand, and it worried him more than a little to imagine how he and Bernice were going to provide a life for her that would be even close to what she deserved.

»»»»»»

Bernice came home at one in the morning. He met her in the kitchen, where she was getting herself a glass of water, her hands trembling. She smelled strongly of beer and cigarette smoke.

"How was your date?" Landis asked. "Get much painting done?"

"I'm too short to bartend," she said. "But one guy gave me a twenty-dollar tip. Of course, he asked to see my tits, too."

"Free market economy," said Landis. "You never know what you might be able to buy."

"Well, he got a big smile and one of these." She turned her head to the side, reprovingly, and made her finger a windshield wiper indicating "no."

They went into the dining room. Landis had been in the chair in the parlor, half asleep, when he heard the rattling of the back door.

"You put her to bed?"

"Yeah."

"She called, right?"

"She wanted to know if I was a criminal. I told her no. She's worried, but I don't blame her, given the situation. Anyway, she has some idea how much to trust you, but with me, she's got nothing."

"That's ironic, isn't it? She needs to decide if she can trust you. Maybe she ought to talk to me about it."

"I just sat here all night with your daughter while you went out on a date. If you don't trust me, you're a fool."

"It wasn't a date."

"What was it?"

She finished her water, then dug out the bottle of Black Bush and poured herself some. He watched her, then got himself a glass and joined her. They sat at the table sipping their drinks in silence. Outside, it had begun to rain again, lightly. "It's him, isn't it?" he asked her. "There was no baker."

She stuck a finger in her drink, then moved it to her mouth and sucked it. "Of course there was a baker. I told you."

"Nope. I'm starting to get it now. Talk about being used. You needed me to help you take her, but all along you were planning to get with this other guy."

"That's not true," she said. "Stop."

But he felt it in the air and in his stomach, even in his teeth. "Your mother's boyfriend? How messed up is that? What—is the age difference between the two of us not enough? You need more? You're completely out of control. Trust. You want to talk about trust? I can't believe I got involved in any of this. I'm going home," he said.

"Home, home? Or just home?"

He looked at her, all that strange beauty, all that deception. He stood. "Do what you want," he said. "You will anyway."

SIXTEEN

The palm reader's parlor was over a magic-and-joke shop, just off Tejon Street and a couple doors down from the salon where Tessa got her hair done. It was decorated simply, with furniture that looked as if it were on its third owner—a green recliner, a yellow-gold daybed, a lamp made of antlers. The walls were painted a comforting dusty rose, and there was a bowl of peanut M&Ms on the table.

"Your hands are shaking," said Madame Marguerite. She had a peculiar accent, but except for that and the orange scarf tied around her head, she seemed ordinary, with a plain face and smallish eyes, one of which wandered a bit. Her eyebrows were drawn on, and her lipstick was the color of wet sand. Tessa had once eaten at a place that featured belly dancing, and the dancer had struck her in much the same way. But what did she expect in Colorado? The belly dancer had been blonde, with a doughy, unappealing stomach and more than a touch of underarm odor. Madame Marguerite was dirty blonde, freckled, attractive in a skinny, too-many-cigarettes way. She had probably gotten her palm-reading certificate over the Internet.

"I have a chill," said Tessa. She took a single M&M from the bowl and placed it on her tongue. It was 9:00 AM and she'd been waiting in her car for twenty minutes for the place to open.

"You are left handed," remarked Madame Marguerite. "That means you are right-brain dominant. Intuitive, not so interested in intellectual things."

"I suppose."

"And you are worried about something."

"Yes, that's right."

She took Tessa's hand and ran an exploratory finger along its edge, then held it open. "The life line is long and deep—that's very good. You have a spade-shaped hand, indicating manual dexterity. You are probably good at fixing things around the house, perhaps even musical?"

"I teach piano," said Tessa. "But that's not what I want to know. I mean, that's something I already know." The M&M had begun to dissolve on her tongue, in spite of her mouth's dryness. She crunched it up.

"Ah," said Madame Marguerite. "You are one of those people who want to know the future."

"Sorry," she said. "But the sign does say Palm Readings. That was twenty-five dollars I gave you. I thought telling the future was part of the bargain."

"The future doesn't exist. That's the big secret. It's now, and now, and now. And now." She smiled. "See what I mean? It just keeps coming."

"Then why am I here?"

"You want to know about *now.* It might seem like I'm being difficult, but I'm just trying to be clear."

Tessa thought she might choke. "Do you have some water?"

Madame Marguerite hurried over to the sink and brought her back a glass. "Are you OK?"

"I'm fine," she said.

"OK, tell me, what is it about your health that concerns you?"

"I'm not able to eat, if that's what you mean. I'm not sleeping very well, either."

"There is someone in your life you are having trouble communicating with?"

"I think I get it," said Tessa. "You could ask these questions of anyone."

"I am asking them of you. Only you."

"Where are you from?" asked Tessa.

"Colorado," she said. "Southern part. This here" — she ran a finger across Tessa's palm—"this is the head line. Very important. Yours is broken, right here."

"I have a broken head line?"

"Exactly." She leaned back in her chair. "There was your life before today, and then there is your life after today. Think hard. There is no future. But from today, every choice you make can shape the next present. Does this make sense?"

"And that's not the future?"

"I told you, there is no future. If you want, I can get out a crystal ball. I have a crystal ball. Children like to see it."

Tessa bit at her lip. Madame Marguerite came around to comfort her, putting an arm around her shoulder. "Your problem is to do with your child. I see that. She is sick, isn't she?"

"I don't know why I came," said Tessa. "I'm sorry." She got up to go.

"The reading isn't over," said Madame Marguerite.

But Tessa was already hurrying out the door.

Emily, she thought, bypassing God entirely. *I know you can hear me. Everything is going to be OK.*

A dark cloud had settled over the peak. In front of the Antlers Hotel, a clown was making balloon animals. She wandered toward her car, picking up her pace when she saw a woman in a uniform getting ready to write her up for an expired meter. "No!" she shouted. "I'm here!"

»»»»»

At the airport, she put her car in long-term parking and rode the shuttle bus to the terminal. It was raining on the mountain, but to the east it was a hot, sunny day, two realities coexisting, as in a dream. She had an hour to kill, so she bought a paper, ordered a coffee at the snack bar, sat down, and pretended to read. The terminal air smelled like something sprayed out of a can. A man with a string tie and a cowboy hat asked if she were alone, said maybe he could join her.

"You don't understand," she said. "I'm married."

"Didn't mean it that way," he said. "Only how you looked like you could use a doughnut, go with that coffee. Bartender." He raised a hand. "Couple of your finest doughnuts."

"What do you do?" she said, after the doughnuts had arrived.

"Manufacture tubing," he said.

"Like for the inside of tires?"

"Nope. More like custom tubing—aluminum. You heard of a Blackhawk helicopter? Well, they couldn't fly one of those things without our tubing. We got tubing that's on space shuttles. Discovery and Columbia. What happened to Columbia, that was foam breaking off and hitting the ship. I guarantee you, the tubing, which is internal, by the way, was fine straight on through."

"Not something I ever gave much thought to."

"Well, you wouldn't. Most people don't." He moved his chair a little closer to hers. "Say, it wouldn't be too forward of me to ask if I might have a little dunk, would it?" He held out a broken-off piece of his cruller. "You mind?"

Against her better judgment, she let him. He dipped the pastry into her cup, held it there for a moment, then extracted it and slipped it quickly into his mouth. She figured him for about forty, and his smoky blue eyes weren't unappealing. He dipped again.

"Nothing like a good dunk," he said.

"You can have the rest," she said, pushing the cup toward him. "I didn't want it in the first place."

He smiled at her. "Then I guess a blow job would be out of the question?"

She jumped up, grabbed her bag and newspaper, and walked quickly to the gate area, where she seated herself beside an elderly woman in a pink pantsuit who was talking loudly on a cell phone.

She had a broken head line. Perhaps people could sense this about her.

Tessa got out her own cell phone and began to dial David's number, but then stopped. Supposedly he'd gone hiking. She didn't know what was right anymore. When she was with him, she thought one way, by herself, another. He was a cheating bastard—she understood this. But he was *her* bastard. She'd promised God, she'd promised Jesus, she'd promised her parents, she'd promised herself. Her marriage wasn't just some part of her life, her marriage *was* her life. If she lost Emily and then lost David, what would she have left? And yet, if she spoke to him, she might never get on the plane. Instead, she called the house and left a message on the machine. She'd be back in two days. There were frozen pizzas in the freezer, or he might even want to pick up something from Szechuan Dragon. She'd try to call again soon.

»»»»»

Inside the BWI terminal, it was noisy, people seemed to speak another language entirely, and every other face was dark. She felt completely out of her element, and it made her worry even more about Emily and what had happened, how she might have already changed into someone unfamiliar. What did she know about people like this? Her life so far had been clean and tidy and American, and yet it had somehow led her here, to this chaos.

When they'd come back from Bear Mountain, it had been in silence. At the house, he'd gone off alone, slept downstairs. She couldn't tell what he was thinking—she never had been able to, only now it scared her. She hadn't seen him at all yesterday—he'd worked, and then his band had had a gig up in Littleton. Robin called in the afternoon and told her that Landis was in Baltimore, and after hanging up Tessa made herself an omelet and some bacon, poured herself a glass of milk. She sat at their kitchen table and ate as slowly and deliberately as she could, forcing it down. She needed her strength. Her body was starting to consume itself, she was convinced. When she was done, she cleaned up the dishes and called Baltimore information to inquire about people named Click. Bernice, who had been living in Atlanta before coming to stay with them, had always been mysterious about her past. There were two listings, so she just chose one. She got Bernice's father on the first try. "Of course," he said, after she'd explained who she was. "I understand completely." Then he gave her another number.

It took Tessa a while to get up the courage to make the call. For much of the afternoon, she stared at the number. And then finally, she dialed it. "Bernice?" she said. "Bernice? Is that you?" For just that moment, she felt the two of them connected not just by a stream of electrons passing through phone lines but also by a mutual cord of love, anger, and regret. Finally, Bernice hung up. When Tessa tried back, the phone just rang and rang.

And then, at last, she'd gotten to speak to her.

She got on line for a cab and had the driver take her to a cheap hotel a few blocks up from the inner harbor. Her driver was Pakistani or Indian or something, intent on being a cheery tour guide, and she barely heard a thing he said, other than that the brother of the new president of Afghanistan owned a restaurant in town. There were strange characters hanging around in the shadows around the hotel entrance, but the doorway itself was bright and the glass and chrome polished and inviting, the entrance floor a pink marble. She announced her presence to the receptionist, presented a credit card, and was given a room on the sixth floor. Once inside, she called Bernice's number, but the phone just rang. After counting to twenty, she hung up and sank into the desk chair, which smelled of old cigarette smoke and Lysol. Then she found Donald Click's number and dialed it.

»»»»»

In the huge, dark apartment, she sat on the sofa. She was surprised at how old Donald Click was, given Bernice's age.

He'd poured her a ginger ale, though he was drinking scotch, and there was jazz music playing. She thought she could hear the sound of a television coming from the other room, too. This seemed a strange way to live.

"I'm very sorry," he said. "You're obviously in distress. At least you can feel better knowing that Pearl is just fine—I've seen her and I can attest to it."

"Emily," said Tessa. "Her name is Emily. After my grandmother."

"Well, the kid I met goes by Pearl," he said.

Her eyes wandered to a painting on the wall—it looked like someone had lobbed paint at the canvas from a distance, then scratched it off with a rake.

"That's mine," he said.

"It's nice."

He sipped his drink. "My wife—Bernice's mother—had what she called her purple days. A purple day could come along just about any time, and there was no real predictor. And on those days, well, let's just say she was unreasonable. It was very hard on me, and on Bernice. Eve—that was her name—left us. In the long run, I think it was better for everyone."

"I'm not sure I understand what you are saying."

"Bernice has it, too, whatever it is. Purple days. It's in her eyes, that distant look she'll sometimes get. This isn't supposed to be an excuse. I'm just telling you."

"There's nothing wrong with Emily." She thought about how the child talked to herself, how she sometimes got up in the middle of the night and wandered the house. But these things were all normal enough—she'd asked their pediatrician. She'd checked the books, like a responsible mother. And not just the ones David had bought her, *Raising an Angel* and *The Godly Child*, but Dr. Spock, too.

"I'm sure you're right." Loud voices suddenly started up outside the window, and he pointed. "Look," he said. "You can see their legs."

She watched. Just visible through the partially closed slats of the blinds, two pairs of legs, one male, one female, had paused on the sidewalk outside. The man was angrily berating the woman about something.

"I'm the troll under the bridge. It's better than reality TV. Last night, a man drank two whole pints of vodka out there—I found the empties this morning. Talked to himself the entire time, too. Kept saying, 'I told you it wasn't like that, but you wouldn't listen. Why wouldn't you listen?'"

"That's—I don't think I could live like that."

"I've decided it's a privilege. Everything is perspective, you know."

"Who do you think he was talking to?"

"His wife? The president? Who knows? Just someone who wouldn't listen. I sympathize with him. I feel like I've been talking to myself my whole life." He gave her a sort of half smile.

Tessa thought he was attractive. She also saw that his age difference must have made it almost impossible for him to relate to Bernice after his marriage broke up. Her own parents were older, too—her father retired air force, her mother a silent homemaker who'd had Tessa when she was forty. Tessa hadn't mentioned anything to them yet about Emily's disappearance because she knew what they'd think, which was that she'd somehow misplaced her, like the bicycle they'd bought her for her twelfth birthday, which she'd left outside school the next day, walking home instead, because that was what she always did. When she'd remembered a few hours later and hurried back, it was gone, its chain lock cut, and nothing around but a few gum wrappers in the dirt.

"I'd like to know where they are," she said.

He tore a yellow sheet of paper off a small pad and wrote something on it. "Here's the address. I'm selling the house. That's what I say, anyway. I haven't contacted a broker. You get attached to things, you know? But it's my retirement, so I'll probably have to cash in soon enough. I said she could stay there for a while, just until she gets herself sorted out. I suppose you've got papers, or whatever, on the child?"

"We don't want to have to go through with all of that. Or I don't, anyway. I'm just hoping she'll listen to reason."

"Oh, sure," he said. "That sounds like Bernice."

»»»»»

After she used his phone to call again, and there was still no answer, he called her a cab. This driver was foreign looking, dark, and didn't talk at all. His radio was tuned to a station in what she guessed was some African language. On the ride north, she passed handsome old stone row homes, a lively area of bars and restaurants, a man playing the ukulele at a bus stop. There was a grand train station, and then the neighborhood grew quickly more dilapidated, some of the buildings still massive, but clearly no longer in use. She saw signs for fried chicken and something called lake trout, and there were other signs in what she thought might be Korean. They passed houses with boards in their windows and concrete where the doors had been, an ancient pharmacy advertising patent medicines, the Anointed Hands of Perfection Beauty Parlor, and a vertical yellow sign that read, simply, "Afro-American." Then they were in a more residential section again, with three-story houses and porches. The driver made a turn and then another. Finally, they pulled up in front of the address and she found some money in her purse.

Excited to be so close, in spite of her exhaustion, she waved to the driver that she was fine, and the cab pulled back out into traffic and disappeared up the block. She mounted the steps to the front porch, noting the peeling paint and sagging wood. As she stood staring at the door, trying to get up the nerve to press the bell, she heard voices behind her.

They all froze for a moment, a tableau of uncertainty: Bernice a bright-eyed, hard-bodied, punk-looking girl in jeans and a green top that left a suggestive few inches of stomach exposed; Landis, earnest and bearlike in jeans and a work shirt; Emily a tiny exclamation mark of attention, her thin legs emerging from oversized blue shorts, her T-shirt decorated with the cartoon image of a one-eyed man with an enormous moustache. Emily came rushing toward her, arms outstretched, and Bernice turned and ran away up the street.

"Hey!" Landis shouted after her.

"Sweetheart," said Tessa, hugging Emily. She held her out to look at her, then hugged her again. Her face was dirty and her nose needed a wipe, but otherwise, she seemed just fine. "Oh," she said. "Oh."

"We had chocolate ice cream," said Emily.

"Go after her," said Tessa to Landis, wrapping the child even tighter in her arms, happy at the familiar way Emily's head locked into the space between her head and shoulder. "It's all right."

Landis was still standing at the gate. "I should probably stay here."

"I won't do anything," said Tessa. "You go on. Where do you think she went?"

"I don't know." He kicked at the sidewalk. "How do I know you don't have a cab coming?"

"The cab left. It's just me. Emily and I will stay here, I promise. Can you let us in?"

He shook his head. "Bernice has the key. Unless she's got one. Emily?"

"Bernice has the key," Emily said, pulling away.

"OK, then," said Landis, uneasily. "I'll be right back." He took off jogging in the direction that Bernice had gone.

"We can sit on the steps," said Emily, the proud owner of all of this, ready to show it off. Tessa sat down next to her, taking her hand.

"I've been so worried. Are you sure you're all right?" She found a Kleenex in her pocket and wiped at the chocolate on Emily's cheek. Then she held it to her nose for her to blow, which she did.

"I had an inspection in my ear. But I took drops."

"Let me see?" She peered in. "Nope. No inspection that I can make out."

"It's gone, now. It wasn't a demon."

"I hope not." Tessa hugged her again, her eyes filling with tears. She kissed her neck, her ears. Finally, she let her go. "You're coming home with me. Back home." She sniffed and peered up the block, but there was still no sign of Bernice and Landis. She could, of course, grab Emily and find another cab, just make a run for it right now, in spite of her promise, and whether or not Emily wanted to come. They'd had battles of will before. Last spring, Emily had gone through a period with her *Veggie Tales* videos when she simply wouldn't stop watching, and David had finally had to lift her and carry her into her bedroom, screaming. For a while, she'd wanted a dog—one of the neighbors had recently purchased a puppy—and when they told her no, she'd refused to eat for an entire day. "You want to, right? You want to come home with me?"

"Of course," she said.

"I promise that sometimes in the future you can come and visit Bernice. OK?"

Before she could answer, they were rejoined by Landis, who was out of breath and sweating.

"She's heading to the coffee shop. She says she won't come back until you're gone." Tessa was pretty sure this was the same person she'd seen back in the Springs. There was something off kilter about his face, as if the two sides hadn't been aligned quite right. He looked strong. "Just you, I mean." He nodded at Emily. "She's supposed to stay."

"Supposed to?"

He looked somewhat embarrassed. "Yeah."

"I need to talk to her," Tessa said. "Where's this coffee shop?"

"Around the corner." He dug the key out his pocket. "At least I can let us in now. We'll call you a cab."

"I can find it myself if you won't tell me."

"You'll see it. I don't know what it's called—Lucky's, Louie's, Lovers. Something."

Tessa kissed Emily on the forehead. "Do you want to come?"

"Yes," said Emily.

»»»»»»

It was Lucille's. She found Bernice seated at a table in the very back, staring at a brownie. "Hello," she said. She helped Emily into a seat.

"Hello, yourself," said Bernice, clearly sulking. "She likes me more."

"This isn't a contest. And anyway, that's not true."

"Is. Ask her. I'm teaching her devil worship. We read *Harry Potter* together, and next week we're getting matching tattoos that say Darwin, with little feet."

Tessa looked around at the few other customers, most of them reading at their tables, apparently not paying attention to this scene. "Why are you being like this?"

"Because I can. Because I don't care anymore. I mean, I'm past caring."

"How will you support her?"

"I'll manage. I'm sure as a single mother, I'm qualified for all kinds of special programs. If not, I'll move to France. They have free health care, I hear."

"She's starting school next week."

"School? Or Bible boot camp? I know what you people are up to with her. She'll start school all right, but it will be someplace normal."

"You've looked into that, have you?"

Bernice's eyes were lit blue, like match heads. "It's on my list."

Tessa took a deep breath. She had been both dreading and longing for this moment. Emily had removed all the sugar packets from their holder and was arranging them in patterns on the table. A waitress came to take Tessa's order, but she waved her off. "You must see that, between the two of us, I'm the one with more to offer," she said, quietly.

"No," said Bernice. "I must not. I used to think that. The whole time I was living with you, and for the next couple of years, that's what I kept telling myself. I bought it—the whole package. Nice house, fresh air, squeaky-clean white people who owned mountain bikes and who would make sure she didn't smoke and didn't screw or do drugs. I almost believed it myself—almost. Then one day I realized it wasn't true."

"What wasn't true?"

She didn't answer.

"What?"

"That you were better than me."

"I never said that."

"You did just now. 'I have more to offer.'"

"I didn't mean it that way."

"Sure, you did. Anyway, it doesn't matter. It's practically leaking out your pores."

"I thought it was the opposite, that you felt you were better than *us*."

Bernice drank some of her coffee, spilling a few drops down the front of her shirt in the process. She dabbed ineffectively at them with a napkin, then tossed it to the table. "I didn't finish college," she said.

"What does that have to do with anything? Finish now. No one's stopping you."

"I'm sorry," said Bernice. "Sorry, sorry. All right? I said it. Now, couldn't you just go home to your husband and forget about us?"

Neither one of them said anything for almost a minute. Tessa did think about David, but for some reason, what she imagined was his running socks, laundered, lying neatly in little white balls in the top drawer of his dresser where she'd placed them. "He's cheating on me," she said, quietly. Emily continued arranging the sugar packets.

"I heard him tell you once that God must have been watching out for him because he'd found a place to gas up for three cents less a gallon than usual. Do you think God cares how much it costs for that creep to fill his tank? It's so . . ." searching for the word, she held her hands out, fingers apart, as if she'd just released an invisible bird.

"Did you hear me?"

"Yeah," she said. "I heard. That's what guys do. They cheat, and they lie. Are you really surprised?"

"As a matter of fact, yes."

"Well, I can't help you there."

"Two weeks ago, everything was one way, now it's another, and I don't see how it can go back. The only thing I'm really certain of is that I have a daughter."

"So do I. Right? Just go ahead and hate me."

"My mother always said to hate the deed, not the person."

"That's nice. My mother always said, 'Fat over lean.'"

"What does that mean?"

"It's a painting thing. For oils, you want to make sure that your outer layer doesn't dry before your inner layer does, or else you'll end up with a cracked surface."

"I still have all of the artwork you did at our house," said Tessa. She didn't mention that David had insisted it be kept in the closet. "There's the still life with the lemons, and the one of the backyard, with Pikes Peak in the distance."

If this made any impression on Bernice, it didn't show. It was a gift to be able to see something and then make an image of it, Tessa thought, and she was envious of Bernice's ability, just as she was envious of the biological ordinariness of Bernice's body, where reproduction had simply happened. Bernice drank more coffee. "This stuff isn't even hot." She pushed the cup away from her. "You look tired. Where are you staying?"

"A hotel," said Tessa.

"Why don't you go back there, get some rest."

"I won't go without her."

"It's OK, Mommy," Emily said. "You can go."

"Maybe tomorrow, we'll go to the aquarium and see the sharks," said Bernice, swiveling in her chair. "What about that? You're a shark fan, aren't you?"

"I'd like to," said Emily.

Bernice touched the girl's hair briefly, then turned back. In the years since Tessa had last seen her, Bernice's features had taken on a new definition, an adultness that Tessa found almost surprising.

"I'm going to think about this, OK?" said Bernice. "Give me tonight. You can do that. I know there's no reason for you to trust me, really, and you shouldn't—you shouldn't trust me. But it will mean something to me if you try. You have to give me status here. I've had one miracle in my life, and that was the day my daughter recognized me. That's *my* religion, and you have to respect it. Without ever seeing me, she knew. Right, honey?"

"We have a photo," Tessa said, feeling a sudden need to hurt her, if only a little. "From just after you first came. You're in shorts and a bathing-suit top, out on the deck. She's seen it—I let her. That's how she recognized you."

"I don't care," said Bernice. "I don't care what you say. I know what I know."

The marbled pattern in the plastic tabletop gave Tessa a sudden realization. "David's drums," she said.

"What about them?"

"Pearl. That's the brand. It says it right on the front of them."

"Well, what do you know?" said Bernice to Emily. "You named yourself after a set of drums. I hadn't put that together. I guess it's better than Ludwig." She leaned forward toward Tessa. "Christian rock? Isn't that like 'military intelligence,' or 'jumbo shrimp?' Aren't you just a little, I don't know, embarrassed?"

"You shouldn't put something down when you don't know anything about it," said Tessa.

Bernice's face flushed. "Look, I'll stay here. You go back and get Landis to drive you to wherever it is you're staying. I won't run away with her again, I promise."

"How do I know that?"

"You don't. It will be an exercise in *faith*."

"Why do you hate me so much? What did I ever do to you? We took care of you, we fed you."

"I was tricked," said Bernice. "We were never friends."

A fire truck passed by outside, its strobing light and blaring siren momentarily pausing time inside the coffee shop.

"You said you didn't want your baby," Tessa whispered. "That's what you said! And you took our money."

"I can't believe you just said that in front of her," said Bernice.

"We could have been friends. I wanted that." She hesitated. "Look, was there anything else that happened? Anything I don't know about?"

Bernice blew her nose into another napkin. "I have no idea what you mean."

"With David."

"Could this wait until tomorrow?"

"Never mind. I already know the answer."

"No, you don't. You don't know anything."

But Tessa was starting to feel a strange separation from herself, a feeling that, had she been in church, she might have attributed to something else entirely. "I will," she said. "Because you ask, and because Emily seems all right, I will go back to my hotel. But I want you to understand something. You may have given birth to her, but Emily is *my* daughter. I changed her and got up with her in the night and held her when she cried. I took her to the doctor and bought her things to wear and taught her to speak and to dress herself, and I fed her and tucked her in at night and loved her. I did that, not you. We did it together, she and I. Now you've changed your mind, and maybe I can understand that—I can even respect it, I guess. But you can't change any of those other things, because they are facts." She reached out for Emily's hand, and the girl took it. She knew each tiny finger. A waiter brought a beer to the table next to them, where a man sat by himself writing in a notebook, and she waited for him to leave. "I don't think I'm better than you. I never thought that. If you thought I thought that, well, then that's some problem you have. I'm not. I'm just a person who really, really wanted a child and couldn't have one."

"And God sent you me," said Bernice.

"That's what I believe," said Tessa.

"Then all I can say is God must really have it in for you."

SEVENTEEN

Bernice saw her mother only one more time after her make-out session with Craney Crow Devereaux. In March, they went to the Woman's Industrial Exchange for chicken salad with tomato aspic and homemade mayonnaise. They talked about Lucian Freud and Francis Bacon and even a little about what Bernice was doing at school. It was all remarkably normal. Afterward, they went for a walk up Charles Street until they were outside an enormous art deco building with the words "Monumental Life" on it, way up high, spelled out in gold lettering.

"Look," her mother said. "Ever notice that?"

Bernice took in the front of the building, where two massive fluted columns were centered inside a larger granite box shape. She did not know what any of this was about, although she felt nervous. Her mother had told the school that Bernice had a doctor's appointment, then picked her up.

“It’s not all it’s cracked up to be,” her mother went on.

“Excuse me?”

“Sex. Or maybe you know already.” She smiled pleasantly. Eve Click was still pretty, prettier than Bernice would ever be, but she was starting to look a little weathered, and at lunch, Bernice had thought she detected a skunky hint of dope smell about her clothes, though she couldn’t be certain, and she’d never known her mom to smoke.

“I’m not having sex,” Bernice said.

“Of course you’re not. But you will. So this is the talk.”

“The talk? What talk?”

“The one we’re supposed to have.”

Bernice said nothing.

“Do you know why the Woman’s Industrial Exchange got started?” her mother asked. “Confederate widows, after the war, needed some way to make money. They worked together. Women helping other women.”

“Hear me roar,” said Bernice.

“No one else was going to help them.”

“Leading directly to that fat old broad who served us lunch,” said Bernice. “She had a monumental ass on her.”

Her mother laughed. “You know,” she said, “I’ll always love you. You’re my little Chili Bean. You can’t weasel out of it.”

“Who said I wanted to?” asked Bernice.

“So, anyway, I just wanted to show you this.”

“Which has what to do with the Industrial Exchange?”

“Nothing.”

“It’s a nice building. I could imagine Superman flying around it.”

“It’s art,” she said, “of the unintentional sort. It’s a big reminder. Monumental Life. That’s something to think about. We might all be better people if we kept that in mind, you know?”

“Unintentional?”

"That's right."

"Mom," Bernice said. "I think it's just the name of a company."

"Does that matter?" she asked.

"I guess not."

"Exactly."

They were both quiet for a moment.

"And that's the talk?" asked Bernice.

"Yup," said her mother. "That's the talk." She stared up at the building, then held one finger out in front of her as if testing the wind.

"What are you doing?" Bernice asked.

"Taking away a letter."

Bernice squinted up at the words, then looked back at her mother, who seemed now to glow in the cold afternoon sun.

"Monumental Life and Monumental Lie," said her mother. "Hardly any difference at all."

»»»»»

That August, once she heard what had happened, even just the stilted, vague version of events that her father gave her, Bernice came to the conclusion that she had killed her mother. Not on purpose, of course—it wasn't the same as bashing her head in with a brick, or poisoning her slowly with arsenic in her soup—but she'd done it nonetheless. *MDMA*, her father said. *It's also called Ecstasy*. Her mother had found out about Bernice and CC. And while perhaps it was CC who had told her, it was more likely that her mother had just *felt* it, in that same way she'd known Bernice had been mean to another girl at school one day, and had made her stand in the closet for twenty minutes when she got home, despite Bernice's protests. The way she'd always known everything, as if Bernice's head were made of glass.

In May, there had been the card that said, "I've moved!" on it, with her new address in Fell's Point, and a ten-dollar bill stuck inside. Then her mother had been accepted to a small arts colony in New Mexico. "Not a real place," her father had sniffed, although Bernice sensed his jealousy. "Just some for-profit crap." An antique linen postcard had arrived for Bernice at the house. On the front it read Driveway Across Elephant Butte Dam, and there was a picture of an old-fashioned road with no cars on it and what appeared to be regularly spaced lampposts receding toward a vanishing point. On the back, her mother had written, "I found this and thought of you." Bernice had no idea what she meant. Found what? The card? The dam itself? And thought of her why? Thought of her how?

And then, in August, a couple of hippies on their way for a soak and a smoke in the hot springs outside of Jemez had found her.

Her father, with whom her mother had barely spoken in years, made calls, made arrangements, flew out there, dutifully fulfilling his role. They were still married, after all. Seeking someone to blame other than herself, Bernice decided he shouldn't have let his wife make the terrible mistake of moving out in the first place, even though at the time it had been a relief. She'd thought this all along—it was part of the distance between them, that and the fact that he was, obviously, completely unsure of what to do with her, and resentful that this responsibility had fallen to him. Her mother had never been up for life without him, not remotely. He should never have pretended otherwise.

Bernice's blood thickened, her brain slowed. She hadn't done it with CC. She *hadn't.* She told this to her mother at night, lying in her room, staring up into the darkness. Why should nothing lead to something? She tried blaming her mother, and sometimes it worked, but more often it didn't. At her summer job selling watches from a cart in the mall, she started stealing money, and was surprised to find that she simply got away with it. There were no consequences. In an effort to change who she was, one night she went out on the roof and burned her envelope-lining collection. Afterward, she felt no different. The ashes floated over the rooftops like tiny insects.

»»»»»

There was another year of high school to get through, and she managed it, dressing in oversized vintage clothes, hanging out in gay bars in Mount Vernon that were unconcerned about ID and in some of the new, grungier clubs opening up near North Avenue, where Ecstasy was as easy to come by as Budweiser. She took it a number of times and it did not kill her, but it didn't make her feel good, either, or inspire the shit-eating grins she observed on other people. She began to suspect they were only faking it. She stayed far away from Fell's Point. She applied to and was accepted at Georgia State—picking it because her gay English teacher, whom she liked a lot, had gone there, and because it was supposed to have a good painting and drawing program, and because it would be warm and far away from her father.

In the fall, through the university, she found an apartment near campus to share with three sorority girls in a complex called Peachtree Village. She knew nothing about Atlanta, but thought it was probably as good as anyplace else. Her first semester, she dated a creative writing student with a bunch of piercings and tattoos, but she had contempt for him and eventually stopped returning his calls. She went shopping for new clothes, a new identity, something more southern and feminine. She dyed her hair blonde. A history grad student asked her out, and tried to reach up her skirt while talking to her about Savonarola. Her father sent her a subscription to

Art in America, which she studied carefully each month, alone in her closet-sized room. It was the only thing she studied. She was failing nearly everything, going to bars nightly, crashing on her new friend Gillian's couch two and three nights a week. But then Gillian moved away. Bernice, abandoned again and convinced by now that what she was experiencing was probably depression of some sort, still managed to suck it up enough to manage a few Ds. She was allowed back for a second year, though on academic probation. The sorority girls were not so forgiving. They politely but firmly let her know that they wished her well but that they were turning her room into an *actual* closet. She found herself another place in Little Five Points, this time with a possibly gay guy named Tim who programmed computers and played video games and lived almost entirely off Wheaties—he consumed bowl after bowl of the stuff. His used bowls sat in the sink, the uneaten flakes hardening and clinging to the sides like barnacles.

In the spring of her sophomore year, she stopped going to class entirely and took a job at Noon Pie Bakers, working the register. Often, she found herself with so little ambition, so little sense of purpose, that it seemed she ought simply to drown herself, too. Then, one day, she'd read in *Creative Loafing* that Texas Flood would be playing at Blue Mondays, and she decided it was a sign. She scrutinized the poor-quality photo of the band. It was definitely him: CC. There was pollen everywhere that week, a light green dusting changing the colors of cars, causing people to sneeze and wheeze. The whole world seemed to be waking up and coming alive.

She didn't tell anyone about the show. Tim surprised her by inviting her to the movies to see *Mission Impossible* (that he was a big Tom Cruise fan was part of her evidence about his sexuality), but Bernice said she wasn't feeling well. She almost didn't go out, because she really wasn't feeling well, but at ten she put on a short skirt and heels and a jeans jacket and walked the half mile to the bar.

She paid her five dollars, managed to find a spot to stand, pretended to be interested in the music. It was violently loud and hurt her ears. She imagined her mother joining her, breathing drunkenly on her as the two of them watched CC, a big leather hat pulled down over his eyes, his guitar reminiscent of a low-slung machine gun. *You see*, her mother said. *You see what got me interested?* Bernice ignored her, just as she'd ignored her on the nights when she would come up to her room, late, and stand in the doorway, a glass of wine in her hand, staring at her. Then Bernice had pretended that she was asleep, modulating her breathing to sound that way, the only other sound in the room the ticking of the ancient steam radiators, the rattle of the windows in their frames.

At the break, she found him. He seemed genuinely pleased about it. They stared at each other, the enormous thing between them something neither of them cared to address. What did it matter? The smoke staining the air was bitter, and the three drinks she'd downed felt like nine. She was conscious of the stares of other girls trying to figure out how this not particularly special-looking chick could have the attention of someone in the band.

"You want to party later?" he asked.

"Your place or mine?"

"You live alone?"

She shook her head, batted her eyelashes.

"Well," he said, "I've got a hotel room." Then he leaned forward and kissed her ear, at the same time slipping a hand around and giving her ass a quick squeeze.

When the band started again, she plugged bits of napkin into her ears to muffle the music. There was an inevitability to this evening that Bernice wasn't going to stand in the way of. Some things were destined, and she and CC were one of them. She'd always known this, and if she resisted, she'd never move forward, never find out what was next for her.

A few yards away, there was a small commotion as two guys started pushing at each other, and then one threw a punch. It was hard to tell what was going on, as the people in their immediate vicinity backed away, blocking her view in a brief retreating wave of sweaty, cigarette-smelling humanity. CC's guitar spat out notes, a high-wire act of shiny, fast noise, and Bernice felt special and chosen and lucky, perhaps the most important person in the room.

She drank a lot—so much she lost count. She had no idea how they got to the motel, or where it was, though later she remembered the smell of the magnolias, and the sound of a highway overpass nearby that hummed with the weight of the occasional truck. She made him take a shower because he was sweaty and his feet stank, and while he was in there, she tore a bunch of pages out of the Gideons Bible and stuffed them into his pillow as a joke. They did it, and she didn't think it went too badly, considering all the alcohol.

"Mistake?" he repeated, after she whispered the word to him.

She nodded. She was crying.

"What the hell?" He pulled the crumpled papers out of the pillow.

It didn't seem all that funny to her, either.

And then it was light and she was in a cab, her clothes unpleasant against her skin, the humidity a damp towel thrown over the city. Downtown Atlanta was visible ahead of her, its shiny buildings like Oz, or a child's vision of paradise. She smacked her forehead with her hand. The stupid shit you did when you were fucked up. She thought back to health class and to her mother's copy of *Our Bodies, Ourselves*, trying to remember how that all worked. The way her head felt, the way every nerve she had was crying out for water and sleep, she doubted she was even remotely capable of conception, anyway.

The driver was a white guy with a shaved head and wraparound sunglasses, and he had the radio tuned to a rock station, currently playing "The Low Spark of High-Heeled Boys." Stripped of everything was exactly how she felt. She thought how there were a million soundtracks out there, going on all the time. How were you supposed to know which one was yours? She thought that when she got home, she was going to sleep until dinner. She thought, *Well that's over with.*

EIGHTEEN

CC Devereaux watched the TV over the bar, on which a reporter was explaining a sinkhole that had appeared in the middle of Cathedral Street, and wondered why it had taken so long for his past to catch up with him. Tucked away in the back of his top dresser drawer there was a small book in which he'd listed the names of every woman he'd had sex with. The total was fifty-one. The last name, written in a year ago, was Fiona Cooper, the former exotic dancer who now worked part-time as a caterer. Sometimes fifty-one seemed like a lot; other times he figured it was probably just about right. He was a man, after all. It wasn't like he'd forgotten them—on the contrary, the very fact that he'd inscribed their names seemed proof to him that he cared about them. Once a year, usually when he'd had a few drinks, he brought out the book and went through them, trying to reassemble circumstances, remember faces.

Some had faded with time, while others, like Eve's, were still vivid as a photograph. He'd known a lot of love, but none of it had stuck and, remarkably, there had been no consequences. He'd always feared that one day, some woman was going to bust in on his life and say, "Here he is; here's your kid. What are you going to do about it?" He'd just never thought it would be Bernice.

"Sinkhole," said Freddy, who was nursing a large Coca-Cola at the bar and smoking a Newport. "What about that? You're walking down the street one minute, the next you're fifteen feet below street level looking into them sewer pipes."

"Big, huh?" said CC.

"You could lose a truck in that thing, man."

Apparently a sewage pipe had broken, and the surrounding sand and dirt, no longer supported, had sifted downward. At street level there had been, initially, a small puckering of asphalt. A smirk. Over the course of several hours, this had developed into a smile, a laugh, and the present deep guffaw.

"How are you feeling?" CC asked Freddy.

"What's that supposed to mean?" Freddy said. He was the house drummer, and moody.

"I mean, tonight, are you going to play like you mean it, or are you going to phone it in like last night?"

"Can't say." He took off the leather baseball cap he wore to hide his baldness—CC never understood why Freddy didn't just shave what remained of his hair—scratched his head, replaced the hat, then stared menacingly at him through the small, midnight-blue disks of his sunglasses. "What are you so touchy about?"

Maybe it wasn't true. He'd seen the little girl, and he'd thought he'd felt something, some connection. But that could just be vanity on his part.

"I'm a sinkhole for you baby," sang Max Lucca, the kid he'd hired to play seven to ten. He was set up about twenty feet away at the front of the bar, in the window, and he currently had an audience of one, a man so drunk—he'd come in that way—that he probably had no idea where he was. "A stinking hole of sinking road."

"'Stinking hole?'" said CC.

"I like this guy," said Freddy. "He's feeling it."

"You got any kids?" he asked. He'd known Freddy seven years, but if it had ever come up before, he'd forgotten the answer.

"Nope, no kids."

"Married, ever?"

Freddy continued to look up at the TV. "Why do you want to know?"

"I'm interested in you. You're a mystery."

"That's a good thing. You want to have some mystery in your life." He tapped out another cigarette from his pack.

"I don't know. Mystery might be overrated."

"Like this sinkhole," he said. "Mysterious. You're just walking along the street one day and then—wham!—sucked right down into the bowels of the earth."

"So you said."

"We have no idea what's down there," said Freddy. "Tunnels and pipes and ducts and wiring—it's like science fiction."

"Not to mention mole people," said CC. "Don't forget the mole people."

"I'm an earthquake, baby," sang Max Lucca.

"Now he's an earthquake," said Freddy. "He's moving up."

"He'll be a volcano, next," said CC.

"Tidal wave," said Freddy. "Hurricane." He pulled a pack of matches from the dispenser on the bar and lit the cigarette, then examined it. "What happened to the old ones?" he said.

"Printing matchbooks is a cost," said CC. "It's an expense. And there's no point, not with the place closing."

"Damn," said Freddy. "You know what? Until this moment, it didn't seem real to me. That fat sonofabitch been saying he was going to close this place for years. But the matchbooks just kept on coming, you know? This seems serious."

"Oh, it's serious."

"I might have to start looking around."

"For what?" said CC.

"Another job."

"You think this is a job?"

They sat in silence, watching the television for a while. "You know who called me?" Freddy asked.

"No. Who?"

"Bootsy Collins. I was on the phone with him this afternoon."

"What drugs are you on?"

"Bootsy and me go back a long time. We're talking about a project out in LA. Maybe I'll just have to go out there."

Freddy needed an ample fantasy life to make up for the rather close horizons of his actual one. CC worried daily about what he, himself, was becoming.

"I'm a manhole," sang Max Lucca. "A hundred pounds of solid steel."

"Now he's a manhole." Freddy tossed the matchbook back into the dispenser.

"I don't much care for the image."

"No, no. He's good. I like him."

"They aren't steel, are they?"

"What?"

"Manholes. Aren't they like iron or something?"

Freddy sucked more smoke. "That new bartender last night was interesting."

"Interesting how?"

"Sassy. You planning on doing anything about her?"

CC shrugged. He'd made a point last night of letting Jimmy do most of the interacting with Bernice, and she'd acted as if this were exactly what she'd expected. But he'd also been aware that she was watching him a lot. It had been a quiet night, with just a few jammers showing up. Around eleven, he'd had to run over to Fiona's to help her kill a mouse. She lived two doors away from the Latin Palace, where it was ladies' night, and the street outside had been full of idling cars with fancy hubcaps and darkened glass.

"Who you got playing bass tonight?" asked Freddy. The usual house bass player, Porkpie, had been banned for life two nights earlier by Mike for pouring a drink out onto the bar, something he'd done slowly, dramatically, and while standing on a bar stool. Last night, the gynecologist guitar player from Hopkins had come down, and CC had played bass on the house instrument, a black Korean item with mismatched strings that looked like a reject from a Kiss video, until an actual bass player had come by and taken over. Then he'd gone to Fiona's.

"Steve Zimmer."

"You did that for me?"

"I called him and he was free." CC was beginning to think that all bass players came with mental problems. Zimmer's prodigious bass chops were matched only by his ego and inability to control himself, which was why he kept losing gigs and was occasionally available to work a job as lame as jam night at the Harborview, where *every* night was now jam night, meaning that Mike got all his entertainment—however amateur—for free. Porkpie had lately been prone to picking fights and stubbing out cigarettes on the walls, and then he'd pulled the stunt the other night. It amazed CC that this was what his musical career had descended to.

"Thank you," said Freddy.

"You're welcome." CC stared at him. "But you think I'd be a good dad, right?"

"Oh, yeah," said Freddy. "You'd be peachy."

»»»»»

At ten o'clock Bernice still hadn't shown up. CC went onstage and led Zimmer and Freddy through a few tunes. As soon as he got a guitar in his hands, he felt more relaxed, more himself. It was as if there were two of him, one the guy who muddled through his day-to-day life trying to pay the bills and keep his girlfriend happy and maybe improve himself a little—to this end he'd recently bought a subscription to the *New Yorker*—but who was basically no one special and who, like the Harborview itself, was simply marking time. The other, exceptional CC, normally unconnected to his corporeal self, stepped into it, wraithlike, when he slipped on a guitar. What troubled him was the lack of a significant audience. When Texas Flood had ended—the gigs for a Stevie Ray Vaughan cover band had basically dried up—he'd settled in at the Harborview. He knew how good he was. He'd played up and down the East Coast, and had once even opened for the Allman Brothers. Tourists wandered in, complimented him, gave him tips. They were full of stories of the blues bars in their hometowns. He should come there sometime! And he grinned and played host. But what he mostly thought was, *These people don't know shit.*

They did "Spoonful," and "Rollin' and Tumblin'," and then a way-too-fast "You Don't Love Me," during which Freddy kept giving him looks. Peering out into the dark, squinting against the hard, bright lights, CC saw the regular faces in their seats, carrion birds waiting for their chance. Tonight the problem was going to be harmonica players. There was the waiflike deaf guy, who honked anemically, occasionally by lucky accident on key. There was Night Train, who had the kind of physique you can only earn in a prison exercise yard. He was an egotist and mean, and always seemed to think he was headlining his own band at a real money gig instead of just sitting in on jam night at a crummy dive that most decent people were afraid to go into. There were two other guys with harps out, too, though CC didn't recognize them. One looked like a college kid—a few wandered down from time to time—and the other looked like a standard over-the-hill stoner: beard, long hair, tie-dyed T-shirt bulging over a pronounced gut. There were a couple of guitar players waiting, too, skulking in the shadows at the back, smoking and pacing.

Mike had descended from his apartment above the bar, the command center from which he looked down onto the street below, monitored the drunks and partiers, and attempted to guide them through the bar's doors by psychic will and the focused power of sheer greed. He stood now near the front, talking to Max Lucca, who had hung around after his set. CC knew that he was interrogating him, asking him who the hell he was.

He and the band finished playing "Cold Shot," and CC mopped the sweat from his face with the tail of his shirt. The air-conditioning was barely doing anything, and with the lights, it seemed as if it were a hundred degrees onstage. Suddenly, Mike was sticking his fat, mutton-chopped face up at him.

"I told Max he has to bring in ten people next time he comes," he said. "He brings in ten people, all of them buying drinks—at least two—he can play here again. That's fair, right?"

"Sure, if you think charging musicians to play in your bar is fair."

Mike chose not to hear him. "Skate is here," he said. Skate Evans, a huge Aussie, stood toward the center of the bar, working on a double whiskey. A regular, he was also part of the investment group that had bought the tax lien on the Harborview. "He's going to play a few songs."

"Let him wait in line with the rest of these guys," said CC. "It's early yet."

"Sure, sure," said Mike. "Only get him up in a song or two, OK? You know how he can get."

"Did he bring a guitar?" asked CC, knowing the answer. The last time he'd loaned Skate his guitar, the man had been so drunk and so involved in the ear-splitting solo he was playing, he'd fallen backward over an amplifier.

"I don't know." Mike looked over his shoulder. "I don't think so."

"Well, then he can't play. It's a jam, Mike. He knows that. You want to play, you bring an instrument."

"Let him play yours."

"We've been through this."

"Please?" Mike looked as if it hurt him to ask, and CC was reminded—as if he needed to be—that the man's situation was not good. Still, he didn't like what this represented, and he didn't like how it made him feel.

"Night Train," he called. Night got up from the table where he'd been drinking a beer with an attractive redhead in a low-cut dress. He hopped up onto the stage without a word and began putting on a bandolier containing all his various harps over his muscle T.

"Send Skate over," said CC to Mike. "It's OK."

A minute later, Skate was onstage, strapping on CC's Tele. He was even drunker than usual, and thanked him profusely for the loan.

"Birthday, mate," he said, with a wink. Something about the way Skate peppered his speech with "mate" and "no worries" made CC wonder if he were from Australia at all.

CC hopped off the stage. Looking up, he saw it starting already. Skate could barely plug in. Freddy was shaking his head at CC, as if to say, *Don't do this*, but he'd done it, and he wasn't backing off. He felt bad for Freddy. Zimmer would hold it together enough to keep him happy, almost certainly. Zimmer was using the short break to run some impressive scales and do some snapping and popping, and didn't seem to notice the drunk across the stage from him.

CC got himself a beer and took a position at the end of the bar, under the television. He felt a tug on his arm, turned, and found Bernice.

"Hey," he said. "You're just in time for the show."

"I saw Max," she said. "He seems pretty fired up."

"He did good. Invents his own lyrics on the spot. You hear about the sinkhole?"

"I came to tell you I quit," she said. "Sorry."

"That's OK. You were never particularly hired in the first place. I mean, there was nothing official about it. And Mike was never going to go for changing the walls."

She gestured toward his beer. "Can I get one of those?"

He went back behind the bar and pulled a Rolling Rock from the cooler, conscious that Mike was watching him. He brought it back to her. "That guy on the left? He's going to hate that guy on the right."

"The black guy?"

He nodded. "They might just kill each other."

"It's like this," she said. "I have a boyfriend."

"So? I have a girlfriend." He looked toward the door, just in case Fiona might come in, but then remembered she had a catering gig in

Cockeysville. "I don't see what that's got to do with anything. Why the hell did you come down here in the first place?"

"I think I just wanted to show you that I'd changed."

"You can tell me anything you want to tell me. You know that?"

Bernice made a face. "Like what?"

"You know."

"No, I don't know."

"Like about how that's my kid."

She wiped her mouth with the back of her hand. "What most men know about reproduction, you could fit on the back of a postage stamp. You honestly believe our one night together knocked me up?"

"It didn't?"

"Think about it like miniature golf. You've got a long, thin stretch of fairway, then a big old windmill with barely enough space between two of the blades for a ball to slip through, and then on the other side, there's more green, with a little tiny cup, except that cup is up on a rise. You think that you took *one putt* and sent that ball right through the windmill and right up onto that hill and into the cup? That's what you think?" She took a big sip of beer.

"You *have* changed," said CC.

Night Train was talking to the audience. "All right now," he said. "I feel the love out there."

"See, this guy, Skate, he plays loud. And a lot of the time he's out of tune, especially when he's drunk. And Night Train, he couldn't tell you what key he's in most of the time, but he does know when things sound bad, and he gets really angry." She didn't seem interested, so he stopped. "I just thought you might like a little background."

"And you set them up together?"

"Yeah."

"Why?"

"Because I'm in charge. Because I can."

"Well, there's a philosophy to live by. So, anyway, it was a mistake, and I'll be going."

He hopped off his barstool when she did, and they stood looking at each other. Her hand was out, and he took it in his; they shook. He wanted her, he thought. Or maybe not. He wanted *something*, he knew that. He felt bad about Eve, didn't entirely understand what had happened there, only knew he hadn't been equal to the task of keeping up with all her moods. When he'd heard the news, he'd walked over to her empty apartment and stared at the door for a while, then decided it was none of his business. Done was done; everyone had to go sometime. But here she was again, in a way, a younger version, one that seemed to show up at regular—albeit infrequent—intervals, and he thought maybe some higher power might be trying to tell him something.

"Listen," he said. "I don't know about this boyfriend, but I'm quitting, too. I've got contacts down in New Orleans. Family. We could go there together." As he said it, he saw a yard with a swing set, saw himself and Bernice on a porch, sipping beers.

"I'm impressed." She looked around her approvingly. "You'd leave all this for me?"

"It's not about you. I need to move on with my life."

"I'm flattered."

"Let me show you something. He walked her over to the front wall of the room, back in the corner. There, hanging somewhat crookedly against the cracking, black-painted plaster wall, was a photo of him in a dark shirt, open at the collar, a leather hat all but obscuring his face.

"I remember that guy," she said.

"Me, at my peak," he said.

The music was already coming apart badly, with Night Train trying to sing "Born in Chicago," and Skate stepping all over his voice with guitar riffs. The deaf harmonica player had surreptitiously found his way onstage and was hiding in the shadows, tooting away in the wrong key. CC saw that Mike, seated at the front end of the bar near the door, was nervously peering back into the other room, trying to get a fix on what was going down.

"That girl is going to need a father."

"You are assuming an awful lot."

"She looks like me."

"She looks like *me.* And what kind of father do you think you'd make, really? You seduce the daughters of your girlfriends."

"I'm still living in the same place. It's just a couple of blocks from here," he said. "You want to take a walk?"

"Aren't you working? Isn't this your job?"

"I told you, I'm done." He looked toward Mike again, but he had apparently removed himself to the upstairs.

"You have anything to drink?"

"Everything," he said. "You name it. Jack Daniels, right?" He noticed the muscle coming up from her shoulder to her neck, thought how he'd like to kiss its graceful curve, considered that he had probably already done this at that hotel—what, six?—years ago, though he couldn't remember for sure.

"What about them?" As she gestured toward the stage, the song they'd been trying to play came clattering to a halt. He heard Freddy smack a few drums with an indifference that told him he'd gone into his I'm-not-really-here mode. Zimmer was at attention, face like a pit bull, framed by his thinning long gray hair, his *Little Shop of Horrors* T-shirt—he'd done a road tour—soaked through.

Skate stepped to the mic. "Now we're going to do some *fucking* blues," he said. He began soloing, without communicating anything to anyone else, leaving his fellow jammers all looking slightly baffled as to what song he was starting, although eventually they managed to fall into a kind of lurching accompaniment behind him. Night Train was clearly at a decision point—he could leave the stage and admit defeat, and possibly appear never to have been in control, or he could ride out this spell of bad weather as if nothing were wrong at all and assume that, somehow, all would be fixed. Choosing the latter, he put his face to his harp, affecting the kind of intimacy CC associated with a Rastafarian and a big spliff, closed his eyes, and breathed away.

"The street is crying," sang Skate. "Look at the tears rolling down the sky."

More than a few of the waiting musicians had their eyes on CC, nervously wondering how he was going to restore order, and if they were going to be on next. It was nearly eleven, and this thing ended at two.

"Take a walk with me," he said. "Come on."

"Do you have a view from that rooftop deck of yours?"

"You were never up there?"

"No," she said. "I never was."

"Of the harbor, yeah. You can see straight across to the Domino Sugar sign."

"*Sugars.* You can see it from your house, and you still don't know what it says?"

There were now three harmonica players onstage, as the guy in the tie-dyed shirt, apparently sensing a free-for-all, had simply climbed up and commandeered a microphone. He was swaying as he played, and ignoring everyone else. CC recognized him as one of Jerry's kids, those lost souls living out their days in search of the perfect drum circle, arguing the merits and fine points of different Dead shows like wine connoisseurs or theologians. Night Train had stopped playing his harp and was standing with hands on his hips, uncertain what to do next. Skate, who had never stopped soloing, was on his knees in front of his amp, back to the audience, encouraging feedback from the thing, Hendrix-style.

"Let's get," said CC, taking her hand, and he was pleased when she followed along. He figured whatever happened, his guitar would probably be all right. Those Fenders were made tough as baseball bats.

NINETEEN

Landis wished there were a television to watch. Emily was in bed, and it was his job to—well, he wasn't sure what his job was. To be patient. To expect Bernice to do the right thing. Which seemed, given her history and their current situation, a fairly thin hope. He'd already combed through the basement. There were some decent power tools, a radial-arm saw and a table saw, and stacks of unframed paintings against the walls. The brick was crumbling, leaving little piles of red dust in places on the floor, and there were cobwebs everywhere. He found all kinds of boxes and old appliances—a toaster oven, a Mr. Coffee that looked like one of the original Joe DiMaggio ones—but no television. He'd tried all the closets. Nothing. He didn't even want to watch anything in particular; he just needed to get outside of himself for a while. A baseball game, an old movie, hell, even the shopping channel. Just something to keep his mind off how Bernice had gone back to see this guy again.

He stared at himself in the mirror over the dining-room mantel. Behind him, he could see the chandelier, and the parlor to one side, the long entrance hall leading to the front door on the other.

He got a beer out of the refrigerator and sat at the large dining table, which was an old, farmhouse kind of thing, very beaten up and not at all in keeping with the grandeur of the room's original aspirations. There wasn't even a radio anywhere. His thoughts echoed in his head. Anyone else would have walked by now. Making him get his own place—this was ridiculous. Earlier, after he'd driven Tessa Harding all the way downtown to her hotel, he'd come back to find Bernice dressed up to go out again, the kid put down for the night.

But for some reason, he'd agreed to stay and babysit.

He just wasn't able to be alone with himself the way he used to be. In the past he'd been so good at it: sitting outside his trailer with a beer, listening as the distant wash of the rush-hour traffic grew thinner in its tidal retreat. But even then there had been a sense that time was running out on him, as on the night when he'd purposely picked a fight at the Old Towne Tavern with a guy who bumped his cue while Landis was getting ready to shoot the eight. It had been an accident, and there was no need to fight, but Landis had been walking around with a knot of frustration in his chest, and so there followed what might best be called a scuffle. He'd pushed the guy, the guy had pushed him, he'd swung and missed (his back sending him a telegram—which he ignored), and then the two of them had hit the floor, Landis on top, his hands around the guy's neck. After which there had been some commotion around them, and a couple of very beefy guys had removed them both to the parking lot.

Although he'd often thought of Bernice as something that had happened *to* him, Landis now wondered if he hadn't been looking for her, just as he had that fight. You got what you wanted in life, his dad had always told him. "If I'd wanted to be rich," he used to boast, "I'd have been rich."

His father had been like that, without any apparent enthusiasm, dutifully going to work and coming home, plugging himself into the television when he had downtime, a full glass of Gallo sweet vermouth on the rocks near him.

There was one place Landis hadn't checked, and that was the bedroom Bernice shared with Emily. It had a closet—maybe there was a TV in it. Of course, if there were a TV, why wouldn't it just be on a table? But Bernice might have stowed it away for some reason. Maybe she thought if she didn't watch the news, there wouldn't *be* any news. Who knew what internal conversations she had with herself? He thought he ought to at least check it out.

He climbed the stairs to the second-floor landing, stopped outside the empty master bedroom. It was dark, though the yellow light of a streetlamp filtered in through the upper part of the big bay window. The lower part of the window was closed off by interior shutters, a medieval-feeling wooden barricade. He stuck his head in and something skittered off into a corner. He'd have to look into getting a few mousetraps.

On the third floor, he paused outside the door and listened for sounds of Emily's breathing. He pushed the door open as gently as he could, then stepped in and tiptoed toward the closet. Something wasn't right.

"Emily?" he said.

He turned on the light. Her bed was empty.

He tried to stay calm and think it through. Tessa Harding was back at her hotel—he'd taken her there himself. How could she have returned, sneaked in, and spirited the kid off? Plus, he couldn't see her doing it. *Don't panic,* he thought. *Maybe she's just in the bathroom.*

"Emily," he said. Then he said it louder. "Hey! Can you hear me?"

He walked through the whole house, calling her name, hoping grimly that at any moment she'd pop out of some little recess and tell him she'd been talking to Jesus, or playing some other game. It was a big house, big enough to get lost in, and to a little kid, it would feel like the ultimate playground. Surely she was around somewhere.

At last, he went out the front door onto the large wooden porch. A couple of moths drew scribbles around the dusty yellow light overhead. He looked out into the street. There was no sign of her out there, either. If she wasn't still in the house, then she must have left it, perhaps while he was in the basement. He went in and climbed quickly back to the third floor and reexamined the room for clues. There were clothes all over the floor, both hers and Bernice's mixed together, and it was hard for him to tell whether anything was missing. Shoes. She had a little pair of blue sneakers she liked to wear. He looked around in the piles, but couldn't find them. He decided that meant she'd put them on.

Maybe she'd just gone for a walk.

He went back downstairs, calling her name every now and then, although with less hope this time. When he was back on the porch, he decided to walk around the block. Leaving the door ajar in case she should return while he was gone, he headed north, resisting the impulse to shout her name as if she were a lost pet. And if she were lost—irretrievably and forever—what would that mean for them? Jail, probably, the way things were going. He'd been thinking maybe, just maybe, if they could get out of their current predicament, send the girl back to Jesusland with her other mother, maybe Bernice and he could see about having their own kid. If Bernice would go along with it. Except what were the chances of that, if they were going to be carrying around the memory of this night from here on out, the night when he lost track of her little girl because he'd been too distracted by looking for a television to watch? He'd need a better story.

A round-bellied man in a wife-beater walking his pit bull materialized out of the haze ahead of him. Some other, smaller dog, probably peering out through a curtain, began a high-pitched, muffled barking. Landis said to himself, "She's OK, she's OK. Nothing to worry about. No big deal." But after he'd made a left at the end of the block and there was still no sign of a precocious five-year-old out exploring the neighborhood, he began to phrase it differently. "Please, let her be OK," he said. Then, after a while, he just started saying "shit," over and over.

He rounded the next corner, past a boarded-up house with turrets on it and an overgrown yard full of flowers and plastic bags and stray advertising flyers. A bus rumbled past, heading north, its elevated exhaust pipe coughing out a cascade of black fumes so thick they momentarily obscured the vehicle entirely.

It began to rain lightly, and he hurried. He was now more than halfway around the block. What next, two blocks? He tried to think it through mathematically, but kept running up against the sinking realization that there was little point to the effort. One person could not effectively search a large area. Being someplace meant not being someplace else, possibly the right place. If he found her, it would be by thinking like her, or by dumb luck. And he really had no idea how she thought, which just left luck, which—in spite of all the breaks he'd caught in his life up until now—was a lousy thing to count on.

He rounded the last corner, hurrying against the big raindrops smacking the top of his head. Safely back on the porch, he tried to remain calm. It was nearly 11:00 PM. The thing to do was not to panic. This was a problem, and problems had solutions. He would fix this, somehow.

TWENTY

Bernice felt she was entering into a dream knowing exactly where it was going and unable to do anything about it. CC's keys in the red door, the slightly musty smell of the living room of the narrow row house, a cat that appeared from nowhere and rubbed up against her a couple of times.

"That's Rooster," said CC. "He likes you."

"When did you get him?"

"He showed up about a year ago."

"He's just marking me," Bernice said. "I know all about it. They have scent glands in their faces. Now he thinks he owns me."

"Well, you figure he must like you if he wants to own you."

"You got anything to drink in this place?"

He hustled around the kitchen and she observed the surroundings, which had changed: an entertainment center kind of thing where before there had been her mother's sideboard. It held a TV and some assorted and mismatched stereo equipment, everything covered in a good layer of dust. A nearly dead cactus poked up out of a small pot, looking like a pickle run through with toothpicks.

She sniffed. She was having an allergic reaction to the cat.

He came over with two glasses of whiskey and ice. "You want to go up on the deck now?"

They climbed narrow stairs from which the brown paint was chipping, and she tried to think of ways she'd cheer the place up if it were hers. Off the third floor, where the bedroom was, they stepped out onto a porch, then from there climbed steep steps to a wooden platform. In front of her lay the water, with boats tied up to a pier, and the other way, to the west, the lights of the inner harbor and the downtown skyscrapers glimmered silver and blue and red.

"It's a little rickety," he said, stomping around in an alarming way. "Like, it should really be torn off. And I know the inside of the house is a mess, too. But even so, I could sell and come away with some serious money. I don't owe. Even for a gut job, the place should bring around one-eighty in this market. It's funny. Most of the things I tried to do in life went no place at all. But the crappy little house I bought seems to have had a successful career all on its own."

"Maybe you should hold on a little longer. You might double your money."

He shook his head. In the dark, he was just a shape. "You want to kiss?" he asked.

"I want to what?"

"Kiss. Me."

"I don't know, Craney Crow. This is sort of sudden. Here we were, talking real estate, and now you want to swap spit?"

"It was just a suggestion."

"Talk more finance to me. That always gets me hot."

He turned and went to the railing, looked down onto the street below. "When we had that big flood, the water came right to the end of the street, but nothing happened here at all. Totally dry. Couple of blocks from here, they were canoeing."

"I don't remember any floods," she said.

"Last year."

"I wasn't *here* last year."

"I wondered then if maybe it was some kind of message. You know, like those preachers go on about on TV. The end time is coming."

"There was a message all right. It was 'Don't live so close to the water.'" She thought it was a bad sign that he didn't seem to realize she'd been gone from the city for years. He clearly saw the world only in terms of himself. "I lived in Florida. You've got these old ladies worrying all fall about how the next Andrew is going to come destroy everything. So don't fucking live there. Go back to New York. People have to take responsibility for themselves." She took a huge gulp of bourbon. "And, by the way, isn't New Orleans below sea level already? That's really your idea of a place to plan a future?"

"Where is Pearl right now?" he asked, clearly trying to change the subject.

"Same place she was last night—home. She's got a sitter. A young man from the neighborhood." *Oh, and there's a woman in a hotel room about a mile from here who plans to take her away from me forever.*

"You sure he's trustworthy?"

"No, not really. But I wanted to come out."

"To see me."

"Yeah," she said. "To see you."

He stepped forward and leaned down, pressing his lips to hers. His tongue ducked in and out of her mouth with a pleasant enthusiasm. When she'd slept with him in Atlanta, she'd felt bad—not unhappy, but *bad*, like she was sneaking a cigarette or had stolen a dirty magazine. And then later she'd felt stupid, the way she did the time she was twelve and spent all afternoon making a frame and stretching a canvas to show her father, only to have him inspect it and point out where the corners weren't right and where she'd left some slack.

"What do you think?" he said, when they broke for air.

"What do you mean?"

"You know. What do you think?"

"You can't ask a person that. What does that mean? What do I think about what?"

"You really know how to hold on to a moment, don't you?" His right hand was on her ass, and he pulled her closer to him. "We could go inside."

"I like it out here. What do you think is going on back at your bar?"

"I don't give a fuck. I'd rather be here."

"You aren't worried? Those people could be beating each other over the head with guitars. The cops could have come."

"It's OK," he said. "I don't care." He looked at her. "I've got a boat."

"You do? Well that changes everything. A boat!"

"It's not mine, exactly, but I can use it. Guy I know keeps it not far from here. We could go there. Maybe you'd like to see it?"

"Oh, I don't think so. I don't like boats so much."

"Maybe Pearl would like to go out on it sometime?"

She pictured the three of them shooting around the bay, standing at attention like some Revolutionary War image, salt spray behind them, the wind in their hair. She wondered what the hell she was doing here. She'd had some idea, thought she *had* to come, had to see, that this was in fact the responsible choice. But she was wrong. She was wrong about everything, all the time. "She doesn't like boats, either," she said. "I have to go."

"Go?"

"Yeah. Vamoose. Hightail it."

"All right," he said. "Forget it. You're just like she was, aren't you? Twisted up in your own knots. You want things, you don't want them, you think you're better than everyone else, you think you're worse. You're going to drown in it someday, same as she did. I can't believe I'd even think about making the same mistake twice."

She pushed him. Later, thinking it over and trying to understand the impulse, she felt as if something mechanical had sprung to action in her, as if she were merely the nerve endings conveying the message from another place, from a brain unconnected to hers and perhaps not even that interested in her dramatic scenes. But of course, it was something *she'd* done, all be herself.

He made a little yelp, not unlike that of a small dog that had been kicked, then toppled right over the railing. It was almost a joke fall. You get someone to sneak up behind the person and—oof!—over he goes. Only this was no joke.

First came the sound of him hitting the tilted roof below. Then he caught for a moment on the large piece of protruding plastic that acted as a skylight over his bedroom, looking almost comfortable there—a man relaxing on a transparent yellow-plastic sofa—then there was a groaning sound as the plastic gave way and tore loose, banging hard against the gutter, popping up, then sailing over the edge and down to the concrete three floors below.

Bernice held on to the weathered railing, peered over and down. There was a huge hole in the roof where the skylight had been, and she did not see a body on the sidewalk. She turned and went back to the narrow spiral stairs at the other side of the deck, spun her way down to the next level and entered the house.

He was lying on the bed, almost as if he had entered it the normal way and not by descending through the roof. Debris littered the comforter: leaves, blackened bits of grout and caulking, bird shit, and feathers. The comforter itself was green, printed to look like a hundred-dollar bill. CC's lips were bright with blood.

"I am *so* sorry," she said. "Is there something I can do?"

He narrowed his eyes at her. Dust motes hung thickly in the disturbed air. He mumbled something.

"What?"

"I *ung*."

"You bit your tongue. Got it. OK. But you can move other things? You didn't break a leg or anything?"

In response, he got up out of the bed, somewhat unsteadily. He picked up a wastebasket from the floor next to him and spat bright blood into it. "Yeah," he said. "Bit it all right."

"You want some ice?"

"I could have fucking died," he said. He spat more blood, motioned for her to bring him the glass of water from the top of the dresser. She noticed the thickness of the dust, the scattering of pocket change, the scraps of paper with things written on them—phone numbers, shopping lists. She had never really thought about Craney Crow buying groceries. She wondered what he ate, and whether he cooked.

"Here," she held out the glass. "Swoosh and spit. I didn't push you that hard, you know. I think this is your fault as much as mine for leaning back like that."

He spat, then surveyed the hole in the ceiling. "Damn," he said. "It's going to rain."

"I'm sorry I broke your house," she said, suddenly aware she might cry. "I'll just go now."

"You can't." He spat again, then picked up a T-shirt, rolled it, and stuck it in his mouth for a few moments. When he removed it, there was an alarming stain.

Downstairs, she found an ice tray in his tiny fridge, the cat working his way between her ankles, and she brought a cube up for him to suck on. "Ice is for everything," she said, remembering the tub they'd filled for Emily in New Mexico. She still wasn't sure that had been wrong. But Landis had thought it was, and that had been enough to undermine her confidence.

CC had a small, moon-shaped scar, she noticed, under one eye, but it was not a result of any of this.

"I think this was a sign," she said.

"A sign you're a crazy bitch. Just like your mother."

"Maybe I am. So what?"

"So, nothing."

"You told her about us, right? That's why she moved out."

"I didn't tell her anything. Why would I do that? She moved out because I asked her to. We didn't get along. Never did. There was nothing to tell, anyway. You blueballed me. Best thing that could have happened. I don't know what I was thinking. That should have been the end of it, too." He spat again.

"Well, the kid isn't yours," said Bernice. "You can relax."

"Then why did you come see me? Why did you come back to tell me you were going to quit? How come she looks like me? Who is her father?" He went again to the sink, then returned to the table. "Jesus. How long does a tongue take to stop bleeding?"

"A guy I met out west. He's nothing in particular. In the music business, like you. Sort of. Anyway, he's the father. So don't worry about this anymore, OK?"

"The music business? I don't believe you."

"Suit yourself. Belief is very personal. You get to have your own."

"What part of the music business?"

She found herself feeling unaccountably defensive on Landis's behalf. "He's a recording and sound engineer."

"For who?"

"Johnny Rainbow and the Thieves. Glutton Stump. The Dead Astaires."

CC spat again. "You're making this up. I've never heard of any of them."

"Well, maybe you should get out more. Maybe you aren't on top of things like you ought to be. Maybe you've been wasting your time babysitting losers who want to play dress-up Dan Aykroyd a couple nights a week, blow a harmonica, and pretend this is Chicago in 1955, or whatever. Aren't you even slightly embarrassed? That kid, Max Lucca? He's got it all ahead of him. I predict great things. You, on the other hand . . ."

"I just don't know why you came out tonight," he said, quietly.

"Me, either."

He came over and stood in front of her, bending at the knees so that his eyes were more or less level with hers. He smelled strongly of the bar, and she feared he was going to kiss her again, bloody mouth and all.

"Look me in the eye and say it," he said. His eyes were pretty and dark, and the stubble on his chin was like spilled pepper. She understood, or thought she did, how her mother had felt looking into them, trying to divine her own future there. He swallowed. "Say that kid isn't mine."

"That kid is from Colorado," she said. "She's got nothing to do with you."

TWENTY-ONE

Landis heard the rattle of Bernice's key in the back door. He'd been pacing around the kitchen for close to an hour, going out every few minutes to the front porch to scan the street. He'd tried drinking a glass of water, but it did little to calm him down. He was out of ideas, and he was a mixture of worried to death and resentful that it was he who had to be in charge of this emergency.

"What's the matter?" said Bernice, reading his face. "Is something wrong? Is she throwing up?"

"What were you thinking going out?" he said. "You went through all this trouble—hauled her all the way across the country—just so you could leave her and go out on a goddamn date?"

Bernice squinted at him. She smelled of cigarettes and booze, and Landis felt once again that he didn't know her at all. "What happened?" she said, quietly. "Just tell me."

"I don't know. She disappeared."

"Fuck." She put a hand to her head. "Fuck, fuck, fuck. What do you mean disappeared?"

"Her shoes are gone. I think she went someplace. I think she just got up and left on her own, you know?"

Bernice went bounding up the back stairs, and Landis followed her. "Emily?" she called. "Emily?" When he caught up with her at the bedroom, he hoped that somehow everything would be returned to normal, that the child would be safe in her bed, but it was still empty.

"She came back and took her," said Bernice. "It's simple as that. I knew it was stupid to trust her."

"I don't think so."

"You don't think so? Why not? What other explanation have you got? Are there other people out there who want to kidnap my daughter? Do you think a five-year-old girl just felt like taking a walk in the middle of the night in the middle of the city? She came and she took her."

"I can't see it."

"Where were you?"

"Right here. I can't explain it."

"You can't? You can't?" Her eyes were huge. "She sneaked in. You didn't notice. Maybe you nodded off."

Landis understood that this thin reed of logic was providing Bernice with just enough air to keep her going. "All right. We can call the hotel. I'll look up the number."

"What good will that do?" Bernice asked. "Even if she answers, which I doubt she will, she'll say she doesn't know what we're talking about. Right? Why would she say anything else? She's probably on a plane back to the Springs right now."

"In the middle of the night? No way. I think we should call."

"You've looked all over the house? In the basement? The closets? Everywhere?"

He nodded. "A couple of times."

She rapped her forehead with her knuckles. "I can't believe this is happening."

"I'm calling."

"Don't."

But he already had the phone book open. "There are a zillion hotels in here."

"You dropped her off. Didn't you notice what the place was called?"

"Belvedere? I don't remember." The drive downtown had seemed to him like entering a big canyon, a descent past ornate sooty buildings, the remnants of a more prosperous past, a full-scale Greek temple, the abandoned carapace of some departed bank staking out its surreal position near the bottom. Tessa's hotel, an unremarkable concrete structure from the 1960s, had been around a corner, just past a liquor store.

"It's not the Belvedere—that's different. That's a different hotel. Look, it doesn't matter anyway."

He scanned the yellow pages, hoping something would jog his memory. "Belmont," he said. "Here it is. I was close." He dialed and the phone rang fifteen times before a male voice finally picked up and mumbled a greeting. He was connected to her room, and within moments she was on the other end.

"Yes," said Tessa, her voice wide awake. "What?"

Bernice stared at him angrily. "Do you have Emily?" he asked. It seemed to Landis that at this point, there was no reason to play their cards any way but flat out on the table, face up.

"No," she said. "You do."

"She says she doesn't," said Landis, hand over the mouthpiece.

"She's lying."

"Then you talk to her." He held out the phone, but Bernice jumped back as if it were a snake. "What are you . . ." he couldn't even finish the question. "We're not exactly sure where she is," he said to Tessa. "But it's OK, we've got the situation under control."

"Not exactly sure?" asked Tessa. "Not *exactly*?"

"No."

"I'm coming back there. I should never have left."

"Right." He hung up. "She's coming here."

"Great. Perfect."

"Maybe she sleepwalks. You know? It could run in the family."

"I don't sleepwalk."

"Yeah, you do. One time, we went to bed drunk and when I woke up in the middle of the night you were gone. I found you standing naked out on the balcony, staring up at the peak. I led you back inside and put you to bed. I just never mentioned it."

"I can't say that makes me feel much better," said Bernice.

He left her on the porch and jogged around the block a few more times, scanning the yards and doorways, but with no luck. Then he rejoined Bernice so she wouldn't have to face Tessa Harding alone. Bernice was seated on the front step, picking at her ankles.

"You want to talk?" he asked.

She shook her head violently. When he tried to put an arm around her, she pulled away. So he just sat there, sweating.

After about ten minutes, a battered cab pulled up and Tessa Harding got out, looking tired but radiant with determination.

"She ever sleepwalk?" asked Landis.

"I've found her in the family room playing a couple of times in the middle of the night," Tessa said. "But in this strange way, with her eyes half closed. She's never gone far, though. Just into the next room. One time—"

"One time, what?" said Landis.

"She urinated. Right on the floor."

"I'm surprised you didn't call an exorcist," said Bernice.

"How long does it last?" asked Landis. "Could she still be asleep?"

"I don't know. I just don't know what happened, but it sounds like she might have wandered someplace. I mean, it's possible she's right around here, very close."

"How was I supposed to know any of this?" said Bernice.

"You weren't," said Tessa.

"Maybe we should go check parked cars?" Landis offered.

"Maybe," said Tessa.

Bernice shook her head. "People lock their cars. There's almost no chance she'd find an open one to sleep in. She's not in a car."

"Well, what do you want to do?"

"I don't know," said Bernice, her voice suddenly a cracked whisper.

"There's tea," said Landis, who had always believed in the restorative power of hot drinks. "Why don't we all go inside and get our heads together?"

He made it, choosing three mugs from the cabinet over the stove, rinsing them and rubbing them out with paper towels, boiling the water in an old kettle that was already out, fishing teabags from a brand-new box he found on the counter. It seemed to him that Tessa, who was seated across from Bernice at the kitchen table, was taking this all fairly calmly. Perhaps she'd already reached the limits of her stress, and this current crisis wasn't particularly worse than the one she'd been living with ever since they'd slipped out her basement door with Emily. He realized with some surprise that he was glad she was here.

"Does she know her way around well enough that if she wakes up, she can simply walk back?" Tessa asked.

Bernice rubbed her temple. "I don't know what she knows. She can spell *pistachio*."

"She can spell a lot of words. I've been teaching her. She'll be way ahead when she starts school," said Tessa.

"I could tell you everyone from my first-grade class, and where they sat," said Bernice. "Lester Diomede, Angela Hall, Bertha Yates, Justin Thomas, whose feet smelled."

Tessa looked at Landis, who looked back at her.

"What is the point of that?" said Tessa. "Why are you telling us that?"

"Katherine Wheeler, Jonathan Dimock, Heidi Grosz, Heather Boccanfuso. Heather sometimes didn't wear panties."

"Your father more or less told me that you were unstable," said Tessa. "But I think I know you as well as he does, maybe better in some ways. And I don't think he's right."

"We have to call the police," said Bernice.

"I don't know," said Tessa. "Maybe."

"Should we pray?" asked Bernice.

"Please."

"I'm serious. I've got nothing better to offer. You people with your megachurches. That's what you do, right? Put a glass of water on the radio and five bucks in the mail, and then drink the water and get cured?"

"You aren't describing me," said Tessa. "Pinnacle Christian is small. You know that. You even came once."

Bernice bit a fingernail. "You want unstable? I almost killed someone tonight. But it didn't happen. Maybe this is the other side of that. There's a balance sheet, right? If I have a debit, then there's a credit due somewhere, don't you think?" She took the remainder of her tea to the sink and dumped it. "I'm going back out on the porch."

Landis followed her. It was raining again, the street reflecting the light in streaks and patches. "You went to their church?" he asked.

"Oh, yeah. She begged me. And I was bored. I didn't have much to do, really. You can only watch so much TV and read so many mysteries."

"So, what are you thinking?"

"That it's over. We have to call the police. That this is my fault for having a sleepwalking gene."

An SUV alive with thumping bass, its windows tinted so it was impossible to see in, roared noisily up the block.

He touched her arm. "We should have planned better," he said.

"I went back to his house," she said. "Then I pushed him off his roof."

"Don't joke."

"I'm not joking. I pushed him off. He fell through a skylight. He's OK—a little bruised up, I guess. I was feeling lucky for a while there. I told him I was with you."

"You did?"

"We'll call the police, and then they'll want to know our names, and they'll want to know where Emily lives, and where she goes to school, and all that stuff. And even if Tessa doesn't rat us out, what difference will it make? They'll get to the truth, anyway, one way or another. You need to get out of here now. Go back to that place you rented and see if you can get your deposit back. I won't mention you. Tessa won't. Hopefully Emily, when we find her, won't." She looked up at him in the yellow porch light. "I'm really sorry," she said. Then she kissed him quickly on the lips, got her keys out, and walked up the sidewalk, headed north.

“Where are you going?” Landis called after her. “Bernice?” But she was just a shadow, and then he saw her getting into her car. He watched the taillights come on, watched her pull jerkily out into traffic. It was amazing she hadn’t been pulled over yet, the way she drove, and those Colorado plates not even registered to that car.

TWENY-TWO

Donald Click approached the hole cautiously, for fear that the asphalt under his sneakers might give way, but the earth held for him, and he was able to get right up to the edge. What he was doing was illegal, he understood, but he doubted the bean counters at city hall had figured out a standard fine for unauthorized sinkhole viewing. Traffic had been rerouted starting one block north, and this whole section of Cathedral was dead quiet. He stood with his umbrella held over him, distinctly disappointed. There were great black hunks of road, broken and almost appetizing, like torn bits of overcooked brownie. He could see a lot of mud, and some sort of enormous pipe, but not much else. He'd hoped for more. Himself a basement dweller now, he felt he was coming closer to the secrets of the underworld, and things like pipes and ducts attracted him. There was a connection here, he thought, with the ancients. On their honeymoon, he'd taken Eve to Arles, shown her the spot on the Alyscamps, that Roman lane of the dead, where Van Gogh and the visiting Gauguin had painted the same day, the two masters taking their easels with them. After, they'd visited the cryptoporticus, a series of underground passages that were all that remained of the forum. She'd hated it, but he'd liked the coolness, the darkness, which was total save for the occasional small area lit from a window cut high above. These nether regions were what endured, what got passed along from generation to generation. Immune to fashion, utilitarian, essential. Sometimes, lying in his bed, he mentally mapped his position with respect to the rest of downtown Baltimore, and it amused him to think he was closer to the steam tunnels and water mains—the arteries and tendons of the city—than to the glassed-in offices of the suit-and-tie crowd.

That long-ago trip, he and his new wife had also visited Italy, staying in the cheapest hotels, playing professor and naughty student nightly, traipsing through museums and churches by day to see frescoes and mosaics, the fingers and preserved blood of saints. He'd been at the beginning of his bad life, slipping casually into the coat of his new identity, corrupter of youth, a man who lusted after his own students. It didn't bother him. He wanted to tell her everything he knew, to fill her with himself. It was the spring of '75. The United States had just pulled out of Saigon. They hadn't told anyone they were getting married, had just quietly gone down to city hall. He lived on Tyson Street back then, in a thin, tall house two hundred years old, painted purple and red. They slept naked together on the small bed, fans arrayed around them, talked about buying a mansion together, about seeing the world, about raising a family.

When Eve died, she'd been reading a self-help book called *You Rock!* He still had it—it had been on her nightstand at Ojo de la

Vaca, the arts colony where she'd won a residency. He'd gone out there, canceling classes, flying into Albuquerque, then driving to the morgue in Bernalillo. Those hot wires so tightly laid inside her head, day after day, fraying a little more and a little more, until finally one melted and sparked. He knew what had happened, more or less. A pill slipped into her hand by another resident. Driving her rental car in the early evening to the parking area—perhaps she'd already been there during the day once or twice—hiking the quarter-mile trail up to where the hot water bubbled out of the ground into three separate pools, each a different temperature. The rock walls and ledges of the largest pool colorfully textured with the wax drippings from years and years of candles. Taking her clothes off and stepping naked and alone into the hottest of the three and settling in and closing her eyes, the Ecstasy having already raised her body temperature dangerously, the water moving the process along. As heatstroke overcame her, she hallucinated, imagined herself not in New Mexico at all, but a guest in the baths of Caracalla, surrounded by high walls of polished travertine, gazed down upon by statues of gods and goddesses, elaborate mosaics of Neptune and dolphins and whales spread out before her, shimmering under the surface of the water. Half an hour turned into an hour, turned into two. The guests of the baths came and went, the sun played through the high windows, sent shadows traveling across the domed ceiling. She slipped farther into the water, let it fill her mouth, her ears, her nose. It grew dark. *I rock*, she told herself, the words seeming to separate themselves from any meaning they might have previously held. Someone called out that the baths were closing. The sound was distant. No one came for her. No one came.

Overhead he heard a helicopter flapping into range of the sinkhole, and he could see its searchlight slicing the mist, hunting some criminal. He imagined a figure running through the streets, ducking into one of the alleys where the old slave houses used to be, and the carriage houses. In Naples, someone had stolen her camera right off her shoulder. He remembered now how angry he'd been—as if he'd failed in some way to protect her—whereas Eve had simply taken it in stride. In spite of her incompetence in so many things, he'd always suspected she might actually understand the world better than he did. Mean dogs let her approach and pet them. Perpetually lost, she somehow always managed to end up where she was going.

But she'd betrayed him, and that was the simple fact of it. Betrayed him for a musician when what she knew about music—well, she didn't know anything about music. Perhaps he'd been too difficult, playing her Coleman Hawkins and Sonny Rollins and saying, *OK, what's the difference?* when it turned out that she had trouble telling a sax from a trumpet. That first year with her out of the house he'd gone over it and over it in his head, trying to pin down the exact moment when things had turned, when she'd gone from being a person with occasional bouts of mania to a mania with occasional moments of personhood.

He wanted to blame it all on her illness, but somehow, he never could. She'd *wanted* to be crazy, had found comfort in it, had found an excuse for all the bad behavior that was bottled up inside her, waiting to get turned loose.

The helicopter circled again, then moved on, the clattering sound of its rotor receding into the distance.

And then the girl had started hating him. He hadn't deserved it, hadn't treated her badly, hadn't even kept her from seeing her mother, at least on the occasions that Eve showed up to do something, go to the movies, eat an ice cream. Bernice blamed him for what happened, sided with her mother—that was natural. But there was something else in her, too, a hostility and suspicion. She knew, as did he, that he was pretty much a fake. He was not a professor: he was a person who played at being a professor. He'd held one visiting position after another, but none had ever turned into a real job. His paintings had sold reasonably well over the years, but in that respect he had failed to come even close to achieving what he thought he deserved. Perhaps if he'd been a little crazy himself he would have had more success. And so he'd simply decided to ignore the facts and live as if he were who he had intended to be, and that persona had necessitated a degree of arrogance—why not just call it snobbery?—that had removed him not only from his wife and his child, but also from himself.

He took a step back from the edge. His knees ached, as did his back and neck. He could hear easy-listening jazz being piped out into the empty street from the front of the Lord Calvert Hotel.

Turning his head, he was surprised to see Bernice standing a few feet from him, her hands on her hips. "On the highway coming here," she said, "we passed a big sign that said Report Suspicious Activity. Suppose this counts?"

"Well, hello," he said.

"A lot of mud down there." She joined him and peered over and down, then whistled. "You think it means something?"

"I think it's a hole in the road," he said. "Of course, you can read it any way you wish."

"Tonight, I'm thinking it's suspicious activity."

He didn't respond. He remembered her roundabout way of getting to whatever it was she wanted to say.

"Do you really think it?" she asked.

"What?"

"What you told that woman from Colorado? That I'm unstable?"

"I don't know how to answer that. I'm not a doctor. Have you been to a doctor? Do you even have insurance?"

She kicked a bit of gravel into the hole. "No, I don't have insurance. I don't have anything, really. I've been living a stupid life, I guess you'd have to say." Bernice sat down suddenly, leaning her head against his leg. "Dad?" she said.

"What? What is it?"

"Oh, Dad. I lost her. I went out, just to see. I had to. I had to think through all the possibilities, not just for me, but for her. So I went, and then when I came back, Landis told me she was gone, and he didn't know where."

"I don't know what you're saying." He put his hand on her head, felt the soft hair, remembered suddenly what she'd been like to hold as a baby, how only he could make her calm down some nights when she woke crying, how he'd walk her up and down the hall, humming "Darn that Dream" until she'd gurgle and smile and drift off. There had been nothing intervening between them back then, no complications. Just the cry and the comfort.

"You don't?"

"Not really. Take a deep breath and try again."

She barely whispered it. "Emily wandered off. She's lost."

"Then what are you doing here?"

"I wanted to see you."

"Why?"

"I don't know. I just did. I was headed for your door, but then I saw you out here."

"We used to find you in odd places. Once, you were under the sink in the kitchen. Your mother was for locking you into your room, but I didn't like the idea. She's probably in the house somewhere, and you just haven't found her. I'll come—I'll help look. I have experience. It's my house."

Bernice stood back up. Her eyes were swollen, but she wasn't crying. "I started all this, and I should never have done it. It's like a scab

I just picked at and picked at, you know. Remember how I'd do that, how I couldn't leave anything alone?"

More than ever, she reminded him of Eve. "Once, on a car ride back from Maine, you picked your mosquito bites so badly you bled all over the backseat upholstery. We had to make an emergency stop at a McDonald's for napkins."

"I'm sorry about that."

"Oh, I got most of it out. Dish detergent and a toothbrush. That was the old Volvo."

"Did you hear what I said?"

"She'll turn up," he promised.

"We're calling the police. I've sent Landis away. I'll never see him again."

"You're being overly dramatic."

"I'm not. It's serious. Can I tell you something?" she asked.

"Is it something I want to hear?"

"No. It's not something I want to say, either. It's something no one knows."

"Then you'd better not." He hesitated. "That's not the kind of relationship we have."

"I want to tell you. It's the worst thing. I want to tell you the worst thing I've ever done." She came over and touched his shoulder. "I've got no one else to say it to."

"I don't want to know."

"You don't?"

"No. What difference will it make?"

"I don't know."

"Exactly. There's no reason, then. Whatever it is, you did it. It's done. Telling me won't change it."

She stuck her hands in her pockets and kicked at a pebble, sending it flying into the hole. He knew she thought he didn't love her, and he wanted to tell her she was wrong, that he did, but he had no idea how to put such a sentence together.

"You really think she's in the house someplace?" she asked.

"I do. I know you want to imagine her scooped up by child slave traders and shipped off to Arabia, but the simplest answers are often the right ones." He didn't even know if he believed what he was saying, but it seemed important to sound calm for her. He could still do it, could still bring her down from her anxious state. "Go home and see. And then call me and let me know, all right?"

"There's this part of me—" she stopped, looked at him in a way that he found alarming. Her voice diminished to a desperate whisper. "I don't know myself."

"You don't?"

"No. Not even a little."

He put his hand out, and she took it and held it. After a few seconds, she released her grip and stepped back, her eyes focused away from him, on the ground.

"Go home," he said. He tried to smile at her in a way that inspired confidence, that said, *You can do this*, just as he'd faced so many undergraduates at crits over the years, their earnest attempts displayed on the wall. "Go home and look again."

TWENTY-THREE

"We need to call the police," said Landis. They were in the parlor, Tessa perched on the edge of the faded green armchair, Landis pacing around in circles. A half hour had passed since Bernice left, and they'd been through the house again twice. Landis' mouth tasted thick and metallic, and he felt as if his nervous system had been attached to a battery charger. "Every second we wait could be a second too long."

"Maybe you're right. I don't like it, but maybe you are. Do we have something to show them? A recent photo? I've got one in my wallet, but it's from last year. She's grown a lot."

"Can I see it?"

She showed him. It was the kind of formal shot you had done at the mall, with Emily in a frilly white dress posed in front of a pastel backdrop. "She looks like an angel," he said.

"I guess that's the idea," said Tessa.

The front door burst open and Landis jumped up just as Bernice stomped in.

"What are you doing here?" asked Bernice, looking at him.

"We didn't call yet. She wouldn't let me."

"You'll get in trouble," Tessa said, still holding the photo.

"Did you pray?" asked Bernice.

"I never stopped," said Tessa.

"Has anyone tried under the sink?" She led them into the kitchen. There was a good-sized space underneath, but it held only a couple of dried-up dish sponges and some mouse turds.

"We've looked everywhere," said Landis. "She's not in the house."

"All right, then. We start walking the streets, looking in parked cars, on people's porches, whatever it takes."

"I think this is beyond us now," said Landis.

The doorbell rang loudly. They all three ran to the front hall. Landis got there first and pulled open the door. On the porch was a thin, grinning, shirtless man, his chest dark with thick hair that seemed unlikely given the pallor of his complexion. His bony, shaved head shone with perspiration. He looked like a concentration camp survivor, but an unusually strong one—perhaps one who had made a deal for food. At the end of one of his long, tightly muscled arms, her hand linked with his, was Emily.

"Does this little girl live here?" he asked.

"Oh, my God," said Tessa. She scooped up Emily and kissed her on the cheek. "Where have you been?"

"No place," said Emily.

"That's all right, I don't need to come in," the man said, peering past them, clearly trying to get a view into the house. "I just wanted to make sure she got back safe and sound."

"Where did you find her?" Landis asked.

"Walking around by herself. I'm Charlie." He held out a long-fingered hand. Landis thought it was like shaking hands with a batch of drill bits. Charlie jerked a thumb over his shoulder. "I live next door."

Landis recalled the flicker of blinds he'd seen the other day. "Walking around where?"

"Out there. On the sidewalk. I was on my way out to practice my tai chi. I saw her just standing there, so I thought I'd bring her over. I think she was asleep on her feet, you know?"

"She's been gone nearly four hours," said Landis.

Charlie smiled at him again. "I don't know about that. I just found her a few minutes ago. I'm sure that must have been scary for you all, though. I don't have any kids myself. Wouldn't mind, maybe, someday. Gotta find the right woman first. You probably ought to keep a better watch on her, you know what I'm saying?"

"Thank you so much," said Tessa. "Oh, we've been worried sick. We won't let her out of our sight."

"Good thinking," said Charlie, tapping the side of his head with a finger.

Tessa and Bernice hustled Emily off to the kitchen, and Landis could hear them back there making happy sounds and telling her how much they loved her. "How'd you know to bring her here?" he asked Charlie.

"I've seen her around, with that other one—the blonde. You, though—you're new, aren't you?"

"Depends. I guess I'm new to you."

Charlie's front teeth weren't any bigger than the surrounding ones. "You're the dad, then?"

"Yeah, I'm the dad."

"And that's your wife?"

"That's right."

He glanced around. "This place was empty for a long time. Then all of a sudden it's like Penn Station."

"Charlie," said Landis, "where have you been the past four hours?"

"In my apartment," said Charlie. "Taking a nap, most of it. Why?"

"I just wondered where you were. I'm wondering about a guy who takes naps at night, then gets up to go practice tai chi."

"Hey, man, I just did you a big-assed favor, OK?" The smile was gone now, and Charlie seemed quite stressed, the tendons in his neck standing out in sharp relief. "You're lucky I didn't call 911, you know? Letting a little girl wander around the streets like that. That's probably criminal behavior. All right?"

"I said thank you."

"Thank you is right. Who knows what could have happened." He scratched at the left side of his rib cage.

"You are a Good Samaritan."

"Son of a bitch," said Charlie. Then he turned and headed off toward the street.

The women had decided, even though it was late, to give Emily a bath. Landis stood just outside the door, listening to the sound of their voices echoing off the tile and around the big clawfoot tub. He heard the water sloshing around, heard the music of their conversation, the tentative sound of Bernice's voice as she asked Emily about the water temperature—too hot? just right?—the flatter, rounder, practiced cadences of Tessa's as she directed the child to move her head a little this way, to sit still and stop squirming, was she a little girl or a wriggle worm? If something were wrong, surely they'd know, these two mothers. If something had been done to her. The child had seemed merely sleepy, not strange—not stranger than usual, anyway—and he took a deep breath and leaned against the wall and tried to simply relax and enjoy the relief of knowing that he hadn't lost her, he hadn't lost either of them.

They brought her out wrapped in a big orange towel, Tessa holding her, Bernice with water all over her pants and shirt.

"Are you sure she's OK?" he asked them.

"She's fine," said Tessa.

"Emily?"

Her eyes were drooping shut, and he was transported by the same feeling himself, the feeling that the adult world was a kind of dreamscape he had wandered into, and all he wanted was to retreat into his own head and sleep.

"We're going to put her to bed," said Bernice.

"I'll just sit here."

There was a chair in the hall outside the bathroom, an old-fashioned one with a high back and almost no cushioning. He sat in the dim light and looked at what he took to be one of Bernice's father's paintings on the wall, a large, two-toned canvas that might have been sky and ocean meeting, viewed at night, or might simply have been some abstraction he wasn't meant to understand. Finally, he heard footsteps, and then Tessa was in front of him.

"You want a ride back to the hotel?" he asked.

"I can get a cab."

"I'm surprised you'd leave us alone with her again."

"I'm trying—I'm trying to do the right thing here. Anyway, you're not to blame. Not for tonight. It wasn't your fault."

"Sure, it was. I could have kept a better eye on her. You don't understand. I was hunting around for a TV to watch."

"I know you think that, but you're wrong."

"Four hours."

"She was sleepwalking. That's all. Bernice is with her now."

"Forget the cab. I'll take you."

"Are you sure?"

"Let me just go up and let Bernice know."

He climbed the stairs. She was sitting in a chair, watching Emily intently, as if her attention were the main thing keeping the child from growing transparent and fading away.

He pantomimed driving, pointed downstairs. Bernice looked at him and nodded, then returned to Emily. Her lips were moving silently—she was having some sort of conversation with herself. Outside, he could hear that the rain had started to come down again. It pattered against the glass of the small skylight in the hall. He left the two of them in the room and moved as quietly as he could back toward the stairs and down to the first floor. It occurred to him that Bernice was probably planning to sit there all night.

»»»»»»

They didn't talk for most of the drive. At one point, Landis wondered if Tessa had fallen asleep, but when he looked over at her, he saw that she had her forehead pressed against the smudged glass of the passenger-side window and seemed to be studying the passing cityscape.

"Your husband's in a band?" Landis said. "I work with bands."

"You probably wouldn't know his."

"Try me."

"They were called Pale Rider, but now they're going by Forty Days."

He nodded, trying to pretend he might have heard of them at some point, though he was certain he hadn't. "In the desert or something, right?"

"It's how long Jesus was in the desert. It's also how long it rained in Genesis. Forty comes up a lot, although I don't think the number really means much. It's more about the wandering—about feeling disconnected from God, at least temporarily."

"You think your praying brought her back tonight?"

"I don't know. I don't think it's possible to say, really."

"I guess that's right." He adjusted one of the air vents on the dash. "That guy looked a little like Jesus, huh? Charlie?"

"I don't think it was him."

"But it could be, right? He could come like a thief in the night."

"That's right."

"You think maybe he *told her* he was Jesus?"

"No."

"Because this kid is waiting for Jesus to come back. Who knows what kind of ideas she's got, right? Don't take this the wrong way—I'm not blaming you. I'm not even sure I know what I'm talking about. I mean, I don't. But I do know that little kids can't keep a story straight, and they make stuff up."

She didn't answer, and he thought maybe he'd gone a little far and somehow insulted her, so he just drove in silence.

"Here we are," he said, pulling over in front of the hotel. "Home sweet home."

"I'm not leaving without her," said Tessa, her head jerking slightly, as if she were just returning from a daydream. "That part is nonnegotiable."

"I never figured it was anything else." He watched her push through the glass doors into the lobby, waited until she was on the elevator before he pulled back out.

»»»»»»

The door was down a couple of cement steps from ground level, with some dusty plastic flowers affixed to the outside. Landis knocked a couple times. Finally, it opened. Charlie was still shirtless, his shorts a strangely baggy affair that might have looked right on a British officer assigned to India. "Can I come in?" asked Landis.

"Nope," Charlie said.

Landis pushed the door open anyway and stepped inside. A distinctly wet-basement smell. A brown sofa was parked up against the long wall of the living room, and on the other wall there was a small television on a metal cart. On the coffee table, six or seven mugs sat out, along with a few scattered pieces of notebook paper.

"You live here alone?" Landis asked.

"That's right."

"You like girls? You like little girls?"

"I don't know what you're talking about."

"Sure you do. Come on, let's talk about it."

"Maybe I should be asking you that same question. You're not that kid's father—you don't look anything like her."

Landis stepped forward so he was fully in the man's face. He sniffed something ugly in his breath. He stepped even closer, to the point where he could feel Charlie's uncertainty—should he back away? Stand his ground? It had been a while since Landis had put himself in such a situation, and he wondered if he could still fight. "I want you to understand something, all right? You will never get within fifteen feet of that little girl ever again. If you see us coming out onto the porch, you will walk the other way, back toward the alley. If you're out front, you will move along down the breezeway until you're by your own front door. You won't talk to her, you won't wave to her, you won't smile at her. And she will never, ever come into this apartment. Got all that?"

"She's never been in this apartment."

"I want to believe that. And until she tells me something different, I'll try."

"I know who you are," Charlie said, his small, rodent eyes unblinking. "And I seen where you're living. Don't act like you're better than me. You're working some scam. Colorado plates. Coming into my house and threatening me. You're worse than the niggers up the block—at least they don't pretend to be what they're not."

"You think I'm pretending?"

"I know it."

Landis noticed that one of the pieces of paper on the coffee table had ballpoint-pen drawings on it. He grabbed Charlie's left arm and maneuvered it quickly up and behind his back, in the process spinning the man around and doubling him over.

"Ouch," said Charlie. "What?"

"What is that?"Landis pushed him over to the coffee table. "You draw that?"

"Yeah."

"Then tell me who it is."

"What do you mean, who? It's just a picture."

"No, it's not. It's a specific person."

"You're fucking nuts. Let me go."

"Thelonius Monk." It was just a child's drawing, and it looked more like a man driving a truck, but Landis knew the truck was supposed to be a piano. "It's Thelonius Monk, from the *Underground* album." Landis yanked harder on Charlie's arm, felt some section of tendon stretch with a small pop. He was inches from breaking his arm. "What did you do?"

"Nothing."

"And my little girl was never in your apartment?" He increased the pressure even more.

"I wanted to teach you a lesson," he gasped. "That's all. I didn't do anything to her. She was standing on the sidewalk. I gave her some chocolate milk. What do you think I am?"

"A lesson?" Landis pushed him to the floor and kicked him in the ribs. Not too hard, but hard enough. It would hurt for a week or two, definitely, probably make it painful to sleep. "Everything I just told you," Landis said, quietly, and with menace

Charlie sat up, rubbing his arm, a sullen expression on his face. "You got lucky, man."

"Tai chi, huh?"

"Don't underestimate me."

"You don't even look at her."

"You should be thanking me," said Charlie. "She could have wandered out in traffic, gotten hit by a bus."

"And every time you see me," said Landis, "I want you to think about that arm. Because if I have to talk to you about this again, I'm going to break it."

»»»»»

Landis walked around to the front and sat on the steps of Donald Click's house, watching as a few cars slipped past in the humid dark before the street fell empty again. He didn't feel particularly good about what he'd just done, and his back hurt now. Chocolate milk. Perhaps the guy was simply lonely. Maybe he was jealous. He was obviously a person with problems, but that didn't make him evil, necessarily. He just stared at the world from his basement window and lived in his head and let his anger get the better of him.

After a while, he got up and let himself in the front door with the key Bernice had given him earlier in the evening and stretched out on the couch in the darkened parlor. He could hear the rain starting to come down hard outside. The key had significance, he knew. He remembered a rainy afternoon he and Pam had spent together a month or so before her accident; she was the only woman he'd ever shared an address with. They'd spent that afternoon in an arcade at Seaside Heights where someone had gathered together orphan games from other arcades into a kind of old-age home for such amusements, moving from machine to machine. Many were so ancient, they operated for a dime. One, which looked to be a hundred years old, with cast-metal soccer players, only wanted a penny. They shot Old West rifles at tin bad guys, fed coins into pinball machines with numbers that clanked around on oversized odometers. Hugh Hefner and 007, Archie and the Green Lantern, the rain falling in dismal buckets.

"I can get rid of it," she'd told him. She was pretty, young, Greek on her father's side, Irish on her mother's, a collector of stuffed animals who sewed her own dresses, talked about someday starting a clothing business. "I can make an appointment tomorrow."

"No," he'd told her. "Don't do that."

"Because of it, or because of me?"

He hadn't answered. He hadn't known. Instead, he'd put more coins into a machine. He'd thought he understood what the rest of his life was going to be like from that moment on. It turned out he hadn't understood a thing.

Outside, an ambulance passed by on its way to the hospital a few blocks north. He stared up at the parlor chandelier, which was dimly visible above him, a cracked rosette inhabiting the shadows above it. Exhaustion overtook him and he closed his eyes.

TWENTY-FOUR

Tessa watched television in the dark from her bed, hoping the infomercials would somehow drown out the noise in her head and let her go to sleep. She understood Landis's suspicion about the neighbor. But the girl was unmarked, and when they'd bathed her, she hadn't acted traumatized or scared, or even embarrassed. Just sleepy. *You're OK, right?* Bernice had asked her over and over. *Yes,* Emily had replied, without elaboration. *Yes.*

On one channel, an Englishman was selling cookware to an enthusiastic airhead of an American woman. On another, a man with teeth that made her think of white tombstones wanted to explain the secrets of buying real estate with no money down. She was missing out, he told her. She didn't know what everyone else knew. The train was leaving the station, and she was not going to be on it without her cookware, without her real estate DVDs. But it was not too late, not if she acted now.

They'd entered a strange isolation, she and David. Their cars, their house, their mortgage, all of them zipped up in a neat little Christian carryall. She'd never questioned this, never wondered if it might be dangerous. They would be good people and God would reward them for it with wealth, and children, and happiness. That was what she'd believed.

The last year of their trying, before it had become clear that she would never conceive, she'd gone with David to a conference of Christian business owners in Boise, where they'd stayed at a resort hotel. In the mornings, he went to sessions while she explored the town and lounged by the hotel pool. Then, at five, he'd return, looking handsome and rugged in his jacket and tie, and she'd meet him wearing nothing but the fluffy terrycloth robe the hotel provided. She'd felt like a kept woman. The sex they'd had on those sunny afternoons had felt dirty and wonderful, and as close to knowing God as she imagined possible.

But again, nothing. She had prayed, taken her temperature, monitored her ovulation cycle, prayed more. Then she went to the clinic for exploratory surgery and the removal of several fibroid tumors, which left her miserable for weeks. The doctor explained her extreme endometriosis to her as a simple matter of tissue growth outside the womb, but she couldn't help seeing it as something worse—a dark matter inhabiting her that she was responsible for. Somehow, unwittingly, she had invited this unhappiness in, this inversion, made room for it, allowed it to grow. Then there was the matter of the womb itself, which was bicornuate, shaped, ironically, not like a pear, but like a heart. It was she who had taken out the ads in various papers around the country, after reading an article about this in the *Gazette.* "Why do you want to raise a stranger's child?" David had asked her, and she'd told him it wouldn't be that way, it would be their child. Eventually, he'd come around on the subject, or had seemed to. They'd joked about it, made up funny names. Alphonse. Zirconia. But he'd stopped looking at her the same way, had retreated into himself, his work, his musical weekends with the band, and she knew that she'd failed him in the one thing he had counted on her for, and that there was no way to change this, ever.

Bernice had arrived carrying just a small wheeled bag, wearing a faded blue-jeans jacket. They'd met her at the airport, and the first thing Tessa noticed was the smell of alcohol—she'd clearly had a beer on the plane. She had a new pimple on her forehead, and Tessa felt bad for her about it. *Pleased to meet you*, she'd said, extending her hand in a businesslike way. She wasn't showing yet, and she was flirting with them. Tessa hadn't seen that then, but she did now.

The ancient air conditioner under the window cycled on again, and Tessa closed her eyes, telling herself she must sleep, though she couldn't imagine how.

The phone rang at 6:00 AM, and she jumped out of bed to answer it, but it was only the wake-up call she'd requested. She turned off the television, then went into the bathroom and stepped into the cramped tub and fooled around with the faucet for a while before finally figuring out how to get the water to come out of the showerhead. She closed her eyes and felt the roar and the steam.

After toweling dry, she got dressed, drank water from the bathroom sink, and since it was still ridiculously early, decided to take a walk to the inner harbor. She brought her phone. The elevator that took her to the lobby shook and shuddered; everything about this building was decrepit. David made a living providing false smiles. The world was full of decay and rot, and what did people do to address that? They stuck a fancy new lobby on the front so you couldn't tell. This one—the shuddering stopped and the doors heaved open—was all marble and glass, with a couple of potted palms framing the desk and a huge American flag in the front window. What was it Bernice had said? Fat over lean. Otherwise, you could end up with a cracked surface. That was what had happened to Tessa. She'd gotten her layers mixed up, let the outer one dry before the inner one had a chance to.

Traffic was light, and she made her way across the wide streets toward the water. At one intersection, an alarming noise sounded in synchrony with the walk sign, which she figured must be for blind people, though the idea of a blind person navigating this particular stretch of streets seemed dangerous. She wasn't blind, and this thought caused her to consider briefly all the other things she wasn't: deaf, poor, stupid, limbless, crippled, or stricken with some terrible disease. Childless—she wasn't even that. Not exactly.

To her left, an enormous industrial building with smokestacks wore a neon guitar like a joke bow tie. Other modern buildings poked and sprawled along the waterfront, sparkling gold off their windows. A tall ship was moored ahead of her, and as she approached she could read the lettering on its side: Cuauhtémoc. It was flying a Mexican flag.

She approached the foot of a huge hill, an oddly fake-looking rise of green that rose abruptly from the southwest corner of the harbor, its top so flat it looked as if someone had sliced it off with a knife. At the bottom of the steep stairway, Tessa noticed what she thought was only a pile of abandoned clothes, but then she saw a woman's grimy face, eyes tight shut, skin sunburnt and cracked, a whiteness of dried spittle at the corners of her mouth.

We're all doing God's work, in our own way, David liked to say. *Even sometimes when we don't know it.*

She had to step over the woman to start up the stairs, and she did so, taking a deep breath first, because she was afraid there would be a smell. After the third step, she exhaled and inhaled again, hurrying upward, imagining she was climbing a pyramid, which was what it looked like, or perhaps some kind of Aztec ruin.

At the top, out of breath, she looked out on the disorderly spread of the city, the stadiums and the water and the boats and rotting warehouses and more distantly the geometric lines of row houses and even, over to the east, the gold ice-cream-cone spires of an Eastern Orthodox church.

He answered on the third ring, his voice thick with sleep. "What time is it?"

"Why don't you look at the clock?"

There was the sound of some muffled movements, and she imagined him turning on the light on his night table, getting up out of the bed. He paced when he spoke on the phone, as if communication somehow made him nervous.

"Where are you?"

"On a hill," she said. "I've seen her."

"Is she with you?"

"No, she's not with me. But she's all right."

"What are you going to do?"

"I don't know. I don't know what I'm going to do."

"Where are you?" he asked again. "I hear birds."

"Gulls," she said. "I'm in Baltimore."

"Gulls? Baltimore? You should have said something. You should have discussed this with me."

"You and I don't talk. Do we? Do we talk? I can't remember it. Not recently, anyway." A small dog ran up and sniffed at her leg, then wandered away to investigate the base of one of the cannons that pointed out over the harbor, toward the city.

"Of course we talk. Don't be an idiot."

"Then let's talk now. Why didn't you insist on calling the police as soon as you knew it was her?"

"I did. Waiting was your idea. *You* said to wait."

"I know, I know. But you didn't even argue. I've been thinking about it, and it doesn't make sense to me. You called the police that time the neighbor kids had a party until three in the morning. You called them when that guy backed into you at King Soopers."

"I was respecting your feelings. You said they'd bring her back. That's what you said. But you're naïve. Admit it—don't you feel stupid now?"

She had said this, though only because she had needed some hope to hold on to. She repositioned the phone and listened, unable to tell static from breathing. "Don't you love our child?"

"Oh, stop it. I'll fly out there and we'll talk to Bernice. I'm sure we can talk some sense into her. We can give her more money. That's what this is about. I can—we can get hold of more money."

"You didn't answer my question. You don't like Bernice. You never liked her. You said she was cheap and easy. Remember? Why would you care what I want to do? You've got the papers, right? We could get her arrested, have her charged. I don't get it."

"Tell me the hotel," he said. "I'll come there. You shouldn't be doing this alone."

"You don't, do you? You don't have the papers. Something is going on. I don't know what. It's a lie. Everything has been a lie. I've been dreaming. All this time I've been dreaming."

"You're not dreaming, Tessa," he said. "Don't say that. You love me, I love you and Emily, and everything is legal. It was all drawn up by a lawyer. Bernice might be able to challenge it, but I don't think she'd win. Tessa? We're walking together. There's nothing to worry about."

But there was something he wasn't telling her. She felt it like a stone she'd swallowed. "Our house?" she said. "Do we own that? Or do we rent? Are our cars leased? What is going on, David?"

"Of course it's our house. There's the mortgage and a couple of loans, but it's ours. I've got a pencil now. I've got a pencil and a pad of paper. Give me the information and I'll write it down. Don't be hysterical. I'm going to take care of everything."

"Here's what I've figured out. I don't think you love your daughter," she said. "Not really. Not the way you should. And I don't think you love me, either."

"Don't say that. That's just a bunch of shit."

"It isn't. You think there's something wrong with us—with both of us. I don't know what, exactly, or why, but I see it now. You judge us."

His voice turned hard. "You are way out of line here."

The scent of coffee roasting someplace came to her on a soft breeze. "You go now," she said. "Just go. I'm letting you off the hook."

"Tessa," he said. "Everything I do, I do for you. And for us."

"I think maybe I've been asleep," she said. "All this time. And now I'm just waking up."

There was a pause. "What did she tell you?"

"What do you mean? What could she have told me?"

"That girl was crazy. We both knew it. Not trustworthy. A liar."

"Are you listening to yourself? Who's a liar?" She was suddenly tired of hearing him, of feeling connected to something she didn't understand or believe in.

He was quiet again for a moment. "I think we should talk about this in person."

"What?"

"What I'm saying is, whatever she told you, it's not true."

"I'm leaving you, David," she said. "We're going to be divorced. It's over. Over." She hung up before he could try to talk her out of it, and when the phone rang a few moments later, she took a deep breath and turned it off.

TWENTY-FIVE

At 7:00 AM, Bernice, finding herself in her childhood bedroom, momentarily doubted that she was awake at all. She remembered this feeling, the way she had sometimes drifted around the house in a half sleep, seeing but not seeing, inhabiting a parallel universe. But she quickly became aware of her adult self, of the fact that she was still fully dressed, of her need to urinate, of her dry mouth. The last thing she remembered was watching Emily sleep. At some point, apparently, she had gotten onto the bed.

Moving as quietly as she could, she slipped out to the hall and into the cramped bathroom. She used to smoke in here, and there were still burn marks on the windowsill. But then her father had figured out what she was up to and started checking on her, so instead she'd taken to going out her bedroom window and sitting on the tiny ledge outside, the fall from which would most certainly have killed her. It seemed funny to her now that no one had ever reported this to her father, or even the police, because she had to have been visible to the houses across the street, even at night, a skinny, girlish figure poised fifty feet in the air like a gargoyle.

Back in the bedroom, she crouched by the other bed. "Get up, honey," she whispered. "We're going out."

Emily stirred, then opened her eyes. Her breath was like sour milk. "To the sharks?" she said.

"Yes," Bernice said. "If we get there early, we'll be first in line."

She helped her up and into some clothes, then into the bathroom for a quick brush and wash. Emily seemed uncertain about any of this, but it was early, and she'd had a long night. Bernice kept seeing her in the bath, with Tessa confidently working a washcloth over her body, the two of them interacting so easily. Because, of course, they'd been doing this for years. Bernice's job had come after the shampoo, filling a pint beer glass with warm water and pouring it over the back of Emily's upturned head, the child's eyes closed, her chin tipped toward the ceiling.

"Your hair looks cool," she said. "You should always go to sleep with it wet."

After stuffing some clothes and other things into her knapsack, Bernice took Emily's hand and led her to the top of the stairs. "You want me to carry you?"

She shook her head.

"OK. But hold on to the railing."

Bernice went down first, so that if Emily took a tumble, she'd be able to catch her, but there was nothing to worry about. She was cautious, taking each step with great attention. Bernice filled with love for her, felt the warmth inside her like a shot of whiskey.

Landis was snoring loudly in the parlor. She wished he'd just returned to his own place, so that she didn't have to be reminded he existed this one last time. She held up a finger to her lips. "We don't want to wake him," she said.

"Why not?"

"He needs his sleep."

"Doesn't he want to come, too?"

"He's seen the sharks." She moved them through the dining room and into the kitchen. The light outside was violet, moist with the promise of another hot day. An early-rising neighbor's car idled on its parking pad across the alley. Some garbage cans had been placed out for collection, and they overflowed with plastic bags balanced two and three high over the top like ice-cream cones.

The kitchen was a mess. Well, she'd never claimed to be a homemaker. Her own mother had gone back and forth between periods of cleaning zealotry, where she Windexed every inch of glass and washed the floors on her hands and knees, and long stretches of absolute indifference, where she seemed not even to notice her surroundings, leaving items of clothing draped over chairs for weeks at a time, letting dust build up on surfaces until you could write your name in it. She remembered her father shouting about this, his face contorted with anger. When Bernice was in high school, he'd hired a cleaning lady to come once a week.

"I want a Pop-Tart," said Emily.

"Shh," said Bernice. "All right." She fumbled in the closet, ignoring the mouse turds everywhere. She removed the box and took out the one remaining silvery-foil-wrapped packet, then noticed that its bottom had been nibbled through. "Goddamnit," she said.

"Don't *say* that," Emily warned.

"Right, sorry." She took out the pastries and examined them briefly. "You want to get something on the way?" she asked. "Like, maybe a croissant? I'll bet we could find a nice croissant, or even a bagel someplace."

"I want a Pop-Tart."

"Right. Of course you do." One corner of each Pop-Tart had been rounded off. How bad could that be? She slid them into the toaster. Heat killed bacteria anyway—by toasting them, she was being responsible. Serving them raw would be something else.

They sat at the kitchen table across from each other. Emily's eyes were still puffy from sleep.

"Did you have dreams?" Bernice asked.

Emily nodded. "I think so."

"Want to tell me?"

She shook her head.

"Were they bad dreams?"

"Not so bad. I don't think I want to talk about them."

"All right," said Bernice. "That's fine."

After a while, the toaster popped and Bernice got up to retrieve their breakfast. She brought them orange juice, too, hers in a coffee mug, Emily's in a plastic cup with flowers on it that she remembered had just turned up one day years ago, but which she now suddenly thought had probably had something to do with CC. Perhaps her mother had left his place with it back when she was cheating, or—even worse—he'd been here, had brought it with him. She even wondered if her mother had viewed it as some kind of a test, had waited to see what her father would say, had only had her feelings about him confirmed when he failed to notice at all.

"What happened to it?" Emily asked, inspecting the Pop-Tart.

"What do you mean, what happened? It went in the toaster. Now it's out. Come on, we don't want to miss the sharks getting fed. I think they throw them live fish and stuff."

"It's all chewed up."

"No it isn't. Let me see." She took the paper towel on which she'd served the Pop-Tart and scrutinized the pastry with a professional eye.

"That's just a little crust damage. Probably happened in shipping."

"Shipping?"

"Not actually shipping. Shipping means trucks. They probably ought to call it trucking, except that would sound strange. 'Contents may have shifted during trucking.' See what I mean? In the olden times, everything went everyplace by ships." She watched the girl watching her, felt suddenly guilty for not knowing what she was saying or why, for filling Emily's head with useless stuff. What were the important things? *Learn who the liars are*, she wanted to say. *Everything else is just getting along*. But how to explain this? "Your ancestors came over here on ships," she said. "Their corners may have gotten a little damaged along the way, too."

"It looks like a mouse ate it," said Emily, continuing to inspect the pastry. "It looks like teeth marks."

"Well, hell," said Bernice, taking it from her and heading for the trash. "You have to admit, though, the mouse didn't eat *much* of it." She dropped the pastry in the bin. "OK, now, let's go. We'll get breakfast later."

She was unlocking the back door when the front doorbell rang. "Mommy!" said Emily.

"Let's go, *now*." Bernice took her hand and hustled her out onto the back stair, letting the storm door close behind them. She didn't want to head up the breezeway between the houses, so instead she directed Emily toward the alley. Once there, they made a right and headed north. She figured they could make a right at the next cross street, then come back down toward the house, approaching the car that way. They walked quickly, but not too quickly, veering to avoid a recently squashed rat, its gray body broken open and bright with gore.

"Where are we going?" asked Emily, struggling to keep up.

"I told you. To see the sharks. And we'll get you a souvenir, too.

Maybe a refrigerator magnet, or a big old eraser or something. You'd like that, wouldn't you? An eraser in the shape of a sea horse, or shaped like a dolphin?"

They made the right, then another right onto their street, heading back south toward the house. The car was on the west side, not far from the intersection, parked away from the curb at a noticeable angle—so what if she wasn't much of a driver? It wasn't much of a car, was it? She hadn't locked it either, it turned out. "Get in back," she said. Farther south, she could see the purple and black taxicab double-parked outside the house. Landis would have answered the door. By now, they'd probably started to put things together. "Go on."

Emily climbed up into the booster seat and Bernice closed her door, then went around the front of the car and got in the driver's side. Her hands shook as she inserted the key into the ignition and turned it. The starter motor whinnied the way it always did, but the engine did not catch. She pumped the accelerator furiously and tried three more times. The smell of gas filled the car.

"You should get a new car," said Emily. "I think this one is too old."

"I had a fine car," said Bernice. "Mr. Landis ruined it." She turned the key again, and again was greeted by failure, except that this time, the starter sounded weak. "Here's some advice: Never let a man drive your car."

"I can't do the straps myself," said Emily, who had been trying.

"Never mind the straps."

She hadn't seen them coming, but suddenly they were outside her window. Landis tapped on the glass. Bernice ignored him and tried again. He was saying something. She rolled down the window, just a crack.

"Flooded," Landis said. "Smell it? With all that rain last night, the plugs probably got wet. You should give it a rest."

She cranked the window tight. Tessa was with him, that earnest, midwestern-pretty face of hers floating outside like a balloon. "Lock your door," said Bernice, and when Emily didn't do it immediately, she reached around and pushed the knob down for her. Then she shut her eyes. *Please don't let this happen.* She opened them again, but rather than look out, she gazed down at her feet and saw that she had only put on one sock. Her left ankle was bare, descending into the top of her sneaker, scabby where she'd scratched mosquito bites. It looked like the ankle of some schoolkid. It did not look like the ankle of someone who could be trusted with the life and future of a child.

There was a second knock on the window. Tessa was staring in at her, another visitor to the aquarium trying to gain the attention of the exotic fish. The air inside the car had grown stuffy, and she wondered how long she could stay like this. "Bernice?" Tessa said, her voice muffled by the glass. Bernice shook her head. What was there to talk about? And yet she knew this was it—the moment she'd been headed for inevitably. Caught red-handed. And still she didn't have to give up. The engine would fix itself, eventually. This stupid car had brought them all the way here, after all. She'd wait these people out.

"Hey," she said, repositioning the rearview mirror so she could see Emily's face. "Remember our big drive together?"

"Of course," said Emily.

"It was fun, wasn't it?"

"Yup."

"What was your favorite part?"

"I think the motel," Emily said. "The one with the pool."

"In Nashville? But, honey, that pool was empty. Remember? It was closed."

"I know," she said. "I just liked how it looked."

"Me, too."

Then, leaning forward, Emily pushed up the lock and opened her door.

"No!" Bernice shouted, but it was too late. A moment later, Tessa had her in her arms and was hugging her tight.

Bernice rolled down her window, just about two inches.

"Come on," said Landis quietly. "Try to be reasonable."

She took a deep breath, let a few moments pass. Reasonable. Yes, she could be that. She removed the keys, unlocked her door, and got out of the car.

"What did you think?" Tessa was saying, her eyes pink and tired. "What did you think was going to happen? Where were you going?"

"The aquarium," she said. "To see the sharks." Even Landis looked more disturbed than she'd ever seen him. "Tell her," she said. "You knew we were going to the aquarium. We'd have been back by lunch."

"You're lying," said Tessa.

"Am not," said Bernice. She looked at him. "Go on."

Landis, unshaven, his shirt half-buttoned, flexed his big hands, then stuck them in his pockets.

"I'm taking her back now," said Tessa.

"The hell you are. Landis?"

"It might be for the best," he said.

"What?"

"You heard me. This isn't about just you. We have to consider Emily and what's right for her."

"What's right for her is being with her mother."

"I *am* her mother," said Tessa.

"Her *real* mother."

At the sound of her name, Emily looked up at Bernice for the first time since she'd exited the car. Bernice was trying hard not to take this personally or read it as an expression of preference. Emily still didn't look entirely awake, but she did look distressed.

"I'm not letting her go back with you," Bernice said. She was conscious of a fat man smoking and watching them from the porch of his house a few doors up the street. Why did everything have to be so fucking *public*? "I made a huge mistake giving her up, and I'm not making it again."

"Bernice," said Tessa, "it's not up to you."

"It's not?"

"No."

She looked at Landis, who had removed one hand from his pants pocket and was studying the back of his knuckles. Then she looked expectantly at Emily. "Pearl?" she said. "What do you think?"

The cab, which had clearly been told to wait, pulled into a spot that had opened up a few yards down from the house, its tailpipe exhaling puffs of white smoke into the humid morning air that rose from behind it like the product of some invisible hookah.

"I don't know," said Emily.

"See? She doesn't know." But looking at her face, Bernice understood that this was not the case. She knew. Everyone knew. The only one in denial was herself.

"You're young," said Tessa. "You can have more children. You should. Instead of trying to change the past, why not try looking to the future?" She glanced over at Landis. Her hand was on Emily's shoulder. "Bernice?" she asked, more quietly. "Are you going to be OK?"

Landis tried to take her arm, but she shook him off, stepping backward.

"Emily is my daughter," said Tessa. "I won't let anything happen to her."

"She's *my* daughter," said Bernice.

"I didn't say you couldn't come visit. In fact, I'd like that. You should."

"Oh, that'll be nice. I can just see that." Bernice moved toward Emily. Where before there had been only the idea of love, now there was the actuality of it, something she found infinitely more surprising. She sank to her knees. "Emily," she said. "You're not going to do this, are you? You're not going to leave me. After all we've been through? Just tell me this. You love me, right? I need to know that."

Emily nodded. But she was already on the back deck of a boat sailing away from Bernice, her image diminishing toward the vanishing point.

"We're going now, all right?" said Tessa. Emily pulled away, went to the back door of Bernice's car, and opened it. Bernice's heart filled briefly with hope. But a moment later she brought out her knapsack, which held the change of clothes Bernice had stuffed into it, the windup crab and the plush penguin, some plastic sunglasses and a cherry Chapstick that Bernice had bought Emily in Tennessee. They had taken turns playing movie star with it, pretending it was lipstick and admiring themselves in the rearview mirror.

Bernice did not kiss her good-bye. She didn't see how she could. Instead, she started walking down the street, fast. She felt dizzy; she felt in danger of splitting in half. She saw the cab pass her on its way south, probably back to Tessa's hotel first, then on to the airport.

Landis jogged to catch up to her. "There was nothing else to do," he said.

Bernice kept her pace. "I'm not talking to you. You abandoned me—you didn't even try."

"Hey," he said. "I'm here, right? Will you think for a change, instead of just living inside your own head? Look around. You didn't lose anything. Do you even know where you're going?"

"This way." They passed more row houses, their porches leaning oddly to one side or the other, some with well-tended gardens bursting with flowers, others with patches of lawn overgrown with weeds and littered with dog shit. The sun was over the rooftops to their left across the street, angling gold against the bay windows, bouncing off the mirrors of the parked cars. "I think I'd like to be alone."

"You say that, but you don't. You don't want to be alone."

"Oh, yes, I do."

"No one does."

"Will you maybe just trust me on this and go away?"

He stopped and grabbed her by both shoulders, and though she tried to get loose, his grip was too strong. "I'm turning around and heading back to your house, and I'm going to see what there is to make for breakfast. I'm going to have some coffee."

She shrugged. "You're just going to leave eventually. It might as well be now."

"I should take you up on that."

"Go ahead. Traitor."

"No one else would have stuck it out this long."

"You're free," she said. "Released. Bye-bye."

As she walked away from him, the neighborhood dropped off quickly. These were parts of town she'd been forbidden to explore as a child, and had for the most part only viewed through a car window. The houses had originally been just as nice as the ones to the north, but now many were decrepit and in need of repair. She didn't care where she was; the sadness in her felt so deep that she thought if she stopped moving she might simply fall into it and disappear forever.

After a few more blocks, she found herself in front of a church with a hand-lettered sign outside that read Solid Rock Temple of God Jesus: Sunrise Service. She stopped and listened. A band was playing inside, and the building was thumping like an overexcited heart. A thin young man in a white T-shirt that came to his knees walked his pit bull past her, the dog an inscrutable gray waddle of muscle. She thought about Tessa and the church she'd gone to with her and David in the Springs, all those shiny white faces reeking of cologne and good wishes. Gathering her courage, she walked up to the doors and pushed them open. Music flooded out. On a low stage, a young man was singing a gospel song, pacing back and forth, dressed in a light blue suit and a gleaming white shirt, with a red hat that looked something like a fez, and a piece of colorful kente cloth around his shoulders. Bernice hesitated, grappling with the feeling she always had upon entering a church, that she was somehow shoplifting. Inside, she quickly took a seat on a folding chair in the back of the room.

There were maybe thirty people in the congregation, and they were all standing and singing along, their voices competing with the bass, organ, and drums, their bodies moving in joyful rhythm.

It had happened only two days before the church visit, on a sunny Friday near the end of her first trimester. For weeks, she'd been batting her eyes at him, teasing him about himself—*You guys play any Black Sabbath?*—and generally testing him, trying to find where he was weak, because everyone was weak. She'd been asleep, dreaming something warm and tropical, and then she'd opened her eyes to see his hands right in front of her, his arms coming around her sides, and she understood that he was curled up behind her on the bed, his lips touching her neck, and she'd thought *What the hell do I do now?* And then she'd thought, *Better lie still. Lie still and don't acknowledge anything is happening at all.* And in that way, she had convinced herself that it wasn't, though of course it was. She was there and not there, and when it was over, he'd simply gotten up and slipped himself back into his pants and tucked in his shirt and smiled at her in a way that said what was growing in her was now his property, too.

God knows you need a miracle

Yes he does, yes he does

She watched a heavyset woman in a green dress in front of her swaying back and forth to the music, her arms held out to the sides as if she were conducting. She thought about how they'd all stood together, David in his tie and navy blazer, Tessa in her yellow A-line dress with lacy trim, and his hand had felt for hers, as if their relationship were some secret high school crush they had to keep from the parents, as if things could just change on their own from ugly to beautiful for no reason at all except that you wanted them to.

God knows you want a miracle

Yes he does, yes he does

A woman sat beside her and touched her arm lightly. "You feel it, don't you?" she asked, her voice raised to compete with the music. She was pleasant looking, with a round, almost childish freckled face the color of light coffee, wearing a blue blouse and shiny gold-button earrings. "That feeling you're having, that's his light shining on your heart. Go ahead and cry. It's a good kind of crying."

Bernice wiped the tears from her cheeks. "I'm sorry," she said. "I can explain."

"Don't apologize. You're welcome here."

"No, really. I can explain."

But the woman was beaming. She knew what was what. "No need for that," she said. "No need to be sorry. Just remember—it's everything in the world you need, right here in this place, right now."

In the moments after she'd given birth, the labor and delivery nurse who had been with her through the whole thing—Bernice had refused to let Tessa or David come into the room—had returned from the little table where another nurse was cleaning up the baby, suctioning out its mouth, tying off the umbilical-cord stump, and wrapped her arms around Bernice and hugged her. "Oh, honey," she'd said. "You did it. You did it. You were perfect, absolutely perfect. No one could have done better." And Bernice, exhausted from eight hours of labor, numb from the epidural, and confused by this sudden feeling of both accomplishment and loss, had had a momentary sense of being flooded with light throughout her body, as if all the mistakes she'd made no longer mattered and her life was beginning anew.

Morning sun angled through the high, mullioned windows. Sitting on the ledge of the nearest one, a small bird that had somehow gotten in patiently viewed the proceedings, head twitching back and forth like a spectator at a tennis match. In a little while, she thought, she'd go back and see what Landis was doing. He probably didn't even know where she kept the coffee.

ACKNOWLEDGMENTS

My thanks to Lee Montgomery and Meg Storey, and all the dedicated staff at Tin House Books, for their intelligence, professionalism, and good spirits. Also to Ellen Levine for her ongoing support and advice.

Thanks, too, to everyone in Nashville involved with the Parthenon Prize: Alice Randall, who picked *Hot Springs* as the 2008 winner; Lily LaBour Catalano, director; the many readers involved in the screening process, including Sheri Malman; and, most importantly, John Spence, founder, for his commitment to promoting and encouraging new literature.